The Princess Companion

A RETELLING OF THE PRINCESS AND THE PEA

MELANIE CELLIER

Luminant Publications
Making Life brighter

THE PRINCESS COMPANION: A RETELLING OF THE
PRINCESS AND THE PEA

First print edition published in 2016
by Luminant Publications

ISBN 978-0-9806963-4-9

Luminant Publications
PO Box 203
Glen Osmond, South Australia 5064

melaniecellier@internode.on.net
http://www.melaniecellier.com

Cover Design by Phatpuppy Art
Main Title Font by CuttyFruty

For my parents who taught me to love words

The Queen

It had only been a squirrel or a deer moving through the forest. Or so she told herself when she heard the noise through the trees. She tried to calm her breathing.

She focused her mind on the image of his face. After all, she was doing this for him. She would do anything for her beloved son.

He would not suffer like… but her mind skittered away from that thought. That wouldn't help her breathing.

Finally she calmed herself enough to recite the words she still remembered so clearly. The words that would summon help.

She hadn't expected an immediate response so was startled into an undignified yelp that she quickly stifled. Her frightened eyes sought the castle but there were no sounds in response to her cry.

She turned back to look at the creature before her. Relief! The face was still filled with the kindly wisdom she remembered. She felt for a moment the lightness that came from not being alone, from not having to be the one with the answers.

"You came!"

"My dear child, of course I came."

The queen laughed, a low chuckle. "Hardly a child anymore. In fact, I have three children of my own."

She received a smile in response. "You still seem like a child to me. It seems only yesterday when I was –"

But the queen cut her off. "I don't want to reminisce. I need your help."

It came out more sharply than she intended so she tried again. "I've called for you because of my son. I'm concerned for him. He needs your help."

Her companion looked around as if she expected to see the prince lurking behind a tree.

The queen shook her head. "He's not here. Doesn't know anything about it. But I'm desperate that he not make the same mistake as his father."

This earned her a sudden, sharp look.

"And we've heard rumours, the king and I. We have to be sure that the ones who come are *true*. That the one who's chosen is," she paused, "the right one. Please, can you help me?"

"True, you say. Hmmmm." Her companion murmured something under her breath and then was silent for a space.

The queen began to look anxious again.

Then with a swift movement something small was pressed into her hand. "She would have to be true indeed, to feel this. Put it under the mattress, only the right one will feel it."

"Under the mattress? Oh, thank you, thank you."

The queen looked so relieved, so buoyant, it seemed for a moment she was the one with wings. She clasped the hands before her, "I must go. But I'm so grateful! You are as kind as you always were." With a final smile, she turned and slipped away into the darkness.

Her companion didn't move but watched her go, long after she seemed to have disappeared from sight. "The same mistake as his father? What is going on in that girl's head? A muddle, indeed. Well, I suppose they'll all learn something from the experience."

And then suddenly she vanished.

The wood was empty again. Except for the silent watcher who was neither a squirrel nor a deer.

The Prince

Every good story I've ever heard has involved a prince. And usually a handsome, intelligent one. Now I have nothing against being handsome or intelligent but I don't want my life to be a story. I want to be free to make my own choices. Not to be governed by the magical whims of some godmother. Sure, I wouldn't be here at all if a godmother hadn't intervened in my parents' life but that doesn't mean I want that for me. I'm willing to do my duty and fall in love with a princess but I don't want magic to help me do it. I'm perfectly fine on my own.

"Maaaaaaaaxxx!"

Groan. Or at least I would be perfectly fine if I could ever manage to actually be on my own.

This is the worst part of my father's bizarre determination to sequester us all in the middle of the forest every winter. Our winter castle is a lot smaller than our summer palace. The castle is still large by normal standards but normal standards don't apply to twin eleven-year-olds. Particularly when those eleven-year-olds are my sisters.

I debated staying put and hoping they didn't find me or trying to slip past them back to my room. Unfortunately, I spent too long considering my options and they burst into the library and immediately saw me in one of the window seats.

"What are you doing?"

My sister Lily's angelic appearance is extremely misleading.

"Nothing."

"Well, what are you thinking about then?"

The fact that Sophie looks exactly like Lily makes them appear twice as angelic. Once again, incredibly misleading.

"Nothing."

"You can't be thinking about nothing! That's impossible."

Lily was starting to look annoyed and I generally try to be far away when she's annoyed.

"Well, I guess I was thinking about being bored."

"Oh." She frowned and sat down on the floor next to me. "We're bored too, what should we do."

I sighed. We'd only been at the castle for a month and we must have had some variation of this conversation twenty times. I ran through the usual suggestions: study, dance practice, talk to your governess, talk to Mother, talk to Father, talk to Nanny. Each one was greeted with an eye roll from Lily and a sigh from Sophie. The nanny suggestion got two eye rolls and two sighs. I added a new suggestion on the end.

"Why don't you play dress ups? I bet Mother has some old trunks full of clothes that you could use."

"Really Max, we're not five."

I now realised what I had missed at the beginning of the conversation. Lily was in a princess mood. (Don't ask me what I consider synonyms for princess.) I decided to get out of there quickly.

"Well, you'll have to work something out for yourself then. I have to go and help Father with some diplomatic communications." I stood before I'd finished speaking and leaped over the twins' heads to land between them and the door. I then walked from the room as quickly as I could without actually running. After all, I'm nineteen years old. Not even the world's most obnoxious twin sisters could make me do something as undignified as running through the castle.

Once out of the room I slowed to a stroll and headed in the direction of my father's office. There weren't any diplomatic communications, of course. Or at least none that my father would want my advice on. But I wouldn't put it past the twins to come and check if I really was with Father. They were probably mad enough with me as it was. I didn't want to spend the next week checking around corners.

When I reached his office I knocked on the door and pushed it open without waiting for an answer. I only got one stride into the room before I realised something was wrong. My father was almost always in this office during the day, it was his favourite retreat. My mother, on the other hand, was never here. It was a manly room, full of oak wood bookshelves stained to match the dark colour of the desk, and free of any decorations or adornments. She looked out of place sitting in one of the leather chairs across from the desk. Out of place and unsettled. My father, on the other hand, looked downright agitated.

I started to back out of the room but was stopped by my mother's voice.

"Max! Perfect timing. Your father and I would like to talk to you."

She sounded excited which was so far from what I was expecting that I froze and missed my opportunity to dash from the room. I began to regret abandoning Lily and Sophie. Even entertaining two fiends disguised as small girls would be preferable to a talk with my parents.

To clarify, a talk with one of my parents would be fine. It was my mother who told me at the age of eight that my parents agreed I wasn't a little child anymore. Which meant I could leave Nanny and the nursery and get my own suite of rooms and a man servant to wait on me. But it was my parents together who told me that my mother was pregnant and I was now going to have to share their attention with two more siblings.

It was my father on his own who told me he had found the perfect thoroughbred to be my first full sized horse and he was the one who told me they'd bought me my own hunting lodge.

But last year my parents together told me that I couldn't spend the winter at that lodge with friends. Even at eighteen I was expected to join the family in our forest hideaway.

So it was with extreme reluctance that I moved forward and sat in the remaining chair. If my mother felt unsettled she no longer showed it. Only the excitement was on display now. My father on the other hand appeared even more agitated and had abandoned his usual stately calm in favour of drumming his fingers on the desk.

"As you know, your father and I have begun to think about your marriage." Only the memory of Lily and Sophie allowed me to hold back the sigh and eye roll. Maybe I should have just stayed in bed this morning.

"And you also know that it is very important to me that you marry a princess. A true princess." The slight emphasis on the true was new but the princess theme was familiar.

"Yes, Mother," I replied, "and you know that I'm perfectly willing to marry a princess." Which was true. Have you ever seen an ugly princess? No. They can come in the annoying variety sure – just look at my sisters – but they don't seem to make them in ugly. And I'd always figured a common girl was at least as likely to be annoying as a royal one. At least this way I'd be guaranteed a wife I could enjoy looking at whenever official receptions started to drag.

"Your father is concerned that just because a girl is a princess doesn't guarantee she'll make a good queen. Or a good wife for that matter." I threw my father a grateful look. With any luck I'd get a wife I could talk to as well as look at.

"Your father feels that we need to consider something more than just their lineage. So we've decided to invite some princesses to come for a visit and I've come up with a test for them."

At this point, if I hadn't been so busy being horrified, I would have started to question my mother's sanity.

My horror must have shown because she hurried to add, "Just the daughters of a few of our neighbours." My horror didn't abate so she added, "Not all at once of course. One at a time."

I started to breathe again, just.

Everyone accepts the fact that their parents are out of touch. But mine really seemed to have gone over the edge. A test? The suggestion was as strange as their behaviour. My father just kept looking more and more agitated, his fingers moving faster and faster. And my mother, usually the epitome of poise, had now started shooting him tense looks. I would have suspected them of being in the middle of an argument but my parents never fight.

"A test?" I finally managed to get out. "What sort of test? And how many princess visits are we talking about?"

I was already trying to tally the number of balls, state dinners and official ceremonies I would have to endure.

"I guess that depends how the first few visits go," my mother said with a smile.

That made me realise the visits would continue until something worse happened – a wedding. I'd counted on at least another couple of years before that.

"When is the first one coming? Surely we could wait a couple of years before we start the parade…"

I could already tell from my mother's expression that things were not going to go my way.

"We can't afford to wait around, dear. What if it takes a couple of years to find the right princess? This is very important to the kingdom. Since you're our only son, you can't delay getting married and having sons of your own."

Children? Children!!! This was getting worse and worse.

"I'm only nineteen, Mother. I don't exactly have one foot in the grave."

Now both my parents were giving me the look and I knew it was all over. Once duty to our kingdom of Arcadia was invoked I didn't have a chance.

"Fine. When is the first princess coming?" Please let it be no time soon. Or at the very least after my annual hunting trip.

If my winters – spent without friends, hunting or any other diversions – were the low point of my year, my annual hunting trip was the high point. I hosted all my closest friends at my lodge and we spent every day in the saddle. With no women around none of us stood on ceremony and for one week of the year I got to forget I was a prince with royal responsibilities.

"As soon as we get back to the capital. But don't worry, you can have your hunting trip first."

I sighed. Small mercies, I suppose.

Part 1

The Winter Castle

Chapter 1

If anyone had told me a year ago that I would find true love through a pea, I would have laughed. I mean, when you live in a forest and never see anyone who isn't related to you, or at least overly obsessed with wood, it's kind of hard to see how a vegetable could lead you to love. But of course it wasn't just the pea. You could also say the light led me there and in this case that wouldn't be metaphorical.

Sometimes I have good ideas, sometimes I have bad ideas and sometimes I have colossally bad ideas. It turns out leaving the merchant camp for an evening stroll was one of the colossally bad ones. At the time, it hadn't seemed like a big deal – I just wanted to stretch my legs after a week of riding in a wagon. Even when it got dark too quickly and I discovered I'd lost my way I didn't realise just how bad an idea it was. And then it started raining.

The rain didn't reach me at first because the forest canopy was too dense. I could hear the raindrops hitting the leaves above me, though, and occasionally a fat drop amassed enough weight to push through the foliage and land on the top of my head. But I certainly wasn't wet - only starting to feel a certain dampness in the air and an utter certainty that I had no idea which direction led to the camp.

"Well, here's where your stupid pride has led you." I muttered to myself.

Ariana, the merchant in whose wagon I had secured passage to Arcadie, our kingdom's capital, had warned me not to go too far but I'd been supremely confident. After all, if I didn't know the woods, I didn't know anything. Turns out I didn't know anything.

In some ways this revelation wasn't much of a surprise. I had been born in my family's remote house and had slept there every night since, except for the last six in the back of Ariana's wagon.

"Should have been paying more attention instead of daydreaming about ArcadieeeEEK!"

My recriminations turned into a particularly embarrassing shriek at a sudden clap of thunder. I instinctively looked around to check that no one had heard me. My brothers would be laughing over my fright for days. But then I remembered that my brothers weren't here – that, in fact, I was completely alone. Three big drops suddenly fell off a branch and ran down the back of my neck and I had to gulp and angle my face upwards to prevent an equally large tear from slipping out of my eye.

As much as I love my brothers, I hadn't expected to miss them after only a week. I could picture them all clearly, sitting around our worn kitchen table or gathered around the fireplace. I wondered if they were thinking of me. Perhaps they were talking of me or my mother was retelling her favourite story – my birth.

My birth had been unspectacular, although I was instantly pronounced beautiful. This was despite the fact that I imagine I was born, like most babies, looking thoroughly displeased with the process of birth. I think my alleged beauty had a lot more to do with my being a girl than my physical appearance. It seems that after four boys this was a delightful change. Some people think that being both the baby and the only girl I must have led a spoiled life. I can only say those people clearly do not have four brothers.

Apparently I was only an hour old when I received my first brotherly poke. Now a poke may not seem like much to you but I'm told I didn't appreciate it then (after all I'd just been through a very traumatic experience) and I still don't appreciate it now.

My brothers weren't intentionally cruel but they just could not understand that their endless pinches, pokes and slaps truly hurt me. They would leave my arms, legs and sides throbbing for hours. I had accepted early on that I was more physically sensitive than others and that my pain threshold was very low but my brothers couldn't seem to accept it.

I quickly learnt that outsmarting them was my only hope of living pain free. That or keeping them too entertained to think of harassing me. That's what got me started on story-telling. I figured if Scheherazade could keep her head attached to her shoulders with her stories, I could at least keep myself free from poking.

Stories were the constant under-current of village life and I discovered at a young age that I had a knack for giving old stories a new twist. And even for coming up with new ones altogether. If I carefully chose the stories I invented for my brothers, who can blame me? And if the stories tended towards the 'young man is polite to unlikely person who turns out to be a godmother and goes on to help him marry a rich and beautiful princess' type then all the better. My stories were more likely to involve a hedgehog princess than a frog prince but they still ended in true love and happily ever after as all good stories should. And if the hedgehog fell in love with a simple woodcutter after observing how lovingly he treated his mother and sisters, who could blame me?

My parents approved of my story telling because they approved of anything that kept us sitting still in a house that wasn't big enough for the rough and tumble of four large boys. Winter nights could be very long and while they may have secretly agreed that I needed a little toughening up – after all, woodcutting is hardly a trade for weaklings – they very quickly lost patience with my brothers' preferred methods.

Thinking of those warm winter evenings and imagining my family sitting around the fire threw my current miserable situation into stark relief.

That's it Alyssa! I thought sternly. No more messing around trying to find the camp. The woods are crisscrossed with roads. Pick a direction and start walking, once you find a road you only have to follow it and eventually you'll find some sort of shelter.

By now more and more drops were making it through the canopy so I started moving at a sort of shuffling jog, trying to cover as much ground as possible while not ending up flat on my face in the dark.

It was hard to tell how much time had passed but I thought it must have been nearly an hour and I still hadn't found a road. Luckily the ground was fairly flat – I had pretty good stamina as long I wasn't going uphill. I had also stayed pretty warm for the first half of my walk thanks to my movement and my warm cloak. The cloak had been a farewell gift from my mother and was the most beautiful thing I had ever owned. It had been a wedding gift, put away in a cupboard as too fine for everyday use. It was much better quality than any of my other clothes.

But the rain was now crashing through the trees and I was thoroughly drenched, shivering violently and with an ache in my eyes and head from the constant strain of trying to see through the darkness.

I had been talking fairly sternly to myself the whole way but was still feeling uncomfortably close to desperation when I finally saw the light. It was just a flicker and was swallowed up by the trees almost immediately but I changed direction to veer towards it anyway. 'Any port in a storm' they say and this was rapidly becoming a very bad storm. The wind was picking up and I could hear branches creaking in the most ominous manner possible. The thought of a branch, or even a tree, falling and pinning me underneath it - leaving me trapped and in pain for endless hours – made me swallow back a sob and start to move faster.

After only a minute I saw the light again and this time it steadied, beckoning me forward. Now that I could see somewhat I began to run and I saw that the trees ended just ahead of me. I had soon run out from under the leaves and was crossing a large garden, the rain almost blinding me with its force. I focused on my feet, to avoid slipping and falling, but cast one quick glance upwards to see what I was running towards. It was a stone building, far larger than any I had seen before, but it was hard to make out any details through the rain.

Sheltered as I had been in my village, I still knew there was only one building this could be. The royal winter castle. Normally I wouldn't have dreamt of approaching it but now I didn't even hesitate as I ran towards the large wooden front doors. When I reached them I lifted the heavy bronze door knocker and gave several hard knocks against the door. Unfortunately these perfectly coincided with one of the loudest, longest cracks of thunder yet. As soon as the thunder faded away, I lifted the knocker and rapped again, even more enthusiastically.

I tried to listen for the sounds of footsteps inside but the rain was coming down too hard and I no longer had even the minimal protection of the trees. I huddled right up against the door, trying to shield myself with the tiny overhang. This turned out to be another bad idea when the door was at last wrenched open, causing me to stumble forward into the entryway. I would have fallen if the footman who opened the door hadn't caught me.

For a second all I could take in was the blissful warmth. Then I looked around and observed a large stone entryway. The only light was coming from the lantern being held by the footman so I couldn't see the whole space. As the footman closed the door behind me, I observed a cold stone floor and impressive stairs that broke off half way up the flight to curve in opposite directions. A red carpet ran up the middle of the stairs and probably along the gallery at the top of them. I thought I saw a flicker of movement in the gallery and strained my eyes, trying to make out some more welcoming person than the footman who was now staring at me in silent surprise. But the movement was gone and I was distracted by the realisation that it wasn't as warm inside as I had first supposed. I began to shiver rather violently.

"Who are you?" The footman had finally found his voice and asked the question with equal amounts of surprise and disgust in his voice. I instinctively stiffened. My parents had always impressed on me the importance of being polite and if courtesy was taught in a woodcutter's cottage, I would definitely expect it to be taught in a castle. I determined to show him a polite way to address a complete stranger.

"My name is Alyssa. I'm so sorry to have disturbed you. I was separated from my group and caught in the storm. I must beg a place to shelter for the night." He seemed mildly impressed by my manner and I congratulated myself on having given him such a gentle and much needed lesson in manners.

"I guess I'd better get Dorkins," he said, his eyes lingering on the embroidered border of my cloak. This statement made no sense whatsoever to me but at least it was said in a friendlier tone.

"That would be appreciated, thank you," I replied, still determined to be polite. But when the footman promptly turned around and began to walk away I felt some stirrings of alarm. I took a couple of steps to follow him but he quickly turned back around.

"You stay here," he said. "You can't go tracking that all through the house." He pointed at the pile of water where I'd been standing.

"But... you can't leave me here," I gasped, my eyes focused on his lantern.

"Oh, right," he said and turned to fumble around in an alcove next to the door. When he swung back towards me he was holding a lit candle in a bronze candleholder. He held the candle out to me and I gratefully accepted it.

This time when he turned to leave I stayed in place, still shivering and hoping he would return quickly, preferably with a warm blanket. I looked around the entryway again, trying to distract myself from the cold. There were tapestries on the walls and it looked like there was a large fireplace in the wall to my left, next to the door that the footman had disappeared through. But I couldn't make out the details of anything, it was much too dark with only a candle.

Again my attention was pulled up towards the gallery but this time with a noise. I wondered again if there could be someone up there but the light of the candle was much too weak for me to see anything. I was just debating whether or not I should call out to my potential company when I heard a louder sound of movement from my left. Before I had time to do anything other than turn around, a tall, middle aged and solemn looking man came through the doorway and moved towards me.

He was also carrying a lantern and was being trailed by the footman who now looked rather sheepish. The tall man gave me a swift glance up and down, taking in my bedraggled state and then, to my surprise, gave a slight bow and spoke.

"I am Dorkins, their majesties' butler. I apologise for your reception – we weren't expecting you." He paused here as if he was waiting for me to say something so I said,

"Thank you. I don't want to be any trouble, I simply need some hospitality for the night."

"Of course," he said. "If you will follow me. I've already sent the housekeeper ahead to prepare the room."

"Thank you," I said again, this time with more feeling.

I expected him to turn back towards that doorway to the left but he began to walk towards the stairs. I followed him and the footman would have followed me if Dorkins hadn't gestured for him to go back the way they had come. Once he had disappeared from sight Dorkins seemed to unbend a little and even smiled graciously at me. Some of my nervous energy began to dissipate and my feet started to drag a little. I was so very cold and tired.

When we reached the break in the stairs, Dorkins led me up the left branch and then down the left gallery. As we walked, he said,

"My apologies for the footman. Naturally he is not in their majesties' confidence and cannot be expected to handle anything out of the ordinary."

I didn't reply to this as I couldn't think of a single thing to say. What did being in their majesties' confidence have to do with anything? His words reminded me that it was winter and the royal family must therefore be in residence at the castle. I began to wonder if I had committed some huge social solecism by coming to the front door.

Luckily Dorkins didn't seem to expect a response but stopped and opened one of the doors lining the gallery to our right. He gave another bow and gestured for me to precede him into the room. I did so and was surprised to hear the door click shut behind me. I whipped around but Dorkins was gone and I was only facing a closed wooden door. I slowly turned back around to face the room and now I began to feel very confused and a bit apprehensive.

The room was large and sumptuously furnished. Across from the door was a row of windows but they were hidden behind thick red velvet curtains. Next to the windows was a set of armchairs, also covered in red velvet and to my right was a small desk and chair made out of pine. In the far corner, to my left was a fire that had clearly just been lit but was already beginning to glow cheerfully. I barely had time to register the narrow four poster bed, on a slight dais also to my left, before my feet were moving unconsciously towards the fire.

When I reached the fire, I heard a noise behind me and once again whipped around. This time I saw a young girl, around my own age emerging from a doorway I hadn't noticed in the wall next to the desk. She smiled nervously when she saw me and dipped a small curtsey. Then she hurried towards me, already talking.

"Why miss, you must be freezing, wet through like that. You'll catch your death!" As she spoke, she took the candle from my hand and placed it on a small table next to the bed. Then she took off my wet cloak. This she allowed to fall into a wet pile on the floor and next she began to undo my dress. I only half noticed what she was doing, much too distracted by the warmth coming from the fire. The whole time she kept up a distracted monologue about the storm outside and the state of my clothes and hair and before I knew what had happened she'd completely stripped me down and was asking me to lift my arms so she could put a long, dry nightgown over my head.

When I obeyed, I found myself enveloped in the softest, most beautiful material I'd ever felt. It was pure white but had elaborate embroidery around the neckline, wrists and hem. I wondered why anyone would put so much effort into a garment that was only worn to bed. And then I began to feel uneasy again. This was not a room or a nightgown for a woodcutter's daughter. It was something more suited to a princess.

"I think there's been a mistake," I said to the girl helping me and she froze, her arms full of my wet clothes which she was gathering up from the floor.

"Oh no," she said quickly, "there couldn't be. Mr Dorkins never makes mistakes." I now noticed the curiosity in her gaze and began to feel even more uncomfortable.

"This room, this gown, it's much too nice. Do all the guests here get treated the same?" I asked.

"Oh yes," she breathed, her eyes shining. "Their majesties are famous for their hospitality.

"Oh, well…" I trailed off uncertainly.

"You just hop straight into bed," she told me. "I've put a warming pan between your sheets so it will be nice and toasty for you." This comment drew my attention towards the bed and the idea of climbing in, between the toasty sheets, began to override my lingering concerns. I took a step towards it and the girl smiled.

"That's right, just climb up and don't worry about a thing until morning. I'll set your clothes out to dry and bring them back first thing." She turned around at that and left the room through the door I had entered, leaving me to climb up onto the bed on my own.

This turned out to be a surprisingly difficult feat as there seemed to be at least two mattresses on top of the bed. But I managed to clamber rather inelegantly up and pulled back the blankets, slipping between the sheets. I was overwhelmed by the warmth of the bed and the tingling relief of my feet now that they were relieved of my weight. I blew out the candle and prepared to fall instantly asleep.

Unfortunately, before I had time to get more than drowsy, my initial comfort wore off. Although the pillow was the perfect density and the sheets seemed to be made from the same soft material as my nightgown, the mattress had an uncomfortable lump in the middle of my back. I rolled over onto my side but the bed was so narrow, I could still feel it. I sighed in frustration. I was sure a normal person would have just ignored it, as tired as I was, and gone straight to sleep. But I'd never been able to cope with physical discomfort. I knew the pain would distract me too much for sleep. I figured it must be a spring that had broken through the covering of the top mattress. I considered getting up, stripping the bed, pulling off the top mattress and putting the sheets onto the bottom mattress. But I doubted I'd have the strength to pull off the top mattress and I had no idea how to call back the girl who had been helping me. The idea of attempting to relight my candle from the fire and then wandering around the cold, dark castle was so unappetising I didn't even contemplate it. Instead I twisted around and curled my body into a C shape. If I did that, I could just fit my body between the spring and the edge of the bed without rolling off. With the digging pain gone I was asleep within seconds.

Chapter 2

This time when I woke up, I stayed awake. I woke up because I had rolled over in my sleep and was once again lying on the spring. I quickly shifted back into my curled position but unlike all the other times, I wasn't able to drop back to sleep. Enough light was coming in around the edges of the curtains to tell me it was well and truly day time and I was now well rested enough that sleep couldn't overcome the stiffness I was feeling. My back and neck were protesting my unnatural sleeping position and my legs were aching from my run through the woods last night. I tried to stretch myself out straight and nearly rolled off the bed. I quickly rolled back into the centre of the mattress and lay on the spring, grimacing as I did so.

"What are you doing?" said a young-sounding and rather beautiful voice. I flinched and quickly scanned the room, trying to find its owner. It definitely wasn't the girl from the night before.

While I looked around, the voice spoke again. "Who are you?" As she finished speaking I finally spotted her and realised it wasn't a 'her' but a 'them'. Two identical girls who looked as beautiful as they sounded were sitting on the floor and gazing up at me. When they saw that I was fully awake, one of them got up and went over to the heavy velvet curtains and pulled them open. The room flooded with light and I groaned and covered my eyes.

When I cautiously inched them open I saw that she had returned to the floor and I was once again being regarded by four large eyes. Very blue eyes above perfect straight noses and beneath perfectly curled bright golden hair. The girls were identical and so beautiful they had to be –

"This is the Princess Room," the one on the left said. "Are you a princess?" I almost groaned again and all the uncertainty from the night before came flooding back. I was certain now that the lofty Dorkins had made a mistake despite the maid's belief in his infallibility. Why would he have put me in the 'Princess Room' otherwise?

"I'm Alyssa," I said, "and I'm not a princess. I just lost my way in the storm last night and the butler gave me this room to sleep in."

"Well, if Dorkins put you in here you must be a princess," said the girl on the right. "Only visiting princesses get this room."

Oh, great. Who knew what sort of trouble I'd be in now. But I definitely hadn't said I was a princess! This was definitely not my fault.

"Well then, there must have been some sort of mistake." I swung my legs off the bed and they dangled down the side, not touching the floor due to the height of the bed and the two mattresses. "There was a girl in here last night. She took my clothes to dry and was going to return them. Have you seen her?" I peered around as I spoke, hoping to see my dress and cloak laid out somewhere for me.

"Oh yes. We sent her away because you weren't awake yet," said the girl on the left. That got my attention.

"Did she leave my clothes?"

"No, we told her to take them away. They weren't very nice," said the girl on the left again. Now I felt angry. I might be a youngest child, and there was the possibility these girls might be princesses, but I knew how to deal with difficult children.

"Well, you'll have to go and find her then and retrieve my clothes yourself. They may not be to your taste but they're the only clothes I have with me. I can hardly walk around in this nightgown." I spoke briskly and with authority and kept my eye trained sternly on the twins.

"Oh no, we have a much nicer dress for you to wear," said the one on the right who I now noticed had slightly paler eyes but slightly brighter hair than her sister.

"One more fit for a princess," agreed her darker-eyed sister, "you just need to come with us to our rooms. It's not far."

These girls might live in a castle but they were still children and my patience had run out. I slid off the bed and stood towering above them to give me added authority.

"That is enough of this talk of princesses. I've already told you I'm not a princess and I will not be going anywhere until you go and fetch my clothes." I crossed my arms and glared down at them.

The darker-eyed one stood up and stepped towards me, smiling sweetly. "I'm sorry if we've made a mistake," she said, "are you really not a princess?"

I relaxed my pose and smiled back at her. She was just a little child after all, not more than twelve years old. "No I'm really not a princess", I replied, "but no harm done, if you could just –"

But before I could finish the girl's expression changed to triumph and she cut me off.

"Well we *are* princesses. And if you're not, that means you have to do what we say!" she announced with satisfaction in her tone. "And we say you have to come with us to our rooms – now!"

I stared at her in astonishment but before I could think of anything to say, her sister leapt to her feet and they each took one of my hands and started tugging me towards the door.

I could have stopped them, of course, but I was now feeling a little unsure. I was probably in enough trouble already without the princesses complaining of me to their butler, or worse, their

28

parents. So I let myself be dragged out of the room and down the corridor. Maybe I wasn't quite as good at dealing with difficult children as I thought.

The twins pulled me further along the left hand gallery and then across to a door coming off the left hand side.

"My name is Lily," said the darker-eyed one so I knew the other must be Princess Sophie. I counted up in my head and realised they must be eleven.

"This whole side of the gallery is for us and Max," said Sophie proudly. "You were on the guest side."

"And their majesties?" I asked anxiously, dropping my eyes to the ground so I wouldn't be in danger of seeing one of my sovereigns emerging from their bedchamber.

"Oh no," laughed Sophie, "they have the whole East Wing to themselves. You know, the right-hand gallery." When she saw how relieved I looked she laughed again. Neither girl seemed angry with me for speaking to them so sternly before.

The door that Lily now pulled open led into a bright and spacious room that seemed to be half schoolroom, half playroom. The opposite wall was lined with high windows and to the left was a large fireplace with a small fire and several armchairs in front of it. To the right were several desks grouped together and behind them was the largest dollhouse I had ever seen. There was a door in both the left and right hand walls and the left door was open showing a large bedroom with two four-poster beds. Both rooms were as elegantly and expensively decorated as my guestroom had been, although the colour scheme here was pink and green and the rooms had a lived in look that the guestroom lacked.

I could see a slipper poking from beneath one of the armchairs, the desks were covered in several layers of paper and four abandoned dolls lay in strange positions around the dollhouse. It looked like the kind of room I dreamt of for myself while I lay in my tiny bed in my family's cottage. Reluctantly I felt myself softening towards Lily and Sophie. They had a beautiful room but they were still eleven-year-old girls and must be bored in this great drafty castle buried in the woods. Perhaps they were simply curious and had no malicious intent. Curious I could handle.

While I was examining the room, both girls had run off into the bedroom and they now returned carrying a dress. Lily was holding the shoulders and Sophie was supporting the long skirt so it didn't brush against the ground.

"This," said Lily reverently, "is our Princess Dress." This made me laugh which earned me two identically reproachful looks.

"Since you're princesses, isn't every one of your dresses a princess dress?" I asked.

Sophie looked surprised but Lily appeared to give this comment some serious thought. "I suppose you could say that," she said, "but this is a grown-up princess dress. So it's different. We thought you could wear it."

"Even though it turns out I'm not a princess?" I asked, struggling to keep a straight face.

"Well, you look like a princess, so we think it's okay," Lily replied.

My amusement changed to shock. "Look like a princess? Me?" Now, I don't normally consider myself to have any kind of false modesty. I know that I'm quite pretty, I've even been called very lovely. But I definitely don't have the classical beauty of the twins.

"You have golden hair and blue eyes. Like a princess," explained Sophie.

Now I felt like laughing again. My hair is blonde but not the pure gold of the twins, in fact the streaks in it are closer to red than blonde. And my hair would be more accurately described as wavy rather than curly. I certainly don't have the twins' perfect ringlets. And my eyes do have a little blue in them but were always described by my mother as green.

"I don't think all princesses have blonde hair and blue eyes. Although many princesses certainly do," I added quickly.

"Well it's the only grown-up-sized dress we have," said Lily, in a practical vein. "So you'll have to wear it."

I considered my situation for a silent moment. If I was right and the princesses were bored, it might be possible to bribe them.

"How about a story?" I suggested. "If you like it, you promise to go and get my own clothes for me." I tried to look calm and unconcerned, like the adult they seemed to think me.

"What sort of story?" asked Lily suspiciously.

"Oh, one about princesses, of course," I said. "Two princesses, in fact. Twin princesses." Both girls' eyes got large.

"Just like us! We've never heard a story about two princesses," Sophie cried enthusiastically and I knew I had them.

Chapter 3

"And they lived happily ever after," I finished, snuggling a little deeper into the comfortable armchair.

"That was the best story I've ever heard," announced Sophie.

I smiled in satisfaction. "I'm glad you enjoyed it. And that means you have to go get my own clothes for me. That was the deal."

"We never agreed to the deal," said Lily. "And anyway, we can't get your clothes, we told Mathilde to burn them."

I stared at her smug look in shock. It seemed princesses were a great deal more devious in person than they were in stories. Even half-sized princesses.

I could feel the anger inside, a tight pressure in my chest, straining to spread and engulf me. How dare these children burn my clothes! What had I ever done to them? I leapt to my feet and began pacing up and down in front of the fire, glaring at the girls.

I opened my mouth to give the two pampered, spoiled little…. *princesses* the harshest scolding they'd ever received in their short lives. Luckily, before I could say something that I would regret, the door opened and a young man came into the room.

The first thing I noticed was that he was looking at me and he looked angry. This was so unexpected that my own anger faded away. The second thing I noticed was that he was clearly the twin's older brother – crown prince Maximilian – and he was extremely good-looking. His features were heavier than theirs, more masculine, but he had the same straight nose and bright blue eyes. His hair was much darker, a brown closer to black than golden, but the family resemblance was still striking. I had heard that our prince was the most handsome in three generations (princes being less exclusively good-looking than princesses) but I wasn't prepared for the effect of seeing so much attractive masculinity with my own eyes. For once in my life I couldn't think what to say but stared at him in silence. Then he spoke and his words snapped me out of my confusion.

"Who's she? You girls shouldn't have a stranger in your room – she could be anyone." My mouth almost fell open I was so surprised at his aggressive words and rude tone. This was not at all how I had imagined a prince would behave. The twins were children and so had some small excuse for their lack of courtesy. The prince, if I remembered rightly, was nineteen and therefore had none at all.

"Excuse me!" I said quickly. "I'm standing right here and can speak for myself, your *High*ness. Just because I was raised in a woodcutter's cottage doesn't mean I don't deserve some basic courtesy. And someone raised in a palace should know that!"

His eyes moved from his sisters to my face and stayed there for several moments. I returned his look challengingly.

"My apologies, woodcutter's daughter," he said formally. "May I know your name and what you're doing in my sisters' room?"

"My name is Alyssa and I'm here under sufferance, your highness," I replied. "Your sisters have basically kidnapped me."

"Kidnapped you! Good gracious!" Although I hadn't meant my words humorously, I seemed to have surprised a smile onto his face. "And how did two eleven-year-olds manage to do that?"

"Very simply," I replied. "They took away my clothes and had them destroyed." I felt my cheeks flushing as my previous anger returned.

At my words, Prince Maximilian's eyes dropped down to the nightgown I was wearing and suddenly I wasn't the only one flushing. But whatever he was feeling, he mastered it quickly, his look of reserve returning.

"I apologise for their behaviour," he said stiffly. "I will speak to the servants and have some replacement clothes found for you so you can be on your way again."

The subtext was clear — the sooner I was on my way the better. Well that was fine by me.

"I would appreciate it, your highness," I said and swept into as deep a curtsy as I could manage with the nightgown. Unfortunately, the nightgown didn't allow for very graceful movement and I heard one of the twins let out a giggle behind me.

For a second a sparkle in the prince's eye made me think he would join them in their laughter but if he felt any amusement it was swiftly quashed. Instead, he gave me a small bow, turned and strode out of the room.

I let out a big breath and collapsed back into the armchair. What an insufferable boy! Even as I thought it, I could feel a smile creeping across my face. Mmmm, he was good-looking, though. My body began to shake with an internal laugh at my own foolishness.

"He's not normally like that," said Lily, frowning at the now closed door. "He's normally pretty nice. For a brother," she added quickly.

I looked at her skeptically and figured maybe he was nice — to his sisters. Apparently just not to strange girls who wandered in from the forest. Actually, when put like that perhaps it wasn't so surprising. Before I could follow this thought any further, I was interrupted by the sound of a bell being rung from somewhere outside the room.

"Quick!" and "Breakfast!" shouted the twins over the top of one another. And before I realised what was happening they had picked their dress back up, deposited it in my arms, pushed me into their bedroom and shut the door behind me.

I stared at the door in surprise and then down at the dress in my hands. For a moment I considered refusing to put it on. I could always just stay here in the princesses' bedroom until the prince had some normal clothes delivered.

But I had no reliance on the twins leaving me be. Besides I was longing to be dressed. Then I could get away from the princesses and find some clothes for myself. With this thought in mind, I pulled off the nightgown, laying it on one of the beds, and slid the dress over my head.

It settled around my neck and onto my hips and I saw with relief that it was the right length for me and wouldn't drag along the floor, tripping me up.

"Girls!" I called and the door popped open, both princesses tumbling into the room. "I need you to fasten the dress for me."

Lily ran to my back while Sophie just stood and gazed at me. "It's perfect," she said, "just how I imagined."

I smiled, finding their delight infectious. It was certainly a very beautiful dress. White and gold with a scooped neckline and a fitted bodice, the material hugged my sides all the way down to my hips before falling away into a full skirt. A golden ribbon rested along the line of my hips and was tacked at the front to form an off-centre V. The two ends fell almost the length of the dress and fluttered when I moved. The dress was accented with beautiful gold embroidery and the whole thing was very heavy. The weight of the material and the swishing of the skirt made me feel like an actual princess. I lifted my head up and straightened my spine. Surely Dorkins couldn't exact too heavy a punishment on me while I wore this dress. Maybe he would even be fooled, like Lily and Sophie, into thinking I was a princess. At least long enough for me to find some normal clothes and slip away into the woods.

The daydream lasted only for a moment. If I did slip off I would be no better than before – still lost in the woods with no idea how to get back to the merchants. No, I would have to tell the truth and ask for help. I had no money on me, what little I had was back in Ariana's wagon. But I was sure my aunt in Arcadie would be willing to pay a fair journey price to anyone who helped me reach the capital. Once I had a job I could pay her back.

While I had been thinking about the best way forward the twins had been herding me out the door and I now found myself back out in the corridor. I was still in bare feet but the length of the dress hid my toes and the carpet was soft under my feet.

"Come on, Alyssa, I'm starving" moaned Sophie pulling on one of my hands.

Lily grabbed my other hand and together they pulled me along the corridor and down the wide staircase I'd come up the night before. I tried to pull away from them towards the door beside the fireplace but they were towing me in the other direction. Now that it was daylight, I could see an open archway leading to a long corridor on the opposite side of the hall to the fireplace. Various doors came off both sides of this corridor but the twins didn't stop until they reached the final door on the left side.

I felt a twinge of misgiving about what might be on the other side of the door but before I could ask them, Sophie had pushed the door open and Lily had walked through it, still clutching tightly to my hand.

My first impression was of light. The opposite wall was lined with windows and the whole room glowed with the morning sun. A large table filled the length of the room and the wall beside me was lined with a long buffet. The smells coming from the dishes lining this bench were so delicious I could feel my stomach grumble. But before I had done more than register my hunger, I felt it transform into nausea. There were three people in the room, sitting around the table and I recognised them immediately.

Seated at the head of the table was a middle-aged man whose face was familiar from royal portraits. He had the same dark hair as the prince but his eyes were a piercing grey and his face was lined and more tired-looking in person than in paint. At the foot of the table was an elegant lady wearing a blue robe and a small tiara.

She was easily the most beautiful woman I had ever seen, her age giving her an elegance and gravity that only enhanced her beauty. It was obvious that all three of her children had their blue eyes from her and although her golden hair was piled on her head, I guessed that it would fall in perfect ringlets. The twins' youthful beauty was startling because they were identical but I suspected that the queen had been more beautiful than her daughters when she was their age.

All of this I took in in the first few seconds and then my eyes fell on Prince Maximilian. He was staring at me with shock and something that looked almost like hunger. His expression was so intense it scared me a little. My unease only grew when his expression changed to the same angry scowl he'd worn earlier.

"That is not the dress I had sent to you," he snapped. "And I thought you were leaving."

The king and queen had been looking at me with expressions of slight surprise but they now turned their surprise towards their son. I felt myself flushing when I realised how his words could be construed.

"Really, Max," said his mother gently. She turned to me, "and who are you? I don't think we've met before."

She stood up and came around the table, holding out her hand to me. "I'm Queen Eleanor and this is King Henry," she gestured at the king.

I took her hand and curtseyed as deeply as I could. "I'm Alyssa, your majesty. I'm so sorry to disturb your breakfast. I think there's been some mistake. I was looking for Dorkins but the princesses brought me here."

The queen smiled and it wasn't until I saw the way her smile lit up her face that I realised how sad she had looked before.

"My daughters certainly know how to impose their will when they want to," she said, her eyes flashing towards the king and then quickly back to me. "A royal trait I suppose. It seems I must apologise for all my children, we are being poor hosts indeed. But I admit, I didn't know we had any guests." Her tone turned the statement into a gentle question.

"No, no, I'm here quite by accident," I rushed to explain myself. "I was travelling to Arcadie with a group of merchants and got lost in the woods. I couldn't find my way back in the storm last night so I sought shelter here. Dorkins kindly gave me a room but I'm not sure..." I trailed off wondering how to explain the mistake I was sure had been made with the room.

"I see," said Queen Eleanor but I could tell from her expression she was still confused. "If you were caught in the storm then that would explain why you're wearing my dress."

I gasped and grabbed at the dress, for one unthinking moment meaning to pull it off and hand it to her. But I could hardly undress in front of the entire royal family! Instead I stammered an apology that the queen quickly cut off.

"It's quite alright my dear, it's an old dress. I gave it to the girls years ago to use for dress ups. It was one of the first dresses made for me after I became a princess. Knowing my daughters, I imagine they forced you into it - would you or wouldn't you."

I smiled at her in relief. "It was a little like that, your majesty."

"Alyssa is our friend even if she's not a princess," said Sophie. "We found her early this morning in the Princess Room and she's been keeping us company."

"Nanny is sick again," added Lily.

"The Princess Room?" The queen looked at me with sharp curiosity in her face.

"As I mentioned, a mistake, your majesty. I'm not a princess," I hurried to explain, "I don't know why Dorkins put me in that beautiful room. I promise you I never said I was a princess."

"I think I know how the mistake was made," she replied, "I'm sure it wasn't your fault. But tell me how did you sleep?"

She was looking at me rather intently but she'd been so nice that I decided to tell her the truth. After all, they would want to fix that spring before an actual princess came to stay.

I opened my mouth to explain about the bed and my poor sleep but out of the corner of my eye I saw the prince, still staring at me. I suddenly remembered my own words to him earlier on polite behaviour. And here I was, after everything that had been done for me, about to complain about the bed I'd been given! I quickly changed my words.

"It was the nicest room I've ever slept in, your majesty. Much too nice for me. And Mathilde even lit a fire for me so I was nice and warm - such a relief after being out in the storm."

There, that was polite and still true.

"Excellent, I'm glad you passed a comfortable night," said the queen, her expression not quite matching her words.

I couldn't tell if she was pleased or disappointed and I certainly couldn't interpret the look she flashed at King Henry. Something was going on here that I didn't understand and I found myself studying them all curiously. They might be royalty but they were still people and nothing fascinated me as much as people. I wondered how long it would take me to understand them. They certainly seemed to act very strangely and not at all how I had imagined royalty would act. Then I remembered that I would soon be back on my way to Arcadie. I couldn't imagine that I would meet the royal family again after this and I suddenly felt unreasonably disappointed. I would never get the chance to understand their behaviour - they would all remain a mystery to me. I hated not being able to figure someone out.

The door opened and Dorkins came into the room followed by a footman carrying a large silver coffeepot on a silver tray. The footman walked over to the king and began to pour his coffee but Dorkins looked my way. I shivered a little. The queen had said it wasn't my fault but Dorkins still made me nervous.

The queen turned towards Dorkins and smiled at him.

"It seems there has been a misunderstanding, Dorkins," she said. "When I asked you to prepare the red room for a guest I didn't mean that I expected an imminent visitor. I merely wanted to review the room's layout and preparedness. We will soon be expecting several royal visitors," this time her eyes flickered towards her son, "but none of them will be arriving until we return to Arcadie. I was merely occupying myself by testing the room." Her voice lingered strangely over the word test and the prince shot her a sharp look.

I also looked over at the prince and almost laughed at the expression of dismay on his face. He looked exactly how I imagined one of my brothers would look if they heard they were to expect a stream of royal visitors. Gaining this small insight into one of them made me feel a little more secure.

Dorkins, meanwhile, looked as horrified as it was possible for such a stately man to look.

"Your majesty, I apologise for the mistake."

The queen cut him off before he could continue. "No, indeed Dorkins, there has been no harm done and I'm delighted we were able to offer shelter to such a charming subject."

While I had been talking to the queen and Dorkins, the princesses had served themselves breakfast and taken seats at the table. They had been listening with apparent interest to our conversation but were now also eating enthusiastically. The king, on the other hand, didn't seem to have been paying us any attention at all. Instead, he had been steadily regarding his daughters. He now addressed them both.

"Did one of you say Nanny was sick again?"

Lily nodded, her mouth full.

"My goodness, old Martha seems to be sick a lot these days."

He considered for a moment, oblivious to the fact that the rest of us were now staring at him.

"I haven't heard a sound all morning. And I'm sure Dorkins would have informed me by now if some silent disaster had occurred." He now turned his considering gaze onto me. "Did the girls say that you kept them entertained?"

I wasn't quite sure how to answer this. "Well, I did tell them a story, your majesty."

"Excellent! You're hired!" he announced and turned back to his breakfast. A strange feeling of unreality crept over me. Perhaps it wasn't all of them who were behaving strangely after all, perhaps it was I who'd gone mad. Or perhaps I was still asleep and dreaming.

"H-hired?" I stammered.

The king looked back up at me. "Certainly. Didn't you say you were going to Arcadie? Looking for a job I assume."

So he had been paying attention to my conversation after all. I filed away the thought that he was sharper than he looked.

"No need to go all the way to Arcadie for a job. You can have one right here. And we'll take you back to Arcadie with us in the Spring."

"Thank you, your majesty. But what do you want me to do?" I glanced around the room. Dorkins looked disapproving, the queen amused and the prince horrified. I wondered if I looked as bewildered as I felt.

"Look after the princesses, of course. Their starched up governess refuses to look after them outside of lesson time and that nanny of theirs is getting too old. Well, obviously she must be, since she can't seem to get out of bed without coming down with some new ailment. And here you are like a gift from heaven. Never met the girls before in your life and kept them quiet all morning." Some of the bewilderment must still have been apparent on my face because he added, darkly "Very early risers, the twins."

Despite myself I began to feel amused. I remembered my own earlier thoughts on how bored the girls must get, stuck in this isolated castle with no other children. And I already had experience of just how much of a handful they could be. I briefly wondered if I would come to regret taking them on. But I couldn't deny that the king's proposal solved all my problems in one fell swoop.

"Thank you, your majesty," I replied, "I would be honoured."

"Excellent," he said and stood up. "Dorkins, could you come along to my study. I have some business to discuss with you." Dorkins nodded his assent and held open the door for the king. In another breath they were both gone.

42

"Mother!" It was Prince Maximilian. "He can't have been serious! We don't know anything about her. How do we know she's a proper person to look after the girls?"

The prince was carefully not looking my way and I wondered why he found me so offensive. Not that his question was entirely without merit...

"Your father has made up his mind," said the queen "and his word is final." Her tone gentled a little, "You know he has excellent judgment. And she certainly seems well-mannered to me."

They regarded each other silently for a moment. The prince clenched his jaw but nodded once before jumping to his feet and striding out of the room.

Sophie looked up from her eggs, "Whatever's the matter with Max, Mother?"

The queen laughed, a deep, musical sound. "Boys, my darling. Who can hope to understand them?"

She smiled around at us all equally and I realised the footman had left some time ago. There were only girls left now. So I allowed myself to smile in response and feel for a moment like I was part of this small group.

"Please get some breakfast and sit down," the queen said, gesturing towards the buffet. "As usual it is left to us females to work out all the practical details." Her smile suggested she was content with this role.

I picked up a plate and took some eggs and fried ham. I poured a glass of water and sat down across from the twins.

"I think we'll have to give you the title of Princess Companion," said Queen Eleanor. "It's been a long time since we had anyone in the role – not since Mina got married. But you certainly don't look anything like a nanny in that dress!"

I vaguely remembered that Princess Mina was King Henry's sister. She had married a foreign prince before I was born and left Arcadia. I felt uneasily sure that her Princess Companion had been a young noblewoman from the court. I opened my mouth to protest but Lily jumped in before I could say anything.

"We're much too old to need a nanny anyway."

"Very true, my darling. Your father was quite right, I should have thought of it before now."

Although they all seemed quite happy with the arrangement, I couldn't help but feel I was a fraud. And they were bound to discover it sooner or later.

"This dress is certainly very beautiful, your majesty, but it's nothing like my own clothes. I'm only a woodcutter's daughter. Surely Princess Companion is too high a title for me. There must be many people more fitted in rank for such a position."

"I suppose there are," said the queen, quietly. "But unfortunately such people tend to bore my daughters. I assure you, it's not an easy position we're offering. And anyway, none of these more eligible companions are here at the winter castle. If you don't like the role, you can always leave after we return to Arcadie. And you'll receive a generous wage in the meantime."

That was an appealing thought. Only half an hour ago, I'd been contemplating arriving in Arcadie with a debt to repay. And now I would arrive with gold in my pocket. I gave an internal shrug. I had made a full disclosure now; if the queen didn't mind I wouldn't cavil further. Most likely they would get rid of me when they returned to the court in Arcadie in the Spring.

The thought didn't bother me, I was sure there would be plenty of other jobs in the capital. And if I worked hard all winter, hopefully I could leave with a royal reference. That would be sure to open doors otherwise closed to an inexperienced woodcutter's daughter from the deep forest.

"Very well, your majesty," I replied.

"And what of these merchants? Will they be waiting for you? Should we send someone to inform them of your whereabouts?" asked the queen.

With sudden dismay I thought of Ariana - how could I have forgotten her? She would be worrying for me I knew. But I also knew that the other merchants would never agree to delay their journey for my sake. I tried to think what Ariana would do.

"I don't think they'll wait for me. I'm not their responsibility and it was my own foolishness to wander off and get lost. I'm sure Ariana will take my things to my aunt as soon as they reach Arcadie, though. If we could get word to my aunt then she would be able to reassure Ariana that I'm alright."

"That's easily done. Royal messengers travel between the castle and the capital regularly. If you write a letter and direct it to your aunt's address, I'll see it reaches her. In the meantime, I'll speak to Mrs Pine, our housekeeper, and get her to put together some clothes and things for you."

"You're very kind, your majesty," I said between bites of my slightly cold but still delicious breakfast.

"I'll be off now to speak to Mrs Pine. And also to Nanny and to Gretchen, the governess. I'll explain the situation to them." I could tell from her rueful expression that my arrival might be somewhat unwelcome to these ladies. I felt relieved that the queen would be preparing the way for me and a little nervous. If the other staff chose to do so, I was sure they could make my life very unpleasant.

The twins had been whispering together while the queen and I talked but as the queen left the room, they fell silent. I looked up to find four intent eyes boring into me.

"Are you finished?" asked Lily.

"Yes, we want to give you a tour," said Sophie.

I quickly scraped the remaining food from my plate, into my mouth.

"Finished!" I announced, and stood up.

Both girls ran around the table and Sophie opened the door, while Lily took my hand. She looked up into my face and smiled confidingly.

"I didn't really tell Mathilde to burn your clothes. I just wanted to see what you looked like in our Princess Dress," she said.

I almost smiled – I should have known. Lily and Sophie liked to get their own way but their imperiousness was put on. Just a game. Nevertheless I forced my face into a frown and reached out my other hand for Sophie. I pulled both girls in front of me and looked at them seriously.

"It was very wrong of you to lie to me. If we're going to be friends, I have to know that you'll always be honest with me. Can you promise that?"

Both girls looked down, embarrassed or ashamed, I wasn't sure which.

"Yes, we can promise," said Lily quietly.

"We really want to be friends," Sophie said earnestly.

"Ok," I said, allowing the smile to appear. "I'll hold you to that!"

The princesses smiled back at me and I dropped both of their hands, gesturing for them to precede me out of the room.

This was what I needed to remember. I didn't have many skills fit for a castle but one thing I could do was work with people. If I studied them long enough, I could understand them, and once I understood them I could always find a way to work with them. Or around them, if necessary. My brothers used to call it my gift. They would often joke that I must have received it from a godmother at my Christening.

They found this suggestion hugely funny because everyone knows it's only princesses who get gifted at their Christenings. If you're a girl you only get one chance - be born in a palace. My brothers on the other hand still held out hope for themselves - after all, my stories were always full of deserving woodcutter's sons receiving gifts.

But I never minded their teasing. I took pride in knowing that my gift was my own and not some magical enhancement. My brothers had spent their time studying trees but I had spent mine studying the people around me. And people were people after all, whether they lived in a forest or a castle.

I straightened my spine. Confidence was what I needed. I could do this.

Chapter 4

Although the winter castle seemed huge compared to the houses I was used to, I knew it was much smaller than the palace in Arcadie. It only took the twins half an hour to give me a full tour that first morning and there wasn't much chance of my getting lost. The layout was simple. The East Wing had the rooms used by the royal family - dining rooms, studies, receiving rooms - on the ground floor, and the king and queen's suites on the gallery. The West Wing had the kitchen and the rooms belonging to the servants on the ground floor while the gallery held both the prince and princesses' suites and the guest rooms.

The tour concluded in the princesses' suite where we found Queen Eleanor and two older ladies. I knew the housekeeper immediately by her air of calm authority – as powerful, in its own way, as that of the queen. Mrs Pine might rule a smaller domain but she ruled it nonetheless. I made a mental note not to cross her. The other lady was clearly the sickly nanny: she had white hair and the motherly look that the queen lacked. Lily and Sophie ran forward to hug her and besiege her with questions, leaving me free to be introduced to Mrs Pine.

"Mrs Pine, this is Alyssa," said the queen. "Please see that she has everything she needs, as we discussed. I'll leave her in your capable hands." Then she smiled at both of us and left the room.

I turned to Mrs Pine, determined not to let my nerves show.

"Thank you very much for going to all this trouble. I'm so sorry to be a bother but I've lost all my things. It's very tiresome of me, I know. But I assure you I'm not normally so stupid."

Mrs Pine looked me up and down. "Well, there's no harm done from the sound of things," she said briskly. "I've plenty of old things, left by various servants and visitors over the years.

It's a bit tricky to know what sort of dresses to give you. You're not exactly a servant but you're not a guest either." She sighed. "I'll manage, I'm sure. Mathilde tells me she's already met you so I'll give her whatever I find. If you have any questions about how things run here you can ask her. Although if you get into any real trouble you'd better come to me. Mathilde's likely to lose her head in a crisis."

I felt absolutely certain that there was no crisis big enough to make Mrs Pine lose her head.

And it was equally clear she didn't really believe my assurance that I wouldn't run into further trouble. If I wanted that reference at the end of the winter, I would just have to show her I could be trusted. And not only to look after myself but also after two precocious princesses.

"I'll be off now, but the princesses are supposed to be in lessons all morning so Gretchen, their governess, should be along soon. Once she has the girls in hand, you come and find Mathilde."

Mrs Pine's voice kept its level calm but something flashed in her eyes when she mentioned Gretchen. I noted it, but merely nodded to show I had understood her instructions.

When Mrs Pine left the room, I went to rescue Nanny. The poor old lady did look ill and both girls were still hanging off her.

"Lily! Sophie!" I said, rather sharply. "Give her some space. Come over here and introduce me."

Both girls let their nanny go and came over to my side.

"Nanny, this is Alyssa, she's going to be our new Companion," announced Lily.

"Doesn't she look beautiful in our dress," asked Sophie. I smiled at their enthusiasm and watched Nanny's reaction out of the corner of my eye. Mrs Pine might rule the staff but unless I was very much mistaken, it was Nanny who ruled Lily and Sophie's hearts. If she decided I was encroaching on her territory...

The old lady seemed torn, so I quickly held out my hand. "It's so nice to meet you, I'm afraid it's all happened rather quickly and I'm a little overwhelmed. I do hope you'll be able to show me how things work in here. I wouldn't want to upset the princesses' routines."

This deference won me a smile and a warm handshake.

"I'm Martha but everyone calls me Nanny, not just these graceless scamps." She smiled on the twins with real affection. "Now you two go and get your books together. You know Gretchen will be here to start your lessons soon."

"Not lessons," moaned Lily, "surely we can skip our lessons today. It's Alyssa's first day!"

"Absolutely not!" said Nanny. "You know what your royal father has said about your lessons."

Lily looked mulish for a moment but then sighed and walked away.

Once both girls had started moving towards their desks, Nanny led me into the bedroom.

"If I'm honest, it's a relief to have some help," she said as she crossed to the opposite side of the room. "My health has been poor for some years now and it's hard for me to keep up with the girls."

She opened a door I had thought was a closet and revealed a small alcove with a bed.

"Traditionally this is my bed but I'm often too sick to sleep up here now. Mrs Pine has a room for me down in the servant's wings and I'm down there often enough. The maids have to take it in turns sleeping up here when I can't and they hate it. This will be your bed now, though, so it's all working out for the best."

The alcove was tiny, literally just room for the bed. There seemed to be two drawers under the bed and I supposed this would be where I kept whatever clothes Mrs Pine managed to find for me. On the other hand, if the maids hated sleeping up here then hopefully they would see me as a rescuer and be predisposed to like me. That made the tiny space worth it.

Mrs Pine had put her finger on the issue when she said I wasn't quite a servant and wasn't quite a guest. I was going to have to work hard to keep the rest of the staff onside. A sudden mental flash of angry blue eyes made me realise that this didn't just apply to the servants. I sighed and reminded myself it would all be worth it in the end.

"I know it's very small but the bed is quite comfortable and you'll share the rest of the suite with the princesses," Nanny said with a worried look at me. She must have thought my sigh was one of dissatisfaction. I hurried to reassure her.

"It will be perfect for me and I'm delighted to be able to relieve you of the burden. It looks very comfortable. In fact, they put me in the princess room last night - a big misunderstanding - and this bed looks like it'll be more comfortable than the one in there. It was such a beautiful room but the bed had a loose spring that kept me awake half the night." I smiled to show this wasn't a complaint but a confidence between friends.

Nanny laughed. "Stick around royalty long enough and you'll learn that the nicer something looks, the more uncomfortable it usually is," she said. "The exception being the bathrooms in these royal suites. They're much nicer than the ones in the servants' wing. The bathroom is through that other door, the one on the opposite side of the sitting room. It's the one perk of sleeping up here."

A bathroom! I grinned at the thought of using a bathroom every day. Our cottage back home didn't have one and I'd been very impressed by all the marble in the guest suite bathroom.

I walked back into the sitting room, intending to go across and have a peek but while we had been gone Gretchen had arrived. She had the twins sitting at their desks and copying something out of two books. When she saw me, she walked over and looked me coldly up and down and back up again. I stiffened and opened my mouth to say something cutting.

But before any words came out, Nanny came into the room behind me and Gretchen turned to speak to her.

"Their royal highnesses were not ready for their lesson when I arrived – as usual. They have informed me that they have a new Companion. I'm glad their majesties have realised that the princesses need some more competent care. I really can't be expected to run around after them. I'm a governess, not a nanny." I stared at her in surprise. She turned towards me.

"I suppose you must be Alyssa, the new Companion. My name is Gretchen, I'm the princesses' governess. You must come and have tea with me sometime – in my suite, of course. My brother is the Baron of Lilton, so naturally I don't frequent the servant's wing. But the guest suite I'm in is just a little further down this gallery. I would love to hear more about your background."

I'd heard enough to read between the lines – what she'd love is to have the chance to figure out where I fit in the social hierarchy. And more importantly, whether I came above or below herself. Clearly my dress had thrown her. I was now relieved Nanny's entrance had saved me from giving her a put-down. I could just imagine her reaction to being insulted by a woodcutter's daughter. And she would find out my background, sooner or later. I decided my best play was to make it sooner.

"What a kind invitation! But I'm only a woodcutter's daughter." I smiled sweetly at her look of surprise and tried to look naive. "I'm sure it wouldn't be proper for me to socialise with a baron's sister. I'm really more of a babysitter than a companion. And you with your own guest suite! I'm only sleeping in the nanny's alcove." I pointed back towards the bedroom and hoped I hadn't laid it on too thick.

I suppose Gretchen thought awe and respect were her due, however, because she seemed to buy it.

"Oh, I see. Well, in that case you'd definitely be better off with Nanny here and the other servants." Her look of disdain now encompassed both of us. "And I must ask you two to leave. The princesses need absolute quiet when they're studying. They will be ready for you to collect at lunchtime." She looked at me doubtfully, "that's in three hours. Someone will ring a bell."

"Thank you so much. I'll be sure to come back then," I said and gave her a slight inclination of my body, just short of a curtsey.

"Phew!" I said as the door closed behind Martha and me. "I can see why his majesty said she was starched up."

"Starched up! Did he now? Well, that she is and no mistake."

I could see from the look of delight on Martha's face that I'd won back any points I'd lost from my respectful behaviour towards Gretchen. I allowed myself to smile. I'd brushed through that pretty well I thought. I had now been commanded by Gretchen to do the very thing I wanted to do - leave her alone and socialise with the much more friendly servants. It was clear that being friendly with Gretchen would have instantly put the servants off side.

"Nanny," I said, turning to her. "Mrs Pine said I should find Mathilde now. Could you point me in the right direction?"

"Of course, dear. Normally at this hour she'd be cleaning the royal suites but not with all the excitement of your arrival. I suspect we'll find her in the kitchen. She'll be getting all your things together, like Mrs Pine said."

The kitchen seemed a strange place to be gathering clothes but the twins' tour hadn't included the servants' wing and I was curious to see it.

The kitchen, as it turned out, was a hub rather than just a place to prepare food. It was a huge room lined with ovens, cupboards and fireplaces and had a huge table, even larger than the one in the royal breakfast room. Various servants were sitting around the table, preparing food, talking or drinking cups of tea. It seemed that any servant not actively working gathered here to socialise and eat. And sure enough, Mathilde was sitting at the table folding clothes into two large canvas bags. At our entrance she stopped working and called out a greeting.

"This is Alyssa, everyone," she said. And then to me, "I'm sorry I didn't believe you last night when you said there'd been a mistake. Imagine us putting you in the Princess Room." She giggled. "But it's very unusual for Mr Dorkins to make a mistake. We've been grilling Claud here," she gestured at a young man I recognised as the footman from the night before. (Was it only last night?) "He says he doesn't remember you saying anything about being a princess..." she trailed off and looked at me, her face asking her unspoken question.

"I heard the queen explaining it to Mr Dorkins this morning," I said. "Apparently she told him to prepare the room for a visitor but only because she wanted to inspect it. Naturally he assumed she was actually expecting a visitor so when I arrived he thought it was me."

Mathilde was nodding vigorously and had also resumed folding the clothes. As I finished she put in the last item and stood up.

"These are for you," she said and picked up both bags, handing one to me. "I'll come and help you put them away. I can introduce you to everyone later."

She led me out of the room, waving a farewell at the various servants gathered around the table.

"Mrs Pine said you're going to be the Princess Companion so you'll be eating all your meals with the twins. Those two are twin terrors for all they're so beautiful." She smiled at me sympathetically. "You can't imagine how glad I am that I won't have to spend any more nights up there. You don't get much time to yourself when you're a maid – night time is about it. We mostly all gather down in the kitchen, so if you feel like being social come down after the princesses are in bed. Most of us will be there. Although some might be off walking."

I shivered at the idea of an evening walk in this season and then noticed her blush. Walking must be the main form of courting here, just as it was in my village.

"And what about you, Mathilde?" I asked with a grin. "Will you be off walking?" I took a guess. "With Claud, perhaps?"

Her blush deepened but she grinned.

"He's awfully handsome, isn't he?" she asked shyly. "He's only asked me a couple of times, though." She seemed uncertain.

"I wouldn't worry," I said. "I was only in the kitchen for five minutes and I already noticed he couldn't keep his eyes off you."

"Really? Do you mean it?" Her steps slowed as she considered this delightful idea.

"Come on." I prodded her. "The quicker we get this done, the quicker you can get back to the kitchen." When she looked up at me I winked which made her giggle.

"What about you, Alyssa?" she asked. "Seen anyone you like the look of?"

Unbidden, a face appeared in my mind. One with dark hair and piercing blue eyes. Not one of the servants and definitely, completely out of bounds. I had no business even thinking about him. Especially not when he seemed to hate me.

"Not yet," I replied. "But I haven't met everyone yet." I forced a smile back onto my face.

"I suppose it's a bit hard. With you being Companion and all. A servant might be a bit beneath you." Mathilde was looking determinedly ahead while she said this and it was easy to interpret her subtext.

"Don't be silly," I replied lightly. "I'm only a woodcutter's daughter. They wouldn't have made me Companion if anyone else was around to do it. I'm pretty sure I've only got the job until they go back to Arcadie."

Mathilde relaxed and looked at me again.

"Oh, I hope not," she said. "The summer palace is so beautiful. More work, of course, but also more fun. There's so much going on in Arcadie and the palace is the centre of everything. Even if they don't want you for Companion anymore, I'm sure Mrs Pine will find you some position. There's loads more servants at the palace."

I smiled noncommittally. I would have to see what my aunt said first. She might already have a place lined up for me.

By this time we had reached the door of the princesses' suite and Mathilde put her finger to her lips. She quietly opened the door and we slipped straight into the bedroom, shutting both doors behind us. Gretchen was drilling the girls on their times tables and although she looked at us disapprovingly as we went past, she didn't say anything. Mathilde went straight to my alcove and pulled open the drawers. She began emptying the bag she was carrying into one of the drawers so I began to do the same with my bag.

Mrs Pine had found me several dresses that were nicer in cut and quality than the simple uniform worn by the servants but well below the quality of the clothes worn by the royal family. They were closer to the dress Gretchen was currently wearing, although I judged them to be slightly inferior. I only hoped Gretchen came to the same conclusion.

Along with the dresses there were undergarments, toiletries and a nightgown that was made out of the same soft material as the one I had worn in the Princess Room, although this one was completely unadorned. I smiled and stroked the material as I laid it carefully in the drawer. It would feel beautiful against my skin. Right at the bottom of the bag were two pairs of shoes. Simple slippers for indoor use and my own pair of boots that had been cleaned and dried since yesterday's adventure.

Mathilde had finished unpacking and had folded the bag itself and slipped it into the drawer.

"I'd better get back," she said reluctantly. "Come visit us tonight." She turned to go and then turned back in a rush. "Was he really looking at me?" she asked.

"Definitely!" I replied with a grin.

She grinned back and then almost ran from the room. I kept smiling to myself for several minutes after she was gone. Apparently my winter was going to include girl talk.

It looked like the colossally bad idea of an evening stroll was turning into the best thing that had ever happened to me. Our house had been very isolated and I had always felt a little jealous of the girls in the village. When we went in to market I would see them, with their heads close together, giggling and whispering. They were always friendly to me but I knew I wasn't one of them. But here – maybe here I could belong.

Chapter 5

My first week seemed to be gone before I realised it had started. The king had been right - Lily and Sophie were very early risers and their first stop in the morning was my alcove. I was on duty until I handed them over to Gretchen for their lessons and then back on duty as soon as they were finished. Those three hours of lessons between breakfast and lunch were my only free time until the girls fell asleep at night. By that point I was ready for sleep myself – my brain and body exhausted and on overload. But evenings were social time for the staff and I didn't want to get a reputation for being anti-social. So each evening, after the twins dropped off, I would drag myself down to the kitchen.

Once I was surrounded by other people, I always started to wake up, fascinated by this glimpse into the complex lives of royalty and their staff. It was amazing how much you could learn by listening to the servants when they felt relaxed. Mrs Pine and Dorkins mostly avoided the kitchen in the evenings. I concluded this absence wasn't motivated by arrogance, as in the case of Gretchen. The butler and housekeeper seemed to realise that their presence cast a restraint on their subordinates and chose to give them space in the evenings to relax. At first I thought this was rather dangerous and felt sure the servants must slack off on their work each day, exhausted from their highly social, late nights. But I quickly reached the conclusion that the opposite was true. The time spent in relaxation seemed to invigorate them and cause them to work harder during the day.

And while I didn't exactly find the company of the servants relaxing, I did leave the kitchen each evening feeling revitalised, my mind awhirl with new and interesting ideas. I also realised that I had overestimated my understanding of people and their motivations. A whole new world was opening up before me and my brain felt like a sponge, whichever way I turned I was absorbing something new.

It's no surprise then that those first few days I used my free hours each morning to catch up on sleep. I certainly didn't have the opportunity to rest while I was with the twins. They were usually happy to spend the morning in their suite – but only as long as I kept them entertained with stories or invented new games for their dolls to play. And in the afternoon they liked to roam around the gardens. They were fascinated by the woods but had been forbidden by their parents to venture further than the edge of the castle grounds. This didn't seem like much of a hardship to me. The gardens were extensive and beautifully maintained. There were several formal garden beds, enlivened by regular fountains and even a small hedge maze.

But the girls were convinced that the forest would be far more entertaining than the garden. So I had to watch them with an eagle eye whenever we were outside. After only a few days of this I started to get nightmares where I was stumbling through the woods again, only this time it was the girls who were lost and I couldn't find them. It's hardly surprising that I looked eagerly out the window each morning, hoping for rain.

On rainy afternoons the girls entertained themselves in the castle, playing hide and seek or tag through the ground floor of the East Wing. Whether inside or outside they would eventually collapse, exhausted and demand a story. Their appetite for stories was endless and I was grateful for all the tales I had invented for my brothers over the years. These old stories had to be modified, of course, but that was easily done. The woodcutter's sons became princesses and the beautiful princesses became brave and handsome princes.

The morals, however, stayed. For all that they were princesses, Lily and Sophie were as much in need of the lessons as my brothers had ever been. At first I was confused by their wild, unpolished behaviour, especially in contrast with the finely honed social graces of their parents. The king and queen were always dignified and their behaviour towards me and the other servants was polite and considerate. At mealtimes I kept quiet but listened intently and their conversations were intelligent. They carried their authority with ease and an appropriate sense of responsibility. I found myself wondering again and again what had gone wrong with their children. As it turned out, I was Companion for several weeks before the answer began to become clear.

Meanwhile, I finally began to adjust to my new routine. Five days after I had arrived, when I dropped the princesses off with Gretchen, I realised I felt far too awake to retreat to my alcove for a nap. I decided to take a walk outside. It would be nice to enjoy the gardens without fear of the twins' adventuring. But when I pushed the heavy front door open, I saw that it had begun to rain. I sighed with frustration and let the door swing back shut.

I leaned with my back against it and gazed at the entry hall, not really seeing it. I could go back to the princesses' suite but the idea of being shut in the bedroom for the next three hours made me feel claustrophobic. If I went to the kitchen I could be sure of finding company but I realised I wasn't in the mood for listening to the idle conversation of the kitchen maids or the under-gardeners who were sure to be there, sheltering from the rain. I wouldn't mind a good gossip with Mathilde but she would be up in the gallery, cleaning one of the suites at this hour. I sighed again. There was a beautiful sitting room in the East Wing but, without the twins, I felt uncomfortable about intruding into the rooms of the royal family.

I was about to give up and go to the kitchen after all, when my brain finally absorbed what I was seeing. There was light coming from behind the grand stairway – daylight – despite the lack of windows on the far side of the hall. I pushed myself away from the door and began to walk towards the stairs and, for once, instead of starting to ascend, I went around them.

Somehow, I had never explored back here before. The twins hadn't included it in their initial tour and since they were always in a hurry, we tended to rush through the hall on our way to our destination. So it was with considerable surprise that I found an open doorway, hidden in the wall directly behind the staircase.

I stepped through the door and my surprise grew. I was in a large room, the largest I had seen in the castle so far. But it was hard to judge the exact size because most of the room was obscured by rows of tall bookshelves. I walked through the aisle of books directly in front of the door and came out into an open space that ran the whole length of the room. It was lined with bay windows and several small tables and strategically placed armchairs were scattered around. My intense focus on the girls was the only excuse I could find for my failure to notice this room during my exploration of the gardens. It seemed obvious now that something must lie behind the entry hall.

My delight grew as I gazed around at all the books. So much knowledge in one place! I breathed in deeply and smiled at the smell of paper, leather and that indefinable 'book' smell. If every book I had ever seen in my whole life were placed together they would fill only one of these bookshelves. What a perfect place and what a perfect answer to the question of where to spend my free hours. Each of the windows had a small but comfortable looking bench, lined with cushions. I could foresee many happy hours spent curled in a window, reading.

I turned back eagerly towards the bookshelves and began to scan them. The books seemed to be arranged by topic and I walked down several aisles trailing my fingers along the spines of the books before I stopped and pulled out a book on economics. Listening to the king and queen converse over every meal had forced me to acknowledge some shortcomings in my education. I had been completely lost at dinner the night before when they had discussed some recent changes in the trade policy of one of our neighbouring kingdoms.

I was determined not to waste this opportunity. I would study each day and listen at each meal and maybe by the end of winter I would be a little more equipped for life in a big city. I turned back towards the windows and passed a section of fairy tales. My eye was drawn to a small volume with gold lettering down the spine. I smiled and picked it up as well. Perhaps, if I read a chapter of economics, I could reward myself with a story. After all, I reminded myself, fairy tales were research too. And more relevant to my role of Companion than economics. I smiled at my internal justifications. These hours were my own and I could spend them how I liked. My mother wasn't here and I had no governess to call me to task for spending my time reading fiction when I should be studying.

Carrying both books, I moved towards one of the windows. But before I reached it, I heard a slight sound and glanced up. Across the room my eyes locked with those of the prince. I must have been very absorbed in my wonder at the library to fail to notice there was someone else in the room. The prince was sitting in one of the windows, holding a book. My presence seemed to have disturbed his reading and I wondered how long he had been watching me.

Several thoughts raced through my head in quick succession. I wondered if the library was only for the use of the royal family and whether I had violated some unknown rule by taking books from the shelves. Then I wondered why the prince was looking at me so intently. Since that first breakfast he had carefully avoided looking in my direction and had sat in silence at every meal. If I was careful not to look at him, I could almost forget he was there. But now he was back to staring at me.

And then he put his book down beside him and leapt from the window. And as he walked towards me I realised that I was, for the first time, alone with him. He wasn't glaring at me, in fact I could read no anger in his face at all, but I felt a flutter of nerves nevertheless. My feet and hands suddenly felt large and clumsy and I froze in place. As he got closer, I raised the books I was holding and hugged them against my chest, a meagre shield.

He didn't stop or speak until he was right in front of me.

"What have you got there?" he asked, holding out his hands for my books. Reluctantly I handed them over, feeling exposed. He stood in silence for a moment, reading the titles. Finally he looked up and smiled but I wasn't sure if it was meant to be friendly or mocking.

"Economics, hey?" he said. "A strange topic of study for a Princess Companion. So you were listening last night, after all. I thought so." I stared at him in surprise. I could have sworn he hadn't so much as glanced at me all night.

"Do you have a problem with that?" I asked, sick of his strangely antagonistic attitude.

"No, Princess Companion, I don't," he replied and again I couldn't tell if he was mocking me.

"My name is Alyssa, as you very well know," I snapped, determined to fight the out of control feeling he gave me.

"Well, *Alyssa*," he placed a scathing emphasis on my name, "just because you've been welcomed into our family fold, don't get ideas above your station." He held up the book of fairy tales. "This is more fitting subject matter for you."

"Look, *Max*," I replied, "I don't know why I offend you so much or why you can't seem to stand the sight of me but I've never done anything to you. Don't you think you could at least try to give me a chance?" I was no longer nervous, instead I felt invigorated by my anger and by the shocked surprise on his face.

"You haven't offended me," he said after a long pause. Now I was the one feeling surprised. It wasn't the reaction I'd been expecting after my intentionally offensive use of his nickname.

"Really? I suppose it's totally normal for you to spend every meal in complete silence, staring at your food." I raised both eyebrows at him.

"It's not that I'm offended, it's just…" he trailed off. I waited for him to continue but he stood there silently. I decided to try a change of tack, softening my voice and expression.

"I didn't ask for this job but I'm trying my best for your sisters. And I don't think it's the best thing for them to have their Companion and their brother not even on speaking terms. So if I promise that I'll continue to do my best for them, and that I won't take advantage of your family in any way, do you think you can try to aim for some basic courtesy towards me?" He continued to stand there in silence.

"Even if you have to pretend?" This sally made him smile so I smiled back and held out my hand. "Truce?"

"I'll tell you what," he replied, leaving my hand hanging. "If you agree to keep calling me Max from now on, I'll agree to a truce. You can have all the courtesy you want." His smile had gotten bigger and he seemed to read agreement in the surprise on my face.

64

"A truce then, Alyssa." This time when he said my name it was soft, almost like a caress. Before I could think of anything to say, he had turned and walked away, chuckling to himself.

I just stood there, in a daze. *What had just happened?* But I could make no sense of his mood swings. As for his soft voice, saying my name, I decided it would be best if I never thought about that again. Best for my mental health that is.

Without consciously thinking about it, I found my feet leading me over to the window seat where he had been sitting. I picked up the book he had left there. *Diplomatic Relations and the Impacts of Foreign Trade Policy*. It seemed I wasn't the only one who had felt out of depth listening to the dinner conversation. I climbed up onto the seat he had vacated but just sat there smiling. It was a long time before I opened a book.

Chapter 6

Having forbidden myself to think about it, it was only natural that I went to sleep that night and woke up the next morning to a soft voice in my mind, calling me Alyssa. I had no idea what sort of behaviour to expect from... Max from now on. Even in my head it felt disrespectful to address a royal prince as simply Max so I tried saying it over and over again in the quietest of whispers. *Max. Max. Max.* Max. There, that had had the right level of comfortable nonchalance.

I climbed out of bed, surprised to be awake before the twins for once, but when I came out of the bathroom they were both up and clamouring for a game before breakfast. The bedtime story last night had been about a beautiful princess who had been trapped by her godmother in a tall tower without doors. She had been locked up because of the arrogant unconcern she showed after one of her imperious orders had caused a young baker's daughter to be crippled. The tower was cold and bare and without comforts. Every day someone different would call to the princess to let down her long hair. The visitor would then climb into the tower to deliver food and water for the day. If she behaved towards her visitor with concern and courtesy, a new comfort would appear in the tower. If she behaved with arrogance, one would disappear. But her godmother had told her that she would only be freed when she learnt true compassion.

Sophie had asked if the princess had ever got out of the tower but I had told her that was a story for another day. Lily had said nothing but had lain awake long after she would normally have fallen asleep. However, if my story had had an impact there was no evidence of it this morning. Both girls were bouncing around, far too awake for this hour of the morning, demanding new ideas for a game with their usual levels of energy. Wanting to remind them of the lesson from the night before, I suggested that they enact the story of the princess in the tower with their dolls. This suggestion found great favour and I was able to sit in peace for several minutes while they rushed around the room, finding a great many unlikely things to pile on top of their dollhouse. Only after their 'tower' had reached a satisfactory height did Sophie notice my abstraction.

"What's the matter, Alyssa," she asked.

"Nothing," I replied, rousing myself from my thoughts with difficulty.

"Well, what were you thinking about?" asked Lily.

I could hardly tell them I was thinking about their brother and wondering for the hundredth time how he would behave towards me at breakfast, so I tried to look stern.

"Adult things." I had a proper look at their creation and had to laugh. "I think you'd better pay a bit more attention to your 'tower'," I said. "It looks like it's about to fall down. I don't remember that happening in the story."

With a shriek both girls rushed towards the dollhouse and the precarious stack on top of it. I decided they might need a little help with their engineering and the three of us spent the rest of the time until breakfast making the structure stable enough to hold their dolls at the top.

Consequently we were a little late for breakfast and when we entered the room it was to see the king and queen with nearly empty plates. The prince had apparently already finished because he was standing beside the buffet serving himself seconds. He looked up when we entered and smiled.

"Good morning, girls." His sisters nodded at him vaguely as they rushed to grab their plates so I cleared my throat loudly. They paused just long enough to get out a "good morning Max, good morning Mother, good morning Father," before resuming their rush towards the food. I looked back towards the prince and forgot my awkwardness in a moment of shared amusement. He stepped closer to me and spoke quietly.

"Good morning, Alyssa."

"Good morning," I replied, considering leaving the greeting there. But his eyes were altogether too aware, challenging me to keep up my end of the bargain, so I added, "Max" even more quietly than him. Judging from his expression, my response had given him great satisfaction, although whether this came from my use of his name or my hesitation I wasn't sure.

I quickly filled my own plate with breakfast and took my usual seat. When I refocused on the room, it was to hear Max and his father discussing some proposed improvements to the stables. Queen Eleanor was looking on with a pleased smile. I guessed I wasn't the only one who had noticed Max's previous mealtime silence. By the time they had finished their conversation, Max had also finished his second plate of breakfast.

"I'll go find the carpenter and give him those instructions then. If you don't need me this morning," he paused and his father shook his head, "I might stay and watch." As he reached for the door, a sudden idea popped into my head.

"Max, wait," I said without thinking and every head in the room swiveled in my direction. King Henry and Queen Eleanor looked startled at my presumption and turned their attention to their son, waiting for the expected explosion. But he merely smiled politely.

"Yes, Alyssa?" he asked. "Is there something I can do for you while I'm out at the stables?"

"Yes," I replied, "yes, there is." I got up and went over to him, making my request in a quiet voice. Only Max and the queen were close enough to hear me and they both smiled and glanced towards the twins. As soon as Max had left the room the girls spoke over the top of each other.

"What is it, Alyssa?"

"What do you want Max to do in the stables?"

"Not in the stables exactly," I replied, "and I'm not telling."

Both girls looked indignant and Lily turned towards her mother so I quickly added, "it's a surprise. For you."

If I had thought this information would silence them, I soon learnt my mistake. The only silver lining was that their continual chatter distracted the family from the unexpected change in behaviour between the prince and me.

By the time I dropped them off with Gretchen, however, even this silver lining had worn thin.

"One more word from either of you about this surprise and I won't give it to you after all."

"You wouldn't!" declared Lily.

"Just try me."

I met her eyes steadily and she frowned but remained silent. As I walked towards the library I decided to view this as a success. If nothing else, the twins had learnt that I wasn't a safe person to cross. I meant what I said and, unlike Nanny, would stick to my 'no'.

When I reached the library door, I paused, wondering if I would find the prince inside. Then I remembered that he was planning to spend the morning down at the stables and I felt a curious mixture of disappointment and relief. After everything that had happened, some space and silence would be refreshing. I picked up the book on economics from the table where I had left it but decided there was simply no space in my mind for new and difficult concepts. Instead it was the book of fairy tales that I carried over to the window. A beam of sunlight was shining in, warming the seat. I smiled, a couple of hours of quiet indulgence was just what I needed to calm my mind.

At lunch, Max replied to my questioning look with a smile and a nod which I took to mean he had had success with my request. I was pleased, excited to think that my first initiative might meet with success. After the meal, while the twins were being grilled on their lessons by the king, I cornered him by the door.

"Thanks for carrying my message," I said. "Did he mind? He must have a lot of work already with your project in the stables."

"No, he didn't mind at all. He said it might take a few days, though. He'll work on it in the evenings."

"Oh, ok," I tried not to let my disappointment show. Patience wasn't my strong suit. "When it's finished could you make sure you bring it to me when the twins are in lessons? I'll be in the library."

"Still studying up on economics?" he grinned.

"Oh, economics. And all sorts of other subjects inappropriate for a Princess Companion," I replied, testing him.

"It's becoming increasingly clear to me that you're not an ordinary Princess Companion," he said and then turned around and left the room, leaving me to wrestle with whether or not this was a compliment.

The question of what, exactly, was behind the rather cryptic things Max said to me occupied my mind off and on over the next few days. Luckily I had plenty of distraction from both the princesses and the increasingly complex saga of Mathilde's love life. I had told Mathilde about my reading sessions and every morning since she'd turned up to 'clean the library' while I was there. Consequently I had a good chat to look forward to each morning to break up my reading. Occasionally I felt a twinge of guilt that I was distracting Mathilde from her work but the cheery unconcern with which she dismissed my worries convinced me that I was over scrupulous.

"He hasn't asked me to walk for a week."

Mathilde was sitting next to me in the window, holding her duster and looking like she was about to cry. With some difficulty I pulled my mind out of the balance of power theory and concentrated on what she was saying.

"You mean Claud?" I asked.

"Of course I mean Claud, who else," she replied, exasperated with my density.

"Maybe he's just been tired," I suggested weakly. She didn't reply this time but gave me the glare that my poor suggestion deserved.

"Well, it has been cold!" I defended myself. "And maybe he wants to take things slowly while we're all here at the Winter Castle. You know Nikki likes him too. She's always making eyes at him. Maybe he just doesn't want things to get too awkward – you've said yourself things can get a bit intense with so few staff and all of us stuck in the smaller space. Maybe he's just waiting to get back to the Palace."

Mathilde seemed momentarily cheered by this suggestion but then her face fell as she imparted her final bit of news.

"But you remember how he wasn't in the kitchen last night?" she asked.

I nodded. It had been hard not to notice since Mathilde had pointed it out to me every couple of minutes, constantly pulling my attention away from the conversations I was trying to follow.

"After you went to bed he came in."

I only had a second to wonder why the thought of this made her so glum.

"And about one minute after he came in so did Nikki. And she had this evil gloat on her face too."

"But they didn't actually come in together, right?" I was clutching at straws and knew it.

"It totally looked like they'd been out walking but didn't want anyone to see them come in together."

"Surely not!" I exclaimed loyally. "He wouldn't do that to you! And anyway, if he was courting her now, instead of you, why would he be hiding it?"

Despite my words I felt a little uneasy. The more I saw of Claud, the more he gave me a squirmy feeling. A sort of shivering up my spine that I had long ago associated with two-faced people. I was becoming increasingly convinced that something was just a little bit off about Claud.

However, I hadn't yet worked up the courage to confide my concerns in Mathilde who was still looking like she was about to cry. I decided to try another angle.

"And anyway, if he's decided he doesn't like you anymore and isn't man enough to tell you to your face, then you're better off without him. You deserve someone better than that."

It was the age-old cry of friendship but it was the first time I'd been required to say it so I put in all the enthusiasm and sincerity I could muster. Mathilde seemed as completely uncomforted as I imagined every other friend had felt throughout those ages.

"Thanks Alyssa, you're a good friend" she said listlessly and raised her duster. "I suppose I'd better get back to cleaning."

I gave her a quick hug before she could escape and then sat there for several seconds watching her wander over towards the bookshelves and half-heartedly run her duster along one of the shelves. Mathilde might be a little soppy and undeservedly obsessed with Claud but she was still the best friend I'd ever had. I decided it was time I started paying a bit more attention to Claud.

Chapter 7

I didn't get an opportunity to observe Claud that evening because he was once again absent from the kitchen. This seemed ominous and Mathilde excused herself much earlier than usual. Consequently I found it hard to focus on inter-kingdom politics the next morning, my mind constantly wandering to various schemes for finding out the truth about Claud. I'd nearly decided the best thing was simply to confront him and demand the truth when I heard the library door bang open.

"I've got it! He's finished!"

It was the prince's voice and he immediately came into view between the shelves, rather precariously balancing a large wooden object. I exclaimed in delight and rushed over to help him. Together we managed to get it down on the ground without harm.

"Thanks," said Max, "it's not as heavy as it looks but it's an awkward shape. I banged it pretty hard against the door coming in but I don't think it's been damaged. He's done a good job don't you think?"

"It's amazing!" I gushed, "so much better than I imagined. They're going to love it!"

I smiled up at him and realised how close we were standing. His blue eyes were laughing down into mine and I suddenly felt the need to back away a little. I disguised my movement by turning to examine his burden.

It was a large wooden tower that had been carefully painted to resemble grey stone. There were no doors and only a single large window. Through the window I could see an empty room at the top of the tower.

"It opens here," said Max, showing me the catch and the hinges that allowed part of the wall to swing away, giving access to the room. "So the girls can get their dolls and things in."

His eyes were alight with enthusiasm and a sudden suspicion crossed my mind.

"You helped the carpenter with this didn't you?" I asked before I remembered that a prince would hardly be doing manual labour.

"Yeah, I did actually." He sounded half sheepish at being caught showing interest in what was essentially a dollhouse but also half proud. "I helped with the design and I painted it. I'm not much good with the actual woodwork."

"Well, it's beautiful, so much more finished looking than I was imagining. It's perfect, actually. Thank you, Max." I couldn't help but smile to see how pleased he looked with my praise.

"Alyssa," he said, letting go of the tower and stepping towards me. But before he could go on we were both startled by a noise between the bookshelves. We both took a step back and I realised I was never going to hear what he'd been about to say. Another cryptic utterance to add to the list. And to make the moment more awkward, it was Nikki, not Mathilde, who emerged from between the bookshelves.

The duster was in her hands and moving along the shelf but her eyes were on us and they were filled with curiosity and a little surprise. I sighed. Nikki might not be as awful as Mathilde thought she was, but she was a gossip. Whatever she'd overheard would be relayed to every servant in the castle by tonight. I replayed our conversation in my mind but couldn't think of anything I'd said that was particularly gossip-worthy.

Max, meanwhile, seemed to have recovered from his momentary discomfort. I could only suppose the gossip of the servants made no difference to him. Instead his attention had returned to the tower.

"Can I come with you to give it to them?" he asked.

"Of course," I replied, "I couldn't carry it on my own anyway."

"You should give it a try," he encouraged, "you really will be surprised by how light it is. It's the way Joe constructed the walls."

He began a detailed and enthusiastic description of the engineering behind the tower design. I tuned him out while I tried to determine the best angle to pick it up from. At last I crouched down and simply put both hands underneath the base. I straightened back up and realised he was right – it was surprisingly light. But as I took a step, the structure shifted balance and the top of the tower, which was now above my head, started to swing towards me. I quickly shifted it in my grip and the edge of the base scraped along one of my hands.

"Ouch!" I exclaimed and put it down. I examined my hand. There was no mark but I could still feel the sting. I gripped the spot in my other hand but not before Max had leaned in to have a look.

"Wow, you're so soft," he said, with a laugh. "There's nothing there."

"Don't even start," I said, more sharply than I'd intended.

He stopped laughing and looked taken aback. I softened.

"Sorry," I said and then, as an explanation, "I have four older brothers."

That brought the laugh back, although this time only in his eyes.

"Ah, I see," he said, "a trial for anyone. Here give it to me, I can kiss it better for you." He held out his hand for mine but I whipped both hands behind my back, cross at his teasing. I was painfully conscious, even if he had forgotten, that Nikki was watching us with interest.

"Don't be ridiculous," I snapped. "My hand's fine. I'm just sensitive. Which, for your information, is not a crime. There are more ways to be strong than just physically, you know."

"How did that argument work on your brothers?" asked Max as he leaned down and picked up the tower. When he stood back up and I saw his face around the bulk in his arms, I realised he was still laughing at me.

"Boys," I muttered to myself and stalked off ahead of him to get the door.

He needed my help balancing the tower as we climbed the stairs and by the time we reached the princesses' suite my annoyance had been swallowed by anticipation. We put the tower down just outside the door and I told Max to wait while I went in to fetch the twins. It looked like Gretchen had just left so we'd timed it well. The girls looked up from their desks where they were packing away their books and papers.

"Alyssa," called Sophie and "There you are!" added Lily.

"Do you remember that I had a surprise for you?" I asked them. "The one that didn't exactly involve the stables."

"Yes! Of course we remember," cried Lily, her eyes alight. "What is it? Where is it?"

Sophie looked wildly around the room as if she expected it to have appeared while they were doing their lessons.

"It's outside the door, with your brother," I said, pointing at the door I'd just come through.

Both girls rushed past me and through the doorway. I followed them in time to hear their indrawn breaths.

"It's beautiful!"

"It's so tall! Much taller than our dollhouse."

"So much better than the stack of cushions we used the other day."

And then, as if suddenly remembering the story that went along with the tower:

"Thanks, Max!"

"Thanks, Alyssa!"

We both received a hug from one of the girls and our eyes met above their heads. As we smiled at each other I had the sudden thought, *is this what it feels like to be parents?* But then I shook it off. Luckily I still had several years before I had to find out the answer to that question.

"Let's get it into the room, I know just the spot."

Both girls rushed back into the room and I could hear Lily bossing Sophie around as they moved their things, making a space for the tower next to the dollhouse. Once it was in position we all stood back and surveyed it in satisfaction.

But the girls stayed still for only a moment, rushing to move their dolls and various furnishings from the house to the tower.

"Now the lesson should stay fresh in their minds," I said quietly.

"Is that why you wanted it made for them?" asked Max, equally quietly.

I looked up, startled to realise I'd spoken aloud.

He answered the question in my eyes. "Lily told us the story. The one about the tower. It was the other morning when Sophie spilled hot chocolate all down her dress during breakfast and you had to bring her back here to change." His voice was even and I couldn't tell whether he disapproved or not.

I flushed when I realised the king and queen now knew I thought their daughters lacked consideration and courtesy. And worse, that I was trying to school them in it. The older members of the family would know the story wasn't a classic fairy tale. I waited to see what else Max would say but apparently he had nothing further to add. Instead he bid us all goodbye and left the room, a departure entirely unnoticed by his sisters who were fighting over which items to put in the tower room. I sighed and headed over to arbitrate. I'd always wanted a sister in the past but these days I was starting to think I'd dodged a bullet.

The tower occupied the girls for most of the afternoon, the spirited arguments that interspersed the happy games seemed to use their energy as effectively as a game of tag or hide and seek. It was significantly less draining for me, however, since I sat back and let them go, only intervening if things started to get out of hand. Mostly the fights seemed to die out as quickly as they started, harmony returned through some mysterious medium I had yet to fathom.

The result of an afternoon's worth of thoughts was that when I left the suite after the girls fell asleep I was wearing my cloak and boots. I went down the back servants stairs as usual but instead of going into the kitchen, I slipped out one of the castle's back doors and began to slowly meander towards the stables. I knew the carpenter lived in a small cottage down there and I thought an evening visit to thank him would make a good excuse to be outside. My real purpose, of course, was to try to get a glimpse of what Claud was doing that was keeping him out of the kitchen in the evening.

I walked as slowly as possible but still reached the carpenter's cottage without seeing anyone. I knocked on the door and was gruffly bid to enter. I pushed the door open and was glad to enter the warm room beyond. When Joe saw me, he stood up from his rocking chair by the fire and gave me a tentative smile.

"You'll be Miss Alyssa, I suppose," he said. "I've heard a great deal about you."

"All good, I hope." I smiled a little uncertainly. "It seems we servants do like to gossip."

I hoped he would relax when I included myself with the servants but he remained standing respectfully.

"It wasn't from the servants," he replied and now I was truly curious. Unfortunately he seemed oblivious to my questioning look and it seemed rude to press him.

"I came to thank you for the beautiful tower you made," I said instead.

His smile broadened and he reached up to scratch his head.

"That's very kind of you, Miss Alyssa," he said. "It was a pleasure to make it. And I wasn't alone. His highness came down most evenings to keep me company. It's a pleasure to see how he cares about those poor little girls."

"Poor little girls? You mean the princesses?" I asked.

I could tell from his uncomfortable look that the words had been a slip of the tongue and he was slow to answer me.

"Well, not really poor, of course. It just seems mighty lonesome for children out here at the castle. No other children to play with. Although they have each other at least."

"That's why they have me." I tried to sound cheerful although his words echoed my own thoughts. "I suppose it must have been worse for the prince when he was a child. He would have been all alone."

"Oh, the royal family didn't spend their winters out here before the princesses were born," said Joe. "Times were less settled then. Kept the young king busy for years after he got the crown."

I wondered what 'times were less settled' meant but concluded he must be referring to King Henry's unexpected ascension to the throne so shortly after he had married Queen Eleanor. No-one could have predicted the hunting accident which had killed King Edward and it must have been a confusing time for the current king and queen. They certainly would have been expecting to have many years as prince and princess before having to take the reins of government.

Joe seemed kind and honest but he didn't seem comfortable having me in his cottage and I felt like an intruder into his rest.

"Well the princesses are certainly delighted with their new doll tower," I said. "Thank you again for all the work you put in. It's so much nicer than the one I imagined."

"Happy to be of service," said Joe and he held the door open for me.

As it swung closed, I thought I heard him murmur to himself, "Now I understand, pretty as a picture she is." But when I turned back around the door had closed and all I could hear was the faint sound of his chuckle as he moved back towards the fire.

As tantalising as his last remark had been, the cold air reminded me of my second purpose for the evening. I began to walk as slowly as possible back towards the castle, straining my eyes to see any movement in the dark around me. Sure enough, I saw a figure striding away from the castle and realised after a moment that it was Claud. He also saw me and checked, changing the angle of his steps to come towards me.

When we met we were close enough to the lights of the castle that I could see his face clearly. He was smiling but it didn't warm me. Instead it made me realise that we were alone for the first time and I felt again the shivering up my spine, heightened now by the night around us and by our aloneness.

"Alyssa," he held his hands out in greeting and I reluctantly put my hand into his. "I've been hoping to have a chance to speak to you properly but you're always surrounded by friends and admirers."

My thoughts flew to Mathilde and it made his attempt at charm seem even more false. I said nothing so he continued, perhaps encouraged by my silence.

"You outshine them all, of course. You have brightened our little world since your arrival." He paused. "You have brightened *my* world."

My hand had been hanging limply in his as he spoke and he now raised it to his lips. Horrified I snatched it away.

We stood silent now, regarding each other, and his expression changed. He looked confused and resentful and I could only assume Mathilde and Nikki responded a little differently to his honeyed phrases. But there was also something darker lurking beneath and I remembered my fear. I forced myself to speak.

"I think you forget, Claud, that I'm friends with Mathilde. Good friends," I said and his face relaxed a little.

"Of course, of course," he rushed to say. "I didn't mean anything by it, I assure you. Mathilde is charming, I like her very much. You won't mention this to her?"

Some of my contempt must have shown on my face because he rushed on. "I really do like her. I was just swept up in your," he seemed to be searching for the right word, "novelty."

I stared at him in disbelief. Was he serious? And he obviously didn't understand how friendship worked if he thought I wasn't going to say anything.

"I'm going back inside now," I said coldly. "I was only out on a short visit to Joe Carpenter to thank him for some woodwork he did for the princesses."

"I'll let you be on your way then, of course," said Claud. "But I hope any misunderstanding has been cleared up and we can be friends. Nothing more, just friends," he hastened to add.

Again I felt only astonishment. Had the man never had a true friend in his life? He should know perfectly well that he and I could never be friendly now. Not after his treatment of Mathilde. But I said nothing, just turned and started for the castle. After a moment I heard his footsteps resume and when I reached the castle door and turned back, he was already out of sight, lost to the night.

Chapter 8

My mind had been so full of my encounters with Joe and Claud that I had bypassed the kitchen and gone straight to bed. If I had gone in and spoken to the other servants I would have had some warning. But I didn't go in and so was totally unprepared for my meeting with Gretchen the next morning.

Gretchen's appearance in the princesses' suite was my cue to depart so I moved towards the door with my usual head nod to the governess. This time, however, her hand shot out and grabbed my arm, preventing me from passing her in the doorway.

"Just who do you think you are, *woodcutter's daughter*?" she whispered angrily. It was clear that to her this was the ultimate insult and also that our cold but peaceful truce was over. I glanced with concern towards the twins but they were too far away to hear, dragging their feet as they moved towards their desks and began to get out their books. Gretchen saw the direction of my gaze.

"You may have the royal family under your spell but don't think the rest of us are fooled," she snapped. "And they'll forget you just as quick when we get back to Arcadie. At the Summer Palace there are plenty of people actually worth their notice. People like my brother and sister the Baron and Baroness."

I couldn't think what had brought on this attack and until I could work out what was going on I thought it safest not to respond. So I wrenched my arm out of her grip and almost ran from the room and to the sanctuary of the library.

I had only been in the library long enough to catch my breath and calm my outraged thoughts when Mathilde rushed in.

"Is it true?" she asked.

I panicked, my mind switching gears. I hadn't expected her so soon, I'd thought I would have more time to work out the right words before I had to tell her about Claud.

"Look Mathilde," I began desperately and then realised she was almost bouncing in her excitement. This was definitely not about Claud. "Wait, is what true?" I asked, confused.

"Everyone asked me if it was true because they know how close we are and so I told them that *of course* it was. You should have heard me defend you, I mean why wouldn't it be true when you're Companion, I said. Practically like one of the family. But I do think you might have told me. I thought we were best friends!"

"Stop, stop!" I cried, interrupting the flow of her words. "I have no idea what you're talking about. Is what true?"

"That you call the prince 'Max', of course," she exclaimed.

The many events of yesterday had driven Max and my overheard conversation from my mind but now I remembered Nikki's curious eyes and listening ears. Gretchen's change in attitude began to make sense. I nodded affirmation for Mathilde, not sure what to say.

"I knew it," she exulted. "You do realise only his family and closest friends call him Max! The royals really must see you as one of them. My best friend!" She suddenly remembered my perfidy. "But you might have told me!"

"Sorry," I apologised lamely. And then, "I suppose the story made it to Gretchen somehow?"

Mathilde nodded and looked contemptuous. "She likes to pretend she's so far above us and would never stoop to our level but I know the queen's seamstress tells her all the gossip." Now Mathilde looked concerned. "The way Nikki told the story it sounded like you were, well, flirting with the prince and I suppose stupid old Gretchen wouldn't like that."

"I wasn't flirting!" I cried, incensed. And then wondered, a little uneasily, if perhaps I had been. I groaned and put my face in my hands. These were dangerous waters.

"It's just that there's no-one else his age for him to talk to," I said, trying to defend myself.

"It's totally understandable," said Mathilde loyally, "You're just as beautiful as all the girls at court." This was the third time someone had commented on my looks in the last twenty-four hours. I should have been flattered but, judging by the uneasy look on my friend's face, my life would be less complicated if I was excessively plain.

"What is it?" I asked.

"Nothing," she replied. And then, after a pause, "there's nothing wrong with a bit of flirting, of course. All the girls do it, even the maids, if they get the chance. He's the prince after all, and so good-looking! But usually he doesn't respond much. And from what Nikki said... And you're so pretty, and the Princess Companion. But everyone knows you're a woodcutter's daughter..."

Her voice trailed away but I understood what was unsaid. The other servants, and people like Gretchen, would accept my short boost in status as long as I seemed to know my place. And with the prince I had somehow crossed a line.

"Thanks for the warning, Mathilde," I said, "I understand. I need some time to think about all this."

She nodded and moved away to begin dusting the shelves.

I pulled myself up onto one of the window seats. I'd reached a crossroads then. I was pretty sure I could pacify Gretchen and keep all the staff onside. I would just need to show them that I knew and respected my true station. That would mean no more special projects like the doll tower, though. And I would have to go out of my way not to connect with the royals. I would have to avoid Max.

I could see the advantages of that course – it would probably be the best way forward if I was hoping for some sort of job at the palace at the end of the winter. But I still only considered it for about a minute. I had left my home for an adventure, not security, and I always had my aunt to fall back on after all. Plus, I felt committed to my personal project of princess improvement. And that was without considering Max who, truth be told, was the most exciting part of my new life. Avoiding him didn't even feel like an option.

So what was my way forward then? How did I make sure the next two months at the castle were livable? I sat, deep in thought.

"Mathilde?" I finally called out.

"Yes?" Mathilde popped out from between the bookshelves and hurried back over.

"You said that the royals are treating me like one of them. If I choose to accept that and embrace my new role how will the servants react? I know you'll stick by me but what about the others? Will they freeze me out?" She was silent for a moment, thinking it through.

"Everyone's had the chance to get to know you. To see that you're not stuck up like Gretchen. I think most people will accept it. But you'll have to stop visiting us in the kitchen in the evenings." Mathilde looked sad at this thought. "As long as you don't start ordering the servants around, they'll follow the lead of the royals. Not Gretchen, of course."

She rolled her eyes and I sighed. No, there was no way Gretchen was going to accept me.

Mathilde still looked sad so I reached for her hand to give it a squeeze. To my surprise she stepped away.

"I guess we can't be friends any more either," she said.

"Don't be silly!" I said, strongly. "I'm not giving up my best friend."

This earned a smile.

"We may not be able to hang out in the evenings but you can still come here in the mornings, right? I'll be relying on you to keep me up to date on all the news."

Mathilde nodded and looked relieved.

Our conversation had completely driven Claud from my mind but I now thought of him guiltily. What sort of friend was I if I didn't say anything? But somehow I couldn't work out the right words. The more I thought about it, the more I realised that nothing concrete had happened. Nothing that Claud couldn't explain away. It would be easy for him to suggest that he was simply being polite and that I had wrongfully read more into it.

I still had no idea what he was doing in the evenings. If I followed him and saw him with Nikki that would be concrete proof. Then I could say something to Mathilde. I was glad to have a plan, and gladder still that I had an excuse to put off the conversation with Mathilde.

Throughout the day I found my mind returning to Claud. I couldn't shake the memory of the darkness I'd seen in his eyes when he realised I wasn't falling for his charm. Something told me someone should be watching Claud and the sooner Mathilde realised the truth about him, the better off she'd be. Tonight was the night.

With this thought in mind, I dressed in my darkest dress. Just like the night before, I walked straight down the stairs and outside. But this time I turned away from the stables and slipped into the garden. Claud's path the night before had been towards the forest, along one of the tall hedges. I positioned myself behind it, out of view of the door. I then proceeded to wait. And wait. And wait.

I was wearing my boots but my feet were starting to ache from standing so long without moving. And the cold had long since seeped through my cloak and into my bones. I was now shivering constantly and spasmodically a deeper shudder would shake my body. What had seemed a great idea inside the castle now seemed foolish. What if he didn't come out tonight? I could freeze to death waiting for him.

I blame the acute physical discomfort for distracting me so badly that I didn't hear the footsteps behind me. I did, however, feel the hand that landed on my shoulder and roughly spun me around. I was too shocked to scream. Instead I wrenched myself away and took one stumbling step backwards, only stopping when I recognised my attacker.

"Max??" I whisper hissed. "What are you doing here?"

"The real question is what are *you* doing here?" he replied, matching my whisper but looking exasperated. "You've been out here for ages and you're freezing, I could feel your shivers through your cloak."

"How do you know how long I've been out here," I asked with suspicion.

He pointed towards one of the castle windows. "I saw you come out of the castle."

I realised that although I was hidden from the side door at the bottom of the servants' stairs, I could be seen from any of the windows along the front of the castle.

Before I could ask again why he had come out, Max continued. "And you still haven't answered my question. What are you doing out here?"

I opened my mouth and then closed it again.

"That's right," said Max grimly, "It's way too cold out here for you to fob me off with some excuse. I want the truth."

There was just enough light from the castle for me to read the determination in his eyes. But I only had a second to wonder how I could possibly explain the truth when I heard a door open and light shone through the hedge. I stiffened and raised my finger to my lips, staring wide-eyed at Max. He looked confused but stayed silent.

Carefully I tiptoed closer to the hedge, straining to hear any tell-tale sounds. There were no voices but I could hear one person heading away from the stables towards the forest. The trajectory of the footsteps convinced me it must be Claud.

Ignoring Max, I began to creep along the hedge, mirroring the person walking on the other side. After a moment I felt Max fall in silently behind me. I was annoyed — there would be no way to avoid telling him the whole complicated saga now. But at the same time, I couldn't help but feel relieved. There was now also no chance of my finding myself alone in the night with Claud.

When we reached the end of the hedge, I paused. The person I was following didn't hesitate but strode towards the forest. We were now out of reach of the castle lights but there was enough light from the moon for me to see the dim figure of a man. It looked like Claud but I couldn't be completely sure in the darkness.

The equally dim figure of Max now grabbed my arm, trying to tug me back towards the castle. I shook him off and started quietly after Claud. In a few more steps he would be hidden amongst the trees and I didn't want to lose him.

I heard a soft sigh and then Max followed me. I moved across the open ground trying to be silent and quick at the same time. I felt horribly exposed now that Claud was hidden in the trees and I was without cover. The tension was rising with each step and I had to force myself not to panic and break out into a run for the trees. I also had to restrain from reaching out and clinging to Max. I was now doubly glad for his reassuring presence beside me.

In spite of my fears, we reached the trees without being accosted. No sooner had we stepped under their leafy cover than we heard the soft murmur of voices.

I knew it! I thought. Claud is meeting someone out here.

I strained to hear if the other voice was Nikki's. But we were too far away for me to recognise it or make out any words. I crept closer. As I moved, I pulled the hood of my cloak low, hiding the white blob of my face and my unhelpfully golden hair.

I continued to slip from tree to tree until I was close enough to see two figures. It was definitely too dark amongst the trees to distinguish Claud's face but I could now recognise his voice. However I was surprised by his companion. The second voice was masculine and spoke with a faint accent.

"You promised me gold." That was Claud.

"You'll get your gold when we get our information." That was the other man.

For a moment my mind was blank, trying to assimilate the unexpected words. Then I realised the nerves I had felt before were nothing. At least, they were nothing compared to the paralysing dread that was now flooding my body. I slowly, quietly turned my head to look at Max. He wasn't looking at me, he was staring at the two men, but seeing the outline of his figure somehow increased my terror. Unwittingly I had led the heir to the throne away from his guards and straight into the hands of two men of unknown villainy.

"I've given you information, I want my gold and the safe passage out of the kingdom you promised."

"We need to know more about the royal family than the servants can tell us. You said there's a new Princess Companion. Get close to her. Find out what she knows."

I could feel rather than hear Max's body stiffen.

"I've already tried. She's suspicious of me, wouldn't give me anything," said Claud in a surly tone.

"What?" His companion's voice rose slightly. "Someone's suspicious of you?"

The second man was standing with his back to us so we could see what Claud could not – the stranger's hand moving towards a lump at the small of his back.

"No, no, she's just suspicious that I'm two-timing one of her friends. A maid. I am, of course."

Claud gave a quiet chuckle and after a moment the other man joined in, his hand slowly drifting back to his side.

"Well, see what you can get through the friend then."

"Ok, I'll give it another week but then I'm out of here."

"Fine, one week and then follow the instructions we gave you. We'll get you out of here."

"And I'll get my gold?" Claud sounded suspicious.

"Yeah, yeah, you'll get your gold. Just make sure you get something good. You know what sort of things we're looking for."

There was a mutual exchange of farewell grunts and a handshake. Then the stranger began to move off through the woods, away from the castle. Claud stood in silence for a long time, gazing off in the direction the other man had gone. Finally he seemed to notice the cold, shivering and rubbing his arms. He turned back towards the castle and I suddenly realised our mistake. We had missed our opportunity to sneak away. We were now standing between Claud and the castle and if he came forward only a few steps he would see us.

In my alarm, I took an unthinking step backward. My foot landed on a twig and the sound of it breaking felt like a cannon blast ripping through the forest.

Chapter 9

Claud's head snapped towards us and in the same instant Max took off running towards the castle. I stood frozen in shock and watched Claud dash after him. Max had only a few steps head start and was hampered by the trees and the darkness. He hadn't made it far when Claud threw himself forward and tackled the prince to the ground. There was a brief scuffle and for a moment I thought Max might throw him off but then both men rose slowly to their feet, Max with his hands held above his head.

Once they were both upright I could see why. Claud had a gun and it was pointing at Max's chest. They were both panting and staring at each other. I wondered, in a panic, what Max had been thinking. And then, for the briefest second, his eyes flicked towards me and I knew. Max had run back towards the castle but he had run at an angle so that the pursuing Claud had bypassed the spot where I stood frozen. In the split second after I had stepped on that twig, Max had moved to protect me. To keep Claud from finding both of us.

The realisation galvanised me. Thanks to Max's quick thinking Claud was unaware that there were two of us in the forest. I couldn't let that advantage go to waste.

"Spying on me, were you?" Claud spoke. "I can't let you go back to the castle now, can I?"

Max said nothing. In the darkness it was unlikely that Claud had recognised Max. I had no idea what would happen if Claud realised who it was he held at gunpoint. I supposed that depended on who he was working for and what they wanted. For now he seemed hesitant to shoot, probably afraid that the gunshot would be heard from the castle.

I began to move through the forest, testing each step before committing my weight, trying to avoid any more treacherous twigs. Luckily I didn't have far to go. I crept to within a few feet of Claud, took a deep breath and lunged forward. With both hands I grabbed his right arm and used all my weight to pull it down. The pistol went off but the bullet lodged harmlessly in the base of a tree. Claud swore loudly and swung his left fist around, punching me in the face. The explosion of pain caused my vision to black out and I slumped down. But somehow I managed to maintain my grip on his arm, my dead weight only pulling the gun further towards the ground.

Before Claud could hit me again, or prise off my fingers, he was suddenly gone. His arm wrenched from my grip and his pistol dropped at my feet. I lay on the ground, confused, my head throbbing and stared at the gun lying on the hard dirt.

"Alyssa? *Alyssa!* Are you ok?"

Max sounded panicked so with a great deal of effort, I pushed myself into a sitting position. The quick movement made me lose vision again but after a moment I was able to reply.

"I'm ok. What happened?"

"Can you pick up the gun? And I need something to secure his hands. Quickly, before he comes around."

My vision had cleared now and I could see Max kneeling over Claud's still body. I realised that while I was clinging onto Claud's arm, Max had knocked him out. I tried to think through the pain. *Rope, rope, where can I find rope.* I looked helplessly towards the castle and then down at my empty hands. *My clothes!*

I had nothing on me but my clothes, they would have to do. I glanced towards Max but he was looking the other way, kneeling over Claud. I carefully stood up, pulled up my skirt and slipped off my petticoat. I began to tear the material into one long strip, ignoring the burn in my hands as I strained to make the initial rip. At the sound of the tearing fabric Max glanced up.

"Good, bring that here and then find the gun." I walked the few steps towards him, the torn garment in both hands. He took it and began to tie Claud's hands in place. I turned back around but could no longer see the gun in the darkness. Getting down onto my hands and knees, I swept the ground with my fingers until I felt the cold metal. I stood up and Max was suddenly there, standing next to me. For a moment I thought he was going to put his arms around me and I desperately wanted to rest my aching head against his chest. But behind us Claud groaned and Max turned back towards him, holding his hand out blindly for the gun. I put it into his hand and he spoke without turning back towards me.

"I'll guard him. Are you well enough to go get help?"

I nodded and then realised he couldn't see me. "Yes."

"Go straight to the guardhouse. As quickly as you can. I should be alright here but if that other man heard the gunshot…"

The pain in my head was clouding my thinking, I had completely forgotten the other man. I wondered if he would double back or leave Claud to his fate. I took off running without another word.

Despite my pain and bruises, I had never run so fast in my life. With each step I strained to hear the sound of another gunshot, imagining Max lying on the ground, bleeding out.

The moonlight turned the garden into an alien place and twice I veered momentarily off course, startled by an unexpected shadow. My breath was coming in short pants.

I had never been inside the guard house but I knew it was on the other side of the castle to the stables. As I neared it, I somehow found the breath to shout.

"Help! Help!" I screamed as loudly as I could.

There was an answering shout from inside and then bright light poured across me from a suddenly opened door. Guards spilled out of the doorway, several carrying lanterns and the rest buckling on swords or shouldering rifles. I was relieved to see them but illogically angered by all the noise they were making. I was still straining to hear the dreaded gunshot.

The first guard grabbed me by the arms, stopping my forward momentum.

"What is it? What's going on?" And then sharply, after he got a good look at my face, "The princesses?"

"No, the prince!" I panted. "In the woods, with a prisoner. But there's another man with a gun."

Several of the guards took off running in the direction I was pointing. The one who was holding me began to follow, dragging me with him.

"You'll have to come with us," he said. "Show us exactly where he is."

I was exhausted but I didn't complain. Each second without a gunshot seemed to give me a new burst of energy. I was anxious to get back. Only the sight of Max, whole and unharmed, would erase the picture I had in my head. The one where he lay on the ground, unmoving in a pool of blood.

The trip back through the garden seemed to take half the time now that I was surrounded by light and people. As the fastest guards neared the forest I called out "to the left" and they veered around to enter the forest at the same spot where I had emerged. I could hear them calling to each other and then a louder shout. I hoped that meant they had found Max. I sped up.

The forest looked completely different now, light spilling everywhere from the many lanterns. At first I couldn't work out what was going on in the chaos of moving bodies. And then I saw him. He was covered in dirt and his clothes were torn from being tackled to the ground but he was standing talking to the captain of the guard. He had never looked so good to me as he did then, coloured by my relief.

He must have felt the strength of my gaze because he turned and spotted me in the crowd of men. He looked concerned but his words were too quiet for me to hear. I suddenly wondered what had happened to Claud and looked around with concern myself. But no, Claud was still there, supported between two guards, his hands tied with my petticoat.

Before I had time to do more than note Claud's presence, a guard approached me.

"I'm to escort you back to the castle, miss," he said.

"No, no," I said, a little wildly, "I need to talk to Max – I mean, the prince."

"It's the prince's orders, miss. You're to wait for him there."

"Oh… ok." I was reluctant to leave but I couldn't think of any useful reason for me to remain in the woods.

I let the guard lead me back to the palace. I was stumbling now from fatigue and the aftereffects of over-stimulation. I kept my eyes on the back of his boots and almost collided with him when he stopped at the castle door. Dorkins must have been lurking in the entrance hall, roused by the noise and lights, because he opened the door at the first knock. I shook my head mutely when his shocked and enquiring eyes fell on me. I figured it was best not to say anything at all until I had had a chance to talk to Max.

The guard began to lead me towards the East Wing but Dorkins objected sharply. After a slight altercation, I learned my objective was the king's office. I wasn't in the least surprised when Dorkins won the bout and the guard retreated back outside, leaving the butler to lead me to the designated room.

I had glimpsed the office briefly during my tour of the castle but had retained only a hazy memory of dark oak. I wondered, with some anxiety, if the king would still be there at this hour. This new fear was overriding the numbness of fatigue and my mind was sharp again when I entered the room.

To my great relief it was empty. The air was still warm and the fire was still dwindling in the fireplace so I had probably only just missed him. Dorkins proceeded to stoke the fire, moving with a stately majesty to remind me that this task was beneath him. I suspected that he was dying to hear what was going on outside but I remained silent. After lighting several branches of candles and straightening the chairs, Dorkins ran out of things to do and reluctantly left the room.

I sank into one of the chairs and stared blankly into the fire. I longed for my bed and even more to talk to Max. To assure myself he really was ok. As the minutes ticked by I looked around and began to wonder uneasily why Max had had the guard lead me here. Max had seen and heard everything I had. He didn't need me to explain the night's happenings to the king.

Unless.

I suddenly remembered that I had never had the chance to explain to Max why I was following Claud. All he knew was that I had led him into the forest, alone, to face two armed traitors. Just as this thought occurred to me, the door opened. Max entered first, closely followed by King Henry. Both looked grim. And two guards were now stationed outside the door.

Chapter 10

I leapt to my feet, knocking over my chair. Max immediately came forward and picked it back up with a small smile. I was relieved enough that my protestations died on my lips. We all took seats and for a moment simply stared at each other.

"My son tells me that the two of you followed a traitor into the woods tonight and apprehended him." It was the king who broke the silence. "Apparently one of our footmen has been paid to spy on us. It seems my son was right - there are some flaws in our recruitment process."

Silence once again enveloped us. I shivered slightly under the king's piercing gaze, acutely aware of the double meaning of his words.

"I confess to some confusion regarding your role. I'm afraid I have to ask what, exactly, were your intentions when you led my son into the forest tonight?"

I straightened, relieved to be given the chance to explain.

"I had no intention of leading Max into the forest at all," I replied. "I certainly wouldn't have let him follow me if I'd known what we were going to find." After a moment's thought I added, "For that matter, I wouldn't have been out there myself if I'd known what Claud was doing."

The king raised his eyebrows. "Are you asking me to believe that you just happened to stroll into a traitorous assignation? And on a night when my son just happened to be following you?"

I could almost feel his incredulity.

"Of course not!" I hurried to say. "I meant to follow Claud. I had to wait in the garden for ages for him to come out. That's why Max was there, he saw me from his window and came out to see what I was doing. Only then Claud came out, too, so I followed him and Max followed me."

I looked to Max for confirmation of my story. He was looking at his father.

"It's true she didn't seem to want me out there but I was hardly going to let her go wandering around in the forest alone at night."

"Given how events transpired, I think that shows a reasonable level of foresight," said the king.

"I wasn't suspicious of her!" Max flushed. "I was concerned for her safety."

"As I said," repeated the king, "given events, that turned out to be a wise assessment. What I still don't understand is why Alyssa was following Claud in the first place."

Clearly I wasn't going to be able to leave Mathilde out of this.

"It was my friend, your majesty," I said.

"Your friend is involved in this treason?" The king tensed and leaned forward and Max spun around to look at me.

"No, no! I was watching Claud because my friend was in lo...well, she really liked him. He seemed to be courting her but was sending some mixed messages. I was worried about her so I was watching Claud and something seemed," I hesitated, "*off* about him. Honestly, I thought he was messing around with one of the other maids behind her back. I thought if I followed him and saw them together then I would have proof for my friend."

There was silence as the king weighed my words.

"It's true." The king and I both looked at Max in surprise. "I'd forgotten but Claud mentioned something about it to his associate. The other man was worried that someone suspected Claud but Claud said that Alyssa only suspected him of two-timing her friend."

"Well," the king said, after another moment's thought, "in that case it seems we owe a debt of gratitude to your instincts, Alyssa. We might not have discovered Claud otherwise."

I felt emboldened to ask, "What will happen to him now?"

"We'll send him back to the prisons in Arcadie. We don't have any suitable lock-up facilities here. My intelligence chief will be very curious to interview him."

"Will he talk, though?" I asked, concerned.

The king shrugged and it was Max who answered.

"From the sound of things out in the woods he owes no loyalty to his employer. If his motivations are greed it'll be easy enough to convince him it's in his best interests to tell us everything he knows."

I felt relieved but the excess energy had well and truly dissipated from my system now and my fatigue was battling with the ache in my head. Max noticed my sagging lids and wrapped up the conversation. Next thing I knew we were all walking up the stairs, the two guards trailing behind us. When we reached the gallery, the king turned to the right with a quick good night and the guards followed him, leaving Max and I to walk up the west gallery alone. We walked in silence but Max stayed by my side until I reached the door to the Princess Suite.

Then he spoke. "You're hurt."

He reached up, as if to touch my bruised face, but then seemed to think better of it and let his hand drop.

"Out there, in the woods," he gestured towards the forest, "I wasn't sure what you'd do. I thought maybe you'd go for help. I know how you feel about pain, I didn't think you'd attack him."

"I wasn't going to leave you there at gunpoint!" I exclaimed, incensed.

"Well, I'm sorry you got hurt," he said. "And I'm sorry I called you soft the other day."

My anger faded and I managed a small chuckle.

"I am soft," I said. "But that doesn't mean I'm not brave. I just save my bravery for when it's actually needed."

He smiled in response. "You know, that doesn't sound so stupid," he said.

"People don't generally accuse me of being stupid," I replied with a smile, "just soft."

"No, I've never accused you of being stupid," he said quietly. And then, "I think you'd better get some sleep, Brave Alyssa, you're about to keel over."

"You'd better get some rest yourself, Max," I replied, "you must be pretty tired too."

When I opened my eyes it was morning. I must have been half asleep as I prepared for bed because I had no memory of doing it. In fact, it took a moment for any of the memories from the night before to return. At first all I could think of was the pounding in my head. When I put my hand up to my head I gasped in pain. But the contact with my bruise brought the events in the forest flooding back into my mind and I leapt from bed.

After waiting a moment for the head rush to subside, I ran into the bathroom. I stared at my reflection in the mirror in shock. My eyes were still green and my hair still red gold but otherwise I felt unrecognisable. Since it hurt too much to touch the real thing I touched the huge black eye in the mirror. If possible, it looked even worse than it felt. What in the world was I going to tell the princesses?

I did a quick inventory of the rest of my body as I completed my morning wash. My only other injury was some minor scratches on my hands from crawling across the forest floor.

When I heard someone enter the suite I went back out into the sitting room, still in my nightgown but at least clean.

The queen was standing there, looking far more alert than I felt. With a sense of surprise I realised this was only the second time I had seen her here, in the princesses' suite. The first time was my first day when she introduced me to Mrs Pine and Nanny.

I barely had time to register this thought before she swept me into a hug. At first the shock of the unexpected contact held me stiff but after a moment I was flooded with thoughts of my own mother and I returned her embrace.

"Thank you," she said and at first I thought she meant for uncovering Claud's treachery. But then she added, "for saving my son."

"Alyssa saved Max?!?" That was Lily from the doorway to the bedroom. Her words were followed by two shrieks when the queen and I turned towards them and the girls saw my face.

"Well, he saved me too," I said. And then, conscientiously, "twice."

But no one seemed to be taking any notice of me as the girls rushed over and began bombarding us with questions.

"What happened to your face?"

"Are you alright?"

"Where's Max?

"Is *he* alright?"

"How did you save him?"

I looked at the queen, unsure how much to tell them. She seemed similarly uncertain but after a moment she gave a resigned sigh and cut across their questions.

"Last night Alyssa and Max discovered that one of the footmen was being paid to gather information on the kingdom. They captured him but he injured Alyssa."

The queen gestured towards my face. "But she's ok, Max's ok, everyone's ok."

"Everyone except the spy, I hope," said Lily.

I raised my eyebrows at her and she gave me a look that clearly said 'I'm eleven, not stupid'.

"He's safely in custody," said the queen repressively.

"Which one was it?" asked Sophie.

"Which one what?" I asked back.

"Which footman?" clarified Lily.

"Oh. Um, it was Claud," I said, figuring this information was hardly going to stay secret.

"Claud? Really?" Lily turned to Sophie, "that's the cute one."

"Lily!" The queen's tone was reproving but her face looked amused.

"Well he is!" said Sophie.

"I hope you girls haven't ever spoken to him!" said the queen, a new worry rearing its head.

"Of course not!" exclaimed Lily. "He's a footman!"

I raised my eyebrows at her again. Claud might have turned out to be a traitor but none of us had known that before last night. Lily bit her lip.

"Sorry, Alyssa, I forgot," she said.

"Forgot what?" asked the queen, confused.

"She forgot that a princess should always be courteous and considerate to everyone, especially to people of lower rank," piped in Sophie, speaking as if she were reciting a lesson. "Alyssa's been teaching us but sometimes we forget. Lily forgets the most."

At this addition, her sister kicked her in the ankle. By the time I had told Lily off for the violence and convinced both girls to go get ready for breakfast, my embarrassment at their behaviour had faded. I turned back to the queen, trying to think

104

of an acceptable explanation for the girls' words but she spoke before I could think of anything.

"It seems it's not just for my son's sake that I need to thank you," she said.

Her words made me acutely uncomfortable.

"Honestly, your majesty, I didn't do much. Max saved me first. If it wasn't for his quick thinking we would probably both be dead right now."

"Please, call me Ella," she said, smiling with pleasure at my praise of her son.

"Ella, your majesty?"

"Yes, it was my nickname once. No one uses it anymore." She sighed. "I didn't have a very happy youth but I do find myself missing my old name. You've proved yourself a true friend to this family – it was a happy day for us when you got lost in that storm."

She paused and I sat in silence, honoured and unsure how to respond to her reminiscence.

"Only when we're alone or with the family, though," she added.

"Of course, your majesty. I mean… Ella," I amended uncomfortably. I could understand the need for a public show of respect more than I could understand my sudden inclusion in her inner circle.

I felt unworthy of being elevated so drastically but I couldn't help my response to the deep sadness I sensed behind her words. I tentatively put my arms around her. She responded with a smile and a hug but stepped back quickly as the girls came pouring back out of their room. The intimacy of the moment was broken and a small, overwhelmed part of me could only feel glad.

Chapter 11

I soon found that my adventure in the woods had changed more attitudes than just the queen's. I no longer had to rely on Mathilde to smooth things over with the servants. Even Gretchen seemed to have, grudgingly, accepted my new intimacy with the royal family. She couldn't quite bring herself to address me as an equal, though, and had settled for ignoring me entirely. Naturally, I was completely happy with this arrangement.

Any surprise I felt at my sudden elevation in the castle hierarchy dissipated within a day. If the stories flying around were to be believed, I had singlehandedly and purposefully uncovered a plot on the life of the prince and had then, with great cunning and skill, risked my own life to save his. I could see little resemblance between the actual events in the forest and the Alyssa in these tales. But any protestations I made were dismissed as modesty. I began to think rather darkly of all my favourite characters and to wonder if there was any truth in their tales.

It was with this thought in mind that I was sitting in the library and glaring at the book of fairy tales I still kept there for light reading. I couldn't seem to settle my mind to any serious study so I was relieved to hear the door open. I wasn't keen to talk to Mathilde – to say she had had a painful reaction to the news about Claud would be an understatement – but I knew my duty as a friend. I just hoped her outrage would soon overwhelm her heartbreak.

But it wasn't Mathilde who appeared between the bookshelves. It was Max.

Without asking permission he strode over and swung himself onto my window seat, positioning himself so that we were facing each other. He smiled with satisfaction and I wondered if he had come in here looking for me. I was mad at him, though, so I refused to speak. After a moment of silence his smile faded and he gestured towards my face.

"Does it still hurt?" he asked.

"Only if I smile or talk or change expressions," I said with a straight face.

He winced and I relented. "It's not that bad," I admitted, "it already hurts less than it did." He looked relieved but his consideration reminded me of my initial grievance.

"I can't believe the stories flying around the castle," I said, "what in the world have you been telling everybody?" He laughed at my angry expression.

"I thought you'd appreciate it," he said with a smug grin, "I figured if you could put aside your aversion to pain for me, I could put aside my pride for you. I actually think I make a pretty good prince-in-distress."

He laughed again and leaned back with his arms behind his head.

I was tempted to punch him in the ribs – the response I would have given any of my brothers if they struck such a pose – but I was actually rather touched by his words. As frustrating as the exaggerated stories were, they had certainly helped smooth my way.

"No-one else wants to hear it, but you and I know that it was your quick thinking that saved us. Why are you going to so much trouble for me? When I first got here, I thought you hated me."

Max sat up at my words and looked at me seriously. But any hope for a real answer died when he suddenly relaxed and gave me an amused smile.

"You have no idea how much the girls used to plague me before you arrived," he said. "Believe me, I appreciate you more and more with each passing, blessedly quiet, moment."

From his expression I had expected a glib response but this rang surprisingly true. I hadn't thought about it in relation to Max but I knew from experience how annoyed brothers got by younger sisters.

"You must have been what – eight? – when your sisters were born." I asked curiously. "Old enough to think of yourself as an only child. What did you think when you found out your mother was pregnant?"

"I wasn't very impressed by the idea of a baby. But I thought a brother might be okay. As you can see, that didn't work out very well for me."

But he laughed as he said it, to show he bore no malice towards his sisters.

"You must have been bored on your own, though. They're so much younger – I can't imagine you ever played together."

"No, but in Arcadie there are plenty of noblemen's sons my age. Wait until you meet Felix and Nate. I don't think you can appreciate the scope of mischief we used to get up to until you meet them for yourself." His eyes gleamed reminiscently.

"But what about out here?" I persisted, "At the Winter Castle? I can see how bored the twins get and there are two of them."

"Yes, you poor thing. You bear all the brunt of their boredom now," he said, and I was surprised to see that there was real concern, not teasing, in his eyes.

They were such a deep blue as they gazed at me that I found myself distracted. I kept losing my train of thought whenever I glanced at them. And it wasn't just the colour. It was something about their steady expression. I had had glimpses of it before but

I wasn't fully prepared for the effect of such a prolonged, concentrated gaze. While we talked he looked at me as if I had his complete, undivided attention. As if nothing else mattered in this moment except for me and my words. I wasn't used to boys looking at me like that, especially very attractive ones, and I felt a little overwhelmed.

"But it was different for me." It took me a moment to focus back on what he was saying. "They never tried to keep me to the gardens. I was always doing something active. Riding or fishing or learning to shoot."

"Not very nice weather for it," I commented.

"Ah well, I guess it was supposed to toughen me up and on rainy days I mostly stayed inside and had fencing lessons."

"But the girls could be doing some of that. They're certainly old enough to ride."

"They can ride," he replied, to my surprise. "If you ever run out of topics of conversation you should ask them about their ponies. They can talk about them for hours."

"I'm surprised it's never come up," I said.

"I guess they're used to it," he replied. "In their minds, riding is an activity for the Palace not the Castle."

"But why shouldn't they ride?" I asked, incensed on their behalf but also slightly terrified at the thought of trying to control them while they were on horseback.

"As you pointed out, it's cold outside and it often rains. Plus the forest is dense here, not like the fields they're used to riding across at home." He smiled and nudged me with his elbow, inviting me to share his next quip. "I guess it's only boys that need toughening up."

I sighed and rolled my eyes. "Pity no-one told my brothers that. Or maybe it only applies to nobility. I'm pretty sure woodcutter's children are supposed to be tough regardless of gender."

"Well I can see why you left," he said. "You're not exactly the woodcutting type." He was looking at me with the same intensity I remembered from my first day and for a moment I forgot to breathe. His words could be taken either way but there was no mistaking the warmth in his tone. I was glad when the bell rang for lunch, removing my need to reply.

Max leapt lightly to his feet and held out his hand to help me up. I took it. It was the first time we had touched and I wondered if he was as acutely aware of this as I was. His grip was firm and warm and I had to force myself to pull my hand away.

"I didn't realise it was so late," I said. "Gretchen will have left by now and who knows what mischief the twins will have gotten up to. I'd better go fetch them for lunch."

I was glad for the excuse to hurry from the room.

Day by day the bruises faded from my face and from Mathilde's heart. Life settled back into routine with just a few significant changes. I still spent most of each day with the twins and every meal with the royal family. I still listened intently to the mealtime conversations which had turned towards the rival merits of our various neighbours. The king was clearly contemplating an alliance of some kind but he seemed undecided on the best choice of ally. For some reason this topic always made Max uncomfortable and I was surprised that the queen continued to introduce it to the meal table. Although the queen rarely gave her opinion, it was she who facilitated all the conversations around the table. She was usually very good at keeping the discussion going, always encouraging her son to contribute. I could only assume the proposed alliance must be important if she was willing to persist despite Max's apparent frustration. I turned my morning study to alliances.

There seemed to be any number of political, military and trade advantages to an alliance. And our kingdom was large and fairly prosperous. If nothing else, our many resources should make us a popular partner. But I sensed there was a driver to this alliance that the royal family were careful not to mention in my presence. That niggling itch of something eluding me drove me to study harder than before. With the kitchen now firmly closed to me by my new social status, I added an evening study session to my morning one.

Fortunately for my sanity, my study was leavened by a daily dose of news from below stairs. Apparently all the staff had been exhaustively interviewed but no further treachery had been uncovered. The most surprising result of Claud's defection was the unexpected friendship that had now grown up between Mathilde and Nikki. They were bound by their shared injury and outrage – and I couldn't help but feel excluded. I was glad my days were absorbed with the royals. The twins and my study kept me so busy I had little time to nurse the small kernel of jealousy I felt as I watched Mathilde grow closer to Nikki. I tried my best to stamp it down and feel glad for my friend. After all, I saw less of her now that I no longer frequented the kitchen.

I reminded myself that this was only a taste of what it would be like in Arcadie – when the microcosm of the Winter Castle was expanded and all the people I had grown close to returned to their old friends. When I imagined Arcadie, I imagined myself abandoned – alone in a sea of strangers. After all, the big city was going to shatter this small community I had become a part of. All the people who had welcomed me with open arms – Mathilde, the queen, the twins, Max – had done so because out here they were separated from their normal networks. As a consequence of these depressing thoughts, I immersed myself in my current world, blocking Arcadie, and the summer, from my mind. A small part of me rebelled – afraid of the pain that would follow the inevitable shattering of my false reality. That part was silenced and it soon stopped rebelling at all.

Despite my drive for understanding, I had to admit that study could get boring – and lonely. I looked across the dark library. The lantern I was reading by was bright and cheery and the fires were still burning, keeping the room comfortably warm. But the sea of bookshelves looked endless in the dark and I had to fight not to imagine someone lurking just out of sight. I was just considering taking my book up to the sitting room in the princesses' suite when a light appeared over by the door. After a moment, Max came into view, carrying a lantern.

"Mind if I join you?" he asked.

"Please do," I said with a smile, "I'd be glad of the company." *And I'm glad I didn't go upstairs after all* I added in my mind.

The eeriness of the large, dark room was dispelled by the presence of another person and the prospect of company brought an instant lift to my mood.

Max sat down in an armchair close to my mine and for a few minutes we read in companionable silence. The first time he sighed I ignored it. The second time I peered at the title of his book. *Ah, that explained it.* I had read that book last week and the author's sentences were so long you often had to read them two or three times over. I went back to my own book. The third time he sighed so did I.

"I'm trying to read over here, Max," I said.

"Sorry," he replied. But after a moment his frustration got the better of him. "I can't stand this guy. Honestly, this book is impossible to read."

He lobbed the book across the room towards the bookshelf on international relations. Despite my horror at this abuse of a book, I couldn't help but admire his aim. The book sailed halfway across the room and hit the correct shelf, ricocheting to the floor with a thud.

"He's pretentious, yes," I said. "But if you can wade through those sentences you'll find he raises some interesting points. I agree with him that it's important to maintain a balance of power but I think he overemphasises military power. This book gives a more balanced view of the importance of trade." I held up the book I was reading. "You should try this one when I've finished."

"Maybe I should try it now. All these books are mine after all, not yours," he replied. I looked over, shocked at his rude arrogance, and was reassured by the smile on his face. He was making a joke.

Before I could think of an appropriate response, he lunged out of his chair and attempted to wrest the book from my grasp. I laughed and attempted to fend him off but he was too strong. After a moment's tussle he had the book in his hand and was holding it above his head. I leapt to my feet and tried to grab it back but I was too short. I attempted to jump up and reach it but he easily pushed me away. I put one hand on his shoulder, using it as leverage, but he used his free hand to fend me off. We were both laughing but suddenly I was aware of the way he smelled – like wood smoke and rain and parchment – and of the feel of his muscles, straining as he wrestled with me. I froze and he seemed to instantly catch the change of mood, sucking in his breath and staring at me. Our faces were so close they were almost touching and for a moment I couldn't remember what we were fighting over.

Max cleared his throat and stepped back, snapping me out of my daze. With an exaggerated, courtly bow he returned my book.

"Your book, my lady, with my apologies," he said, with a ridiculously large smile.

I could tell he was trying to recreate the stupid, joking mood of a moment ago and I was grateful to him for covering my momentary lapse. The royals might treat me like one of the family but I couldn't allow myself to forget the truth. Otherwise there would be more embarrassing incidents like this one.

"Thank you," I said, my graciousness equally over the top. And then, tentatively, "I could explain the main concepts to you." I gestured towards the discarded book. "Then you won't have to wrestle with those sentences."

"Really, would you?" Max flopped back into his armchair and smiled at me gratefully. "As long as you promise not to tell anyone what a study dunce I am," he said.

"Deal," I smiled, "as long as you promise not to sigh while I'm trying to explain."

"That's what I said to Alyssa!"

Max looked over at me in triumph. We were sitting at lunch and the king had just unknowingly backed up Max's argument from the night before. Max and I now read in the library every night and often we discussed what we were reading, debating the various theories presented by the authors.

I glared back at him, angry at being brought into it. He must know I couldn't argue against the king!

"You told Alyssa that you think Lanover got cheated in their trade deal with Northhelm?" the king asked in surprise.

"Yes. But she agrees with Silvester," he said, naming the author I was currently reading. "She thinks it was deep dealing on Lanover's part. That it's not really about trade. That Lanover want to ensure Northhelm becomes economically reliant on them."

The king regarded me steadily and I glared at Max again.

"It's nice to hear you taking an interest in such things," the king said to his son. "When exactly did you have this deep discussion?"

"Last night," replied Max. "We study in the library in the evenings. We don't agree on much, although we do agree that Rangmere won't like it if Northhelm and Lanover form a stronger alliance."

"Ah," chimed in the queen, "that explains where you've been disappearing to."

"Sounds boring," piped in Sophie.

"I wish we didn't have to study," added Lily, sounding depressed.

I smiled at her encouragingly. I knew she was having trouble with her mathematics and had been attempting to help her with it for several days. Unfortunately mathematics wasn't my strong suit either.

The interjection from the twins turned the conversation to the latest report from Gretchen and the rest of the meal was spent discussing the princesses' progress in their studies. I was extra supportive in all my comments, glad to have the king and queen's attention turned away from me.

When the king appeared in the library that evening I was reminded of my first impression of him. His attention wasn't as easily distracted as it sometimes appeared to be. Before the incident with Claud he had seemed oblivious to my presence, I wondered now if that had actually been the case. Either way, he certainly wasn't oblivious to it now.

His presence made me constrained and uncomfortable. It was an honour, of course, but an honour I would have preferred to do without. I enjoyed discussing my reading material with Max but I hardly felt free to set up an opposing opinion to the king.

But it turned out the king was practiced at putting people at their ease. The observer in me noted his techniques and wondered if I could emulate them, even as the rest of me fell under his spell. By the third evening he joined us I was completely relaxed and easily immersed myself in the debate – grateful now for my hours of study.

But as flattering and stimulating as these conversations were, I still preferred the nights when the queen came. She came less frequently than the king, and never on the same nights as him, but when she did come the library would echo with our laughter. I already knew she was skilled at conversation but I hadn't guessed at her hidden gift for humour. She entertained us with stories of her youth and of court. She drew skillful, amusing sketches of the people who made up her world while always maintaining an underlying kindness. Her anecdotes might gently mock but only in the case of her stepmother and stepsisters did she truly ridicule. And I couldn't judge her for that – the whole kingdom knew the stories of their self-absorbed cruelty.

These lamp lit evenings were the only times I could truly think of her as just Ella. With only the three of us she seemed to let go of her role as queen and even as mother. In the pool of light and warmth we were just three people, whiling away a winter's evening.

Max loved hearing humorous stories about his father, especially, and laughed heartily at his propensity to misplace important documents. "Always at the worst possible moment," the queen assured us and launched into an anecdote about the first trade agreement the young King Henry had attempted to negotiate.

I suspected the occasion had been less humorous at the time but since the king had managed to salvage the situation I felt free to join in the laughter.

"He could never forgive me for roasting him in front of the ambassador," said Ella. "So at my next birthday he hinted that he was getting me a beautiful pearl bracelet. But when I opened the jewelry box, there was only a key inside. He said that since I was such a superior organiser he was handing over the key to his desk. I'm pretty sure he meant it as a joke but I kept it and he's never lost an important document again. Not with me organising his study! Men!"

She rolled her eyes at me and we both laughed at Max's expense.

Both Max and I were spurred on to relate our own humorous tales and I suspect the queen learned a lot more in those evenings about her son's youthful activities than she had previously been aware.

But even more than the nights with the queen, I preferred the nights when Max and I were alone. I never thought too deeply about the reason for this, never analysed my greedy desire to be the sole focus of his attentive gaze. Dimly I knew that danger lay there so I turned my focus resolutely away and simply enjoyed myself.

Chapter 12

Slowly the weather began to warm up and the twins and I were able to spend an increasing amount of time outside. Luckily my dread of clear days had faded. Lily and Sophie were as tireless and mischievous as ever but we usually had company for our garden excursions now.

"They really like you, you know," said Max after the girls had finally exhausted him and wandered away for other entertainment.

I smiled. "They like you more," I said.

"Well, I'm fresh meat," he replied easily.

"I'm surprised you come to visit us," I teased, "I thought they plagued the life out of you."

"They do," he replied with a grin, "but they're still my sisters. And they've actually gotten a lot less annoying since you arrived."

I flushed with pleasure, glad that someone else had noticed the effort that the girls were making.

"Well, I appreciate your visits," I said, "the girls seem much less inclined to make a break for freedom while you're here."

"Glad to be of service," he said, his eyes smiling warmly at me.

"Lily! Sophie!" I suddenly called out. "Don't go any further!"

The two girls looked around guiltily and turned away from the forest.

"You were saying?" laughed Max.

"I said, less inclined, not completely disinclined," I defended myself, also laughing.

The girls wandered into the rose garden so I took a seat where I could keep an eye on them while I chatted with Max. My mind wandered through our usual conversation topics but for once we were both content to simply sit in companionable silence.

I had already explained to Max that my afternoons were strictly study free and he seemed perfectly happy with this, instead talking on and on about Felix and Nate and their adventures together. When he ran out of stories, he would ask me question after question about my childhood and life in a forest village. He seemed strangely fascinated by my older brothers.

I was equally fascinated by life in a palace. Gradually my confusion over the gulf between the behaviour of the king and queen and the behaviour of Lily and Sophie fell away. Max never spoke badly of either of his parents but I could read between the lines. This winter was no aberration. The queen had never taken an active role in raising her daughters. Outside of meals they barely saw her. I could tell this saddened and confused Max. She seemed a much more constant presence in the stories of his own childhood.

I tracked the girls with my eyes, unable to fathom the rules of whatever game they were now occupied with.

"They hardly speak when it's just the two of them," I said after a long silence. "It's like they're so in tune they don't have to say anything out loud."

Max nodded agreement. "They've always been like that," he said. "It comes from being twins, I guess. They hardly talked at all when they were small but they don't have that problem around other people anymore. It's only when they're by themselves that they fall back into their old silence."

"It must be nice to be so perfectly in tune with another person," I said. "But I feel sorry for them sometimes."

Max turned to me in surprise. "What do you mean?" he asked.

"Because they're princesses," I explained. "It would be alright if they'd only been born to a merchant or an innkeeper or even a woodcutter."

"Most girls envy them for being princesses," said Max.

"Yes it's fine for them now, but what about when they get older?" I asked. "Everyone knows princesses are expected to make marriage alliances. Not only will they have no choice in their husbands but they'll almost certainly be separated. It will make it all so much worse for them."

Beside me Max was silent, no longer looking at me but gazing across the garden at his sisters. I wondered if I had offended him.

"I don't mean anything against your parents," I said. "It's just the way of the world. But the more I read about alliances and diplomacy between kingdoms, the more I feel sorry for all the princesses. Personally I've always been grateful to be a girl, but if I had been born a royal I think I would wish myself a boy."

Still Max was silent and I stared at him in concern, trying to read the strange expression on his face. After a long pause, he spoke.

"Maybe you should feel sorry for the princes, too," he said, unexpectedly. "After all, the princesses aren't alone in those marriage alliances. The princes they marry have no more choice than their brides."

"I suppose that's true," I said. "I hadn't looked at it that way." I thought about it for a moment. "I still think the princes have it better off, though, at least they don't have to leave their family and friends and kingdom."

"Well that depends," said Max, "sometimes younger sons will go to live in the kingdom of their bride. Especially if that kingdom has only princesses."

"That's true again," I said. "And after all, maybe I'm taking too melancholy a view. Perhaps you'll be able to find another pair of royal twins for them to marry. Or perhaps they won't need to make a political marriage at all. From the sound of things, the king is already planning one alliance. Perhaps it will be enough."

"Yes," said Max, his tone unusually brooding, his eyes following his sisters as they played in the garden, "perhaps it will."

That was the last time we saw Max in the garden that week. Each day that he failed to appear I wondered again if my conversation had offended him and whether I should ask him about it. But he still came to the library every evening and, when he did, he seemed so much like his usual self that I shrugged it off. I didn't want to be demanding. And he must have been neglecting his usual afternoon activities to spend so much time with us.

The next week he joined us again and life resumed its usual rhythm, except the weather was now improving each day. Soon it hardly felt like winter at all.

As the weather got warmer the servants got busier, packing all the things that were going back to Arcadie and preparing all the rest for storage. An astonishing number of carriages and carts were wheeled out of the carriage house and cleaned. But I quickly realised they would all be needed. Mathilde assured me there was nothing unusual in the number of belongings being transported between the castle and the palace but I found it hard to believe. We argued, laughingly, for a full five minutes on the necessity of carting all the royal mattresses back and forth. Finally I conceded, only commenting wryly that they would be better off leaving the mattress from the Princess Room behind.

"It was shockingly uncomfortable," I told her. "There was a loose spring in the worst possible spot."

"I don't believe you," Mathilde laughed at me, "no royal spring would dare pop out of place!"

I attempted to whack her but she danced out of reach and I laughed with her, glad that she was smiling and laughing again.

The royals were shielded from the preparations as much as possible but I felt a growing sense of sadness as all the trappings of my happy winter were slowly removed. From the twins' chatter it was clear that they were expecting me to return to the Summer Palace with them. I felt increasingly inclined to do so, swayed by their expectation. But I was still torn. Would it be worse to remain with the royal family as a servant, outside their circle, or to be removed from them entirely? It was hard to think of either option without feeling depressed so I encouraged the twins to spend as much time outside as possible. Nothing was being removed from the garden, instead it grew more beautiful each day, so it was easier to thrust the thought of Arcadie from my mind when I was out of the castle.

The day before our departure arrived and I still hadn't made up my mind. Instead I took the girls outside, determined to enjoy myself for one last day. I told myself I would have plenty of time to make up my mind on the journey to the capital.

It was the warmest day we had had so far. The birds were singing madly, as if to make up for lost time, and green was springing up everywhere I looked. It wouldn't officially be spring until tomorrow but apparently the world hadn't got that missive. Out here it was already spring.

The twins were playing in the maze, their interest in it revitalised by our imminent departure. I was taking advantage of the weather and was lying on my back in the grass. My head was pillowed on Max's jacket and he was sitting beside me, pulling apart blades of grass. He already had a small pile of shredded greenery beside him. We were mostly silent, soaking up the rays of the sun, only chatting idly when some thought occurred to us.

"I just had a thought," I said, rather dreamily because I was half asleep. "The night I arrived, the queen had had the Princess Room prepared for visitors. But we haven't had any royal visitors all winter."

"I guess she got a bit overexcited. Probably thinking of this summer." There was unexpected resentment in his voice.

"What's happening this summer," I asked.

"Haven't you heard?" he replied, "apparently it's time I was getting married and producing heirs."

"Married?" I sat up abruptly, no longer sleepy.

"Once we get back to the Summer Palace we'll be having a stream of royal visitors. Foreign princesses to be courted and feted. And they won't stop coming until I pick one."

I stared at him in shock but he wouldn't meet my eyes. We both sat in silence as he shredded two more blades of grass.

"I should be getting back," he said, eventually, rising to his feet. "There's still lots to do before we leave tomorrow."

I couldn't think of any packing the prince was expected to do, but then I could hardly think at all. When I didn't move, he shrugged and started back towards the castle alone. I stared at his retreating back and wondered when the birds had stopped singing.

You hear people talk of a summer idyll but mine had been a winter one. And now I was suddenly confronted with the brutal honesty of my own feelings. And my own foolishness. Only now could I see how far I had let myself fall. I tried to picture a whole day during which I didn't see Max, didn't speak to him. I could see only bleak emptiness. I berated myself silently. How stupid I had been in this secluded castle, to let myself forget that this was not real life.

I felt a crack in the middle of my heart. It inched further and further along with each step Max took away from me. I could have sworn my blood was seeping out, running down my body and soaking into the ground.

Soon he would disappear into the castle and the crack would finish its journey, ripping my heart apart. I wondered, with detachment, if I would die when that happened. Could you survive if your heart was in pieces, all your blood drained away?

"Alyssa? Alyssa?"

I could hear two young voices calling me and I turned my eyes away from his retreating back and clamped down on my heart, holding it together. I reminded myself that it wasn't really broken; I wouldn't let it break. All my blood was where it was supposed to be, pumping through my veins. I was stronger than this and two girls needed me.

Or at least they needed me for a few more days. Because I was certain of one thing. There was no way I was staying at the Summer Palace to watch Max fall in love with a beautiful foreign princess.

Part 2

The Visiting

Princesses

The Traitor

The open wagon bounced along the forest path, making fast progress at the expense of comfort. The single passenger bounced miserably against the floor of the cart, unable to brace himself because his hands and feet were bound with thick leather.

The soldiers who rode on either side of the cart ignored him, focusing on the surrounding forest and the path ahead. The prisoner grunted in pain as the cart lurched over a deep pothole and thought longingly of his warm bed back at the Winter Castle. He silently cursed the prince. He had been so close to the large bag of gold that would have secured a life of ease and comfort.

He was angrily contemplating his lost riches when the first arrow found its mark. The soldier toppled off his horse and the other soldiers spurred their horses in alarm, circling in closer to the wagon and looking wildly into the surrounding trees. Claud looked up briefly and, realising what was happening, pressed himself full length against the floor of the cart. He was no fighter and while he mentally urged on the attackers, he had no desire to catch a stray arrow.

The cart lurched strangely and then sped up, Claud guessed that the driver had been hit. After only a few seconds of the sickening new pace, the cart swerved wildly and came to an abrupt stop, throwing him against the side of the wagon. Cautiously Claud lifted his head up.

The cart was resting against a tree and the two horses were long gone. The body of the driver was hanging off the edge of the front seat, held in place by one of the feet which had caught against something in the foot well. Feeling nauseous, he turned his head to see the fight, which was now taking place behind the wagon.

The bodies of several guards and two horses had fallen in the road but the remaining guards were fighting hard against a larger contingent of men dressed in black leather and armed with swords, crossbows and pistols. The attacking force were driving the soldiers back down the path, away from the cart.

Claud barely had time to assimilate all of this before the cart was rocked again by a black-clad man who climbed over the edge and pulled Claud to his feet. Looking up at his face, Claud felt a rush of relief. It was his employer.

The newcomer cut the cords binding Claud and gestured for him to climb out of the cart. Stumbling from the stiffness in his legs and feet, Claud ran into the forest, his rescuer following close behind him. When a horse appeared and Claud was ordered to mount up he shook his head in refusal.

"I can't ride," he said, panting from exertion and adrenaline. "And my legs are too stiff – they've been bound and jolted in that cart for hours."

"Fine," barked his rescuer, vaulting onto the back of a chestnut gelding. He reached out a hand, "you can ride with me." Relieved Claud took the proffered hand and allowed himself to be hauled onto the horse's back. Once they were both in place, the other man pulled out a horn and sounded a long, low blast.

The already distant sound of fighting broke off but Claud and his rescuer didn't wait for the other attackers. Instead they set off immediately into the forest, wheeling between the trees. Claud hung on grimly and hoped the journey wouldn't be long.

He was disappointed. After fifteen minutes they paused in a large clearing but they didn't dismount. As soon as the rest of the black-clad men joined them they were off again, plunging through the forest. Claud's rescuer was silent, refusing to answer questions and finally Claud stopped asking them.

The ride through the forest felt like a nightmare to him, his relief at being rescued giving way to the pain spreading through his body. When they finally stopped, he fell more than dismounted, taking several stumbling steps away from the horse.

They were in another clearing and Claud looked around in confusion. There was no sign of a wagon or carriage, or even a path.

"Why have we stopped?" He meant to sound strong and assertive but the words came out tired.

"What did you tell them?" asked his employer.

"Look, it wasn't my fault I got captured," said Claud defensively. "There was a whole company of guards." This was stretching the truth a little but he was desperate to justify himself. "They must have overheard us in the forest that last day."

"What did you tell them?" repeated his questioner, ignoring his attempts at justification.

"Nothing!" replied Claud. "There wasn't much of an interrogation. When I wouldn't talk they were happy enough to leave me for the Intelligence Chief in Arcadie."

There was a long pause while the man weighed Claud with his eyes.

"Fortunately for you our spies at the Summer Palace corroborate that," he said finally.

Claud breathed a sigh of relief. Already the pain was fading from his mind, replaced with his previous dreams of gold. He didn't hear the second man who approached from behind and he didn't feel the bullet that pierced his skull.

The questioner looked down impassively at the body, sprawled at his feet.

"Fortunate because otherwise your death would have been more painful," he said to the dead Claud. Signaling to the other men to remount, he turned and swung back onto his horse.

The King

The king rested his forehead on his fingertips, gently massaging his temple. Eleanor was implacable, determined to see this princess business through, but he felt uneasy. He reread the report on the desk in front of him. It reported only failure – again. Failure to find and recapture Claud, failure to find his rescuers, failure even to identify their nationality. It took all of the king's self-control not to ball the report up and throw it in the fire. Instead he placed it in one of the drawers and locked it, placing the key in his pocket.

So far he had avoided telling Max or the Princess Companion of the escape of their prisoner but Max was sure to notice the increased guard when they started their journey back to the capital the next day. And he had decided to speak to Alyssa that night. With no idea who had hired Claud, or why, he needed all the allies he could get.

As if summoned by his thoughts, there was a quiet knock at the door. When the Princess Companion appeared, he stood politely and beckoned her to a seat in front of his desk. Seeing her sitting across from him reminded him of the night they had captured Claud. He sighed. Scrutinising her face, his discomfort grew. She was pale and he could read pain in her eyes.

She had missed dinner, complaining of a mild headache, but from the look of her the headache must be severe. He wished he could send her back to bed but they were leaving first thing in the morning. This was his last opportunity to talk to her.

"I'm sorry to bother you when you're sick," he opened.

"Sick?" she looked confused for a moment and then, "Oh yes, my headache. That's ok, your majesty. I'm at your service."

She sat up straighter and focused on his face, showing her first sign of curiosity.

"Mrs Pine tells me you're well-liked by most of the servants," he continued. "And you're certainly popular with my family."

"That's nice to hear, your majesty," she said quietly.

She sounded a little choked up and he wondered what he had said that could possibly have distressed her.

"But Mrs Pine also says that you're intending to leave our service when we reach Arcadie."

"Yes, your majesty," she replied. "I have an aunt who's expecting me. She runs the Blue Arrow Inn."

"I know the Blue Arrow," said the king. "It's one of the biggest inns in the capital. I don't want to cause any trouble for your aunt but I need you to stay with us, Alyssa."

She frowned now and gave a small, involuntary head shake. The king pressed on.

"You have an intelligent mind," he said, "but more importantly, you have good instincts with people. You suspected Claud when no one else did."

"Thank you, your majesty, but I can't stay."

"Claud's escaped."

"What! When? How?" She was leaning forward now, gripping the armrests of her chair.

"When he was being transported back to the capital. My intelligence chief never had the chance to interrogate him. We can find no trace of him or his rescuers. We still have no idea who he was working for or why they were gathering information on the royal family."

"But…" her voice trailed away and the king could almost see her brain working furiously.

"I'm sure you've heard that a marriage alliance is being planned for my son," said the king. "We'll be having a series of royal visitors. And the princesses will be bringing retinues with them. If our unknown enemy comes from one of the kingdoms sending a delegation, my family may be at risk." Now it was the king who was leaning forward. "But the delegations also present us with an opportunity to identify our enemy."

"That makes sense," she replied, "but what does it have to do with me?"

"People act differently around servants than they do around royalty," said the king. "I need someone I can trust, someone with your instincts, to observe them."

"Surely you have other people who could do that better than me?"

"My intelligence chief will have his own people of course. But I want a spy of my own. And it was you, not my intelligence chief, who discovered Claud. I can't think of anyone better."

"So you want me to come back to the Summer Palace with you. To remain as a servant?"

"No, not a servant. I need you closer to the delegations than that. I want you to remain as Princess Companion, of course."

"But I'm only a woodcutter's daughter. I can't be Companion when you're at court."

"Of course you can! It's an assigned role, not a hereditary one. I can give it to whoever I want." There was silence for a moment as Alyssa considered his offer.

"I'm sorry, your majesty, I want to help but I can't stay on. I just can't."

She rubbed her face with her hands and the king felt guilty for exacerbating her headache.

"I need you Alyssa, my family needs you," the king pushed. "What if it's an assassin they send next time, instead of a spy? What if it's Lily they target? Or Sophie? Or Max?"

She sucked in her breath and her pale face got paler.

"Alright," she said, finally. "I'll do it – for the girls. But as soon as you find out who's targeting you I'm going to my aunt."

The king smiled in relief.

"Thank you Alyssa. I'll see you're well compensated." She hadn't even asked about payment and that only increased his trust in her. "All I need you to do is to stick close to my children. Observe everything and report anything to me. Even if it's just a bad feeling in your stomach, I want to know about it."

"My spine," she said with her first smile of the night, "it's down my spine that I feel it, not in my stomach."

"You feel anything strange in any part of your anatomy and I want to know about it," said the king firmly. "But for now you look like you should be in bed. There'll be time enough for further conversation in Arcadie, before the first delegation arrives."

He stood up and came around the desk, accompanying her to the door with all the courtesy he would have shown a duchess.

Once she was gone he collapsed back into his chair and pulled a piece of paper towards him. He had one last report to read before he could seek his own bed. He glanced at the title. Another of the southern villages had suffered a bad harvest and had now exhausted their winter supplies. They were seeking aid from the capital to make it through to the next harvest. He sighed.

Chapter 13

Arcadie was so much bigger than I had imagined that I couldn't stop gawking out the window of our carriage like the country bumpkin I evidently was. The girls found my incredulity hilarious and spoke over the top of each other, rushing to point out all the sights of interest. Up until now I had spent the journey trying to stop myself looking out the window. King Henry, Queen Eleanor and Max had been riding beside the carriage and I knew I only wanted to look out because I was hoping to get a glimpse of Max. However, once we hit the outskirts of the capital, they rode up ahead and I let myself stare out at the unfolding city.

I already knew it was built on a low hill, with the Summer Palace at its centre, but I hadn't anticipated the size of it or the noise produced by so many people and animals crowded together. Our carriage was travelling along the wide, main road that cut through the layers of the city and led directly to the Palace. At first the houses were small, built in long, connected rows. And the side streets we passed were small and winding.

Before long, though, the branching streets began to widen and the houses became more elaborate, their wooden fronts painted in bright colours. Twice I could see a bustling market place opening off of a side street. I stopped just short of sticking my head out the window, breathing in the tantalising smell of meat pies and roast chestnuts. Occasionally there would be someone watching us from an upper window, waving a handkerchief or throwing flowers.

As the road climbed upwards, the houses got bigger and bigger. These larger homes were surrounded by spacious gardens and were made from stone and decorated with pillars or arches.

There were fewer people on the road here and I missed the sight of the bustling men and women and the playful children who had darted between the vehicles. I had been imagining I could glimpse my own family amongst them but I immediately knew my family would be out of place in this fancier part of the city.

At last the carriage passed under an enormous archway that cut through a thick wall made of white stone. A footman opened the door and the princesses tumbled out, leaving me to climb out more slowly and, I hoped, more gracefully.

The Summer Palace rose before me and I gasped in shock at the sight. It was built from the same white stone as the surrounding wall but with dark slate for the roof. The soaring towers with their graceful spires mirrored the fairy tale castles of my imagination. I had never even dreamed of living in such a beautiful place and I felt overwhelmed by the thought that this was my new home.

"It's beautiful, isn't it?" asked a warm, familiar voice in my ear.

My pleasure at hearing his voice and my delight in the beauty of the palace made me forget I was trying to keep my distance.

"Absolutely gorgeous! Even more beautiful than I imagined!"

"I wish you could see your face," he chuckled. "I think a bug's going to fly into your mouth any second now."

I snapped my teeth shut but couldn't hold back the smile.

"I can't believe you never told me about it!" I said.

"I can't believe you were planning to leave us," he replied, his voice reproachful now. "And without saying anything. Father told me that he only just convinced you to stay – that you were planning to go work for your aunt at the Blue Arrow."

I shrugged.

"I never expected to keep my position once you all returned to Arcadie," I said. "I assumed that once you got back to court

136

the queen would find a more appropriate person to be Companion."

"But Lily and Sophie love you! I can't believe you were going to abandon them. Abandon us."

He looked angry and I wished I could explain that abandoning him was the last thing I wanted to do.

"No-one is being abandoned," I snapped instead. "And I still think your court is going to be less than pleased to have a woodcutter's daughter thrust on them."

I could tell he hadn't thought of this and I could see concern on his face. I wondered if he was picturing me embarrassing him in front of his friends.

Before I could find out, Lily and Sophie rushed towards me and grabbed both of my hands. As they towed me away, I looked back at Max. He was watching me leave, the same worried expression in his eyes. My heart sank.

My very real concern about being introduced to the Palace's inhabitants, now reinforced by Max's reaction, distracted me from the tour that followed. It didn't help that Lily and Sophie led me through the rooms so fast that I felt hopelessly lost. I wouldn't be going anywhere without the twins for a while. Not if I actually wanted to end up at my destination, that is.

I had known the Winter Castle was much smaller than the Summer Palace but I hadn't appreciated just how much smaller until now. The Palace seemed to be an endless maze of rooms. Inside, the white marble was softened by beautiful rugs and wood accents. The style was elegant and simple but the furnishings and decorations conveyed a sense of age and wealth. I was impressed and wondered who was responsible for the interior decoration of the Palace.

We passed lots of people in our whirlwind tour, mostly servants cleaning or moving quickly through the rooms. But a few were dressed like nobles and I was relieved when the princesses didn't stop, moving through these rooms as quickly as the others.

I was still feeling overwhelmed and nervous so I was relieved when the twins got bored of their tour and decided to show me their rooms instead.

"Of course, they're your rooms now, too," reminded Lily.

"And we have a whole tower at the Palace," Sophie announced. I thought ruefully of all those stairs and wished for some of the twins' boundless energy. Luckily their tower turned out to be one of the shorter ones. When I got a look at the rooms inside of it, I realised that the princesses' suite at the Winter Castle had been modeled on this tower. The rooms were all decorated in the same style using the same green and pink. It felt like unexpectedly finding a small piece of home in an unfamiliar place and I felt unreasonably cheered.

As well as a large bedroom, the twins had a huge bathroom, a classroom, a playroom and a formal sitting room. And best of all, there was a small separate bedroom opening off the main one. I went into my new bedroom and walked straight over to the window. The tower might have been smaller than some of the others but it still gave an amazing view over the city and –

"The ocean!" I exclaimed, loud enough to bring the twins into my room.

They both came over to me and peered out the window.

"What is it?" asked Lily. "I can't see anything."

"It's the ocean!" I replied. And when they still looked confused, I added, "I've never seen it before."

"You've never seen the ocean before?" asked Sophie in astonishment.

"No, of course not," I said, amused. "I grew up in the middle of the forest remember."

"Sorry, Alyssa," said Sophie, "I forgot."

"That's ok," I said, gathering both girls into a spontaneous hug. "It's beautiful, don't you think?"

"Yes, it is and I have a great idea," said Lily. I looked down at her enquiringly and she dimpled at me mischievously. "Why don't we go down to visit the ocean tomorrow. Wouldn't you like to see it close up?"

It was a nice thought but I examined her expression suspiciously.

"You're not allowed down at the docks are you?" I asked.

"No," sighed Lily, disappointed.

"Apparently it's dangerous," added Sophie.

I knew I should be angry with them – I thought I'd broken them of the habit of trying to trick me – but I couldn't muster up the emotion. I got the feeling Lily was testing the boundaries for old times' sake rather than with any real expectation of success. And I was feeling more than usually affectionate towards them both. Faced with all these new people and places, it was a relief to feel sure of the twins' childish affection.

Apparently it was normal for the court to give the royal family a day to settle in before descending on them. So it was with great relief that I followed the twins down to lunch in one of the small, private dining rooms. Only the king and queen were there to eat with us and I tried to convince myself I was glad of Max's absence. With only the five of us present, it should have felt like a normal lunch at the Winter Castle. But my roiling internal landscape reminded me that lots of things had changed.

I started obsessing over Max's whereabouts, wondering if he was avoiding me after our earlier conversation. Then I caught the king's eye and was reminded of a bigger worry. What if a spy or assassin came with one of the delegations? What if I didn't sense them – betraying the king's trust in me? Or worse, what if they hurt Lily or Sophie or Max? And finally, guiltily, what if they hurt me? Suddenly Max's absence felt insignificant and I was embarrassed by my earlier thoughts.

Luckily there was no need for me to contribute to the conversation – Lily and Sophie talked nonstop about their ponies and all the summer activities they had missed while in the forest. I had already heard all this ad nauseam on the journey through the forest so I didn't even feel guilty for ignoring them.

"No, visiting your ponies can wait until tomorrow. I think Alyssa would like a break from the two of you. She's been looking pale lately and no wonder, shut up in the carriage with you two chatterboxes for a week!"

I tuned back into the conversation in time to realise that my inattention had nearly resulted in an afternoon visit to the stables. I smiled gratefully at the queen. I needed some time and space to arrange my thoughts and regain some equilibrium.

It was only after the king and queen had swept the twins out of the dining room that I realised I had been relying on the girls to be my guides. I wasn't sure I could even find the way back to the princesses' tower on my own. I wondered if I should just start walking and rely on running into someone who could give me directions. This thought was unappealing so I remained in my seat, hoping another solution would present itself. Luckily for me, it did.

"I see I've missed lunch," said Max, coming through the door and plonking himself in one of the seats. He began to pick over the leftover food in the platters. "But I'm glad you're still here, Alyssa."

He smiled at me and I felt the old comfortable feeling from nights in the library and afternoons in the garden but laced now with a new excitement.

140

"I've got something I wanted to show you."

I smiled at him in return. How foolish of me to think I wanted an afternoon to myself. I now realised that an afternoon with Max was just what I needed.

Chapter 14

"Close your eyes," said Max, excitedly.

I looked at him suspiciously – I had four older brothers after all.

"Should I be worried?"

"Of course not – you're going to love it."

His easy assurance didn't entirely reassure me but I closed my eyes anyway. I heard the sound of a door being opened and then felt a hand on the small of my back propelling me towards the doorway. I put my hands in front of me instinctively and shuffled forwards.

"Come on, Alyssa, take bigger steps," said Max, "otherwise we're going to be here all day."

I sighed and lengthened my stride slightly.

I could tell when we entered the room because the light changed and I stopped, expecting to be told to open my eyes. Instead Max continued to push me forwards.

"Where are we?" I asked, my curiosity increasing.

"You'll see," he replied, a smile in his voice.

We took several more steps and then he said, "You can open them now."

I did. And for the second time that day, my mouth fell open in shock.

"It's amazing!" I cried. "I can't believe how big it is!"

I was standing in the middle of the largest room I had ever seen. It was at least two stories high and the walls were lined with bookshelves. There was a mezzanine balcony running around the room, but even so you would need to use the ladders provided to reach all the books. I had been astonished at the library in the Winter Castle but it was nothing compared to this one.

"We would have to live a thousand years to read all these books," I exclaimed.

"Well, it's a good thing we don't need to read them all then," Max replied, "because I don't think either of us is going to live to be a thousand."

I revolved slowly on the spot, taking in the shelves and the tall windows. Scattered here and there were chairs and tables and I was itching to explore. I wanted to find a niche somewhere I could claim as my own – a replacement for my window seat back at the castle.

"This library is incredible but not a place to read at night," I said. "It would be so big and echoing. It's definitely a place that needs daylight."

"At the height of summer there'll be plenty of hours of daylight after dinner," Max replied, "but we're at the Summer Palace now – there won't be time for reading in the evenings. Once the court returns tomorrow there will be parties and balls and entertainments of all sorts. You'll see."

He was smiling as he said the words but I felt my heart sink. Another reminder that things were different now. He didn't belong to me anymore.

He would spend his time at parties and I would spend my time up in the princesses' tower. The sooner I remembered that, the better off I'd be. Suddenly I lost energy for exploring the library. Perhaps I would come on my own tomorrow.

I turned towards the door and Max seemed to pick up on my desire to leave. His cheerful smile had disappeared and I wondered what was running through his mind.

"I wanted to show you the library before we did anything else but I actually thought you might want to go out into the city this afternoon," he said. "To visit your aunt at the Blue Arrow. I've never actually been in there but I've ridden past many times so I know where it is."

"That sounds great, actually," I said, surprised. "I need to see my aunt – to check if she got my letter and if Ariana delivered my stuff to her."

"Excellent!"

Max led me out a side door and into the large yard between the palace and the palace wall. It was a busy, noisy place full of rushing people and animals. When we'd arrived, I'd been so distracted by the palace itself that I hadn't looked around the yard. I examined it now with so much interest that I nearly ran into Max, who had come to a sudden stop in front of me.

"I never even thought," he said, turning around to face me, "do you even know how to ride?"

I realised that we were standing in front of the stables. "Yes, I can ride," I said. "My mother's father was a merchant. He wasn't very happy when she decided to marry a woodcutter but my mother's a pretty stubborn person." I grinned at certain remembered instances of this stubbornness. "In the end he gave his reluctant blessing and let her take her horses, books and jewels with her. The jewels got sold off pretty quickly but she kept the horses and books for me."

"That explains a lot," said Max, looking at me with a quizzical gleam in his eyes.

"What do you mean?" I asked.

"Well it explains why a woodcutter's daughter from the deep wood has an aunt who runs the busiest inn in Arcadie. And it explains why you love books so much."

I shrugged. "Reading at least is no big deal. Most people in our village could read. The baker's wife was originally from Arcadie and she used to teach all the children. She would have taught me, too, but our house was too far from the village. It was easier to learn at home."

"Being able to read and loving books are two different things" Max replied. "When Father became king, Mother insisted that every village have someone who could teach reading and writing. But most villagers seem to lack either the time or the interest for more than the basics."

"There were a couple of others in my village who were interested in further study," I said. "But they left for one of the cities as soon as they were old enough."

"Well, I'm glad you decided to head for Arcadie," he said. "And I'm glad you can ride. It'll make the trip to the Blue Arrow a lot quicker."

As he talked he made a gesture in the direction of one of the grooms who had just emerged from the stables. I could only assume the prince was a regular visitor at the stables since the groom seemed to find this vague movement comprehensible. He disappeared back into the stables and soon reappeared leading two saddled horses.

"Good afternoon, your highness." The groom bobbed his head respectfully. "I've got a nice gentle ride here for the lady."

He gave me a sidelong glance as he spoke and I could read the questions in his eyes.

I smiled. "I'm no lady," I said, "I'm Alyssa, the new Princess Companion." I held out my hand in a business like way and he shook it tentatively.

"I'm Harry, miss," he replied.

"Feel free to watch me mount up and ride out, Harry," I said. "That way you can feel confident to bring me a more... interesting... ride next time."

Max was watching this exchange with amusement and now answered Harry's enquiring eye with a nod. "If I know my sisters

145

at all, you'll get to know Alyssa pretty well, Harry. I'm sure they'll have her out here every day."

Harry gave a gruff laugh. "Their highnesses do love those ponies of theirs," he agreed.

I examined the mare he had brought out for me while the two men exchanged further reminiscences. She was an older chestnut and her eyes were dull. I sighed and let my gaze drift towards a beautiful palomino being led into the stables. She was a young mare, beautifully proportioned, and as I watched she threw up her head, dancing sideways in playful fun.

Harry must have followed my gaze because his next words mirrored my thoughts. "She's a beautiful one, isn't she? Her name's Starfire. If you can ride as well as you say you can, you can ride her when you go out with the twins."

"Thank you!" I exclaimed, startled. "That would be wonderful."

As I spoke, I moved towards the chestnut mare, eager to show my proficiency. But when I turned towards Harry, ready to be put up into the saddle, I found myself facing Max. His unexpected nearness made my heart speed up and I forgot all about being graceful as he threw me up onto the mare's back. Only once I was settled in the saddle did I remember my audience. I glanced over towards Harry and found him assessing my seat with a critical eye.

Apparently he liked what he saw because he nodded at me and said, "I'll let the other grooms know to have Starfire saddled up whenever the twins want their ponies."

"Thank you!" I repeated and waved at him as we swung our horses around and headed for the palace gates.

I kept my mare close to the prince's horse as we made our way down the main road we had ascended that morning.

"This is the Palace Way," explained Max. "We're riding through the Noble's Circle now but we'll have to go down into the Merchant's Circle to get to the Blue Arrow."

I nodded, pleased. The Noble's Circle still made me feel uncomfortable and I was glad when we rode out of it. My spirits lifted even further once I was surrounded by the bright, cheerful colours of the Merchant's Circle.

Despite my interest in the busy Palace Way, I was glad when we turned off onto a wide side street. The straight main road, lined as it was with buildings, created a breezeway and the wind was strong enough to make me shiver.

"I can't wait until it warms up," I said to Max and he nodded his agreement.

"It'll start to heat up quickly," he said, "Spring is usually pretty warm in Arcadie. If you don't have summer clothes in the packs you sent to your aunt's, Mrs Pine can get some for you."

I smiled at his oblivion. I would definitely need to speak to Mrs Pine about a summer wardrobe – none of the clothes I had brought with me from the forest would be suitable for my current position.

When we reached the Blue Arrow, I was impressed. It was a large stone building, set back from the road in its own yard. When we rode through the gates a groom appeared and took our horses. As we walked through the front door, I saw a carriage pull in and two more grooms appeared and ran to the horses' heads. Aunt Corilyn must be even more prosperous than I had thought.

We entered into a large room full of tables and chairs, with a long bar against one wall. Although it was only early afternoon, the room was already partially full. Most of the occupants were men, although a few women were scattered amongst them. I noticed I wasn't the only one looking around with fascination this time, so I lightly touched Max's arm. When he looked at me, I gestured towards a free table by the fireplace.

We had hardly seated ourselves before a serving maid appeared.

"What can I get for you?" she asked.

Max ordered a beer but I shook my head. "I'd like to see the proprietress please," I said instead.

"Corilyn's a busy woman," she replied, "but I'll let her know you're asking for her."

"Thanks," I said, "let her know Alyssa's here to see her."

"Her niece?" the maid asked sharply and I nodded in reply. She gave us both a closer scrutiny this time and looked thoughtful. "I'll let her know," she repeated and moved away towards a door on the far side of the room.

I wondered with some unease what kind of reception I should expect from my aunt. Would she be frustrated at having a niece thrust on her and glad I had already found a job? Or had she been holding a position for me, in which case she might resent my desertion?

Before I could get too wound up in these thoughts, my attention was caught by a rowdy group of men sitting several tables away from us. They had obviously been drinking for some time, despite the early hour, and they had a ring of empty tables around them. From the looks of things the other customers were giving them a wide berth.

"What does the king ever do for us?" exclaimed one of them, loudly and there was a round of agreement from the others.

"The drought is getting worse and worse," another one chimed in, "haven't had a good harvest in three years."

"And the bandits are out of control," agreed a third. "It's gotten so that you can't travel from one town to another without getting attacked by black-clad men. Unless you have a platoon of

guards with you, of course, like those noble-folk up on the hill."
He gestured away towards the palace.

"And what does the king do about it?" demanded the first
man. "Nothing!"

I looked over at Max with concern and saw that he was
staring fixedly at the table of men.

"We ought to do something about it!" continued the first
man. The expected round of agreement came but it seemed
more hesitant this time. "We should make an example of one of
them, show them that if we're not safe – they're not safe." A
couple of the other men nodded enthusiastically but the others
seemed slightly alarmed at this suggestion of action.

Despite their hesitancy, I began to feel nervous and looked
around at the other people in the room. The rest of the
customers were pointedly ignoring the table of men and no one
spoke up against them. I looked back across at Max. His hands
were now balled into fists but it was hard to read the expression
on his face.

My pulse began to beat in my neck and I could feel all my
muscles tensing. How well did the locals know the face of their
prince? If they glanced this way, would the men recognise who
was sitting in the room with them?

Once again, I had unwittingly led Max into danger. I hadn't
even thought to question our lack of escort but I now felt certain
that the prince shouldn't be wandering the streets of Arcadie
without guards. He'd even told me that he'd never been into the
Blue Arrow before. It hadn't occurred to me to ask why not.

I looked back at the group of men. One of them was now
looking at us with an intent expression on his face. While I
watched, he nudged the man next to him and nodded his head
towards us.

I turned to Max and spoke in a rush. "Maybe we should get going. I can come visit my aunt another day."

"What? No!" Max seemed startled and I suspected he had forgotten me in his absorption with the neighbouring conversation.

The two men looking our way were whispering now and I lowered my own voice to an urgent whisper. "I really think we should go."

Max shook his head emphatically and started to rise to his feet. I grabbed his arm, pulling him back into his seat and whispered even more urgently. "What are you thinking? Don't you dare go over there! There are seven of them!"

The man who had spotted us opened his mouth to say something to his companions but was interrupted by a forceful woman who strode into the room and stood in front of their table, hands on hips. We were effectively blocked from view by her solid bulk.

"I've told you before, Hans, and I'll tell you again. I won't have you causing trouble in my inn. You lot clear out and don't come back until you're sober."

There were murmured protestations from the men at the table but two burly serving men had now come to flank the woman and they followed the group as they reluctantly started to leave.

As soon as the men were up and moving, the woman spun around to face us.

"Come on," she said briskly, "you'd better come out back." When we stared at her in surprise, she gestured imperiously and spoke again. "Hurry up!"

As she chivvied us through the door on the far side of the room, I glanced back and saw the last of the men filing out through the front door. I sighed in relief and examined our saviour.

My initial impression now hardened into certainty. This was my Aunt Corilyn. Her face was sterner and she wore her blond hair in a tight bun instead of wound around her head in plaits like my mother. But they were clearly recognisable as sisters.

"Your highness," said my aunt with a brisk curtsey and a respectful head bob to Max. She then turned her gaze onto me and gave me the same critical examination I had just given her. After a moment she pulled me into a hug.

"Alyssa," she said, a little gruffly, "you turned out better than could have been expected." I grinned over her shoulder at Max's startled expression. Her voice and tone were so similar to my mother's that it was easy for me to hear the hesitant affection behind the words.

"Hello, Aunt Corilyn. I'm sorry I'm so much later than expected," I said, when she released me. "Did you get my letter?"

"That I did," she replied. "It got here two days before Ariana did so I was able to set her straight. In a right worry she was. Seemed to think she wouldn't be able to show her face in your village again after losing you."

"I'm sorry," I repeated. "Is she still in Arcadie? I'd like to apologise to her myself."

"No, she's long gone," replied my aunt. "They were planning to winter somewhere down south so they pushed on almost straight away. But I passed on your apologies. She said she should have known you'd land on your feet."

I smiled. "Did she leave my luggage?" I asked.

"Yes, I've got it safe enough. I would have sent it up to the palace when I heard the royal family were back but I wasn't sure what you were planning." It wasn't a question but she looked enquiringly between Max and me.

"Their royal majesties have been kind enough to ask me to stay on as Princess Companion," I said, flushing a little. "I'm not sure how long it will be for but…" I glanced at Max and trailed away.

The question hadn't left my aunt's eyes but she also glanced at Max and stayed silent.

"Well, that's a right honour for the family. I'm glad to hear you've been doing us proud. If you write a letter to your folks, I'll include it next time I write to my sister."

"Thank you!" I cried, delighted.

"And I'll have one of my grooms drop your bags off at the palace. You won't want to be bothered with them now. Which reminds me, you're welcome to come visit me anytime, Alyssa. But with all due respect, your highness, you shouldn't be out wandering the streets on your own. And you're better off staying out of my inn altogether."

She bobbed a quick curtsey as she said 'your highness' but it did little to soften her words.

Max stiffened and his face took on the arrogant look I remembered from my first few weeks at the winter castle. I realised with surprise that it was a long time since I'd seen that look.

"As I said, I mean no disrespect," my aunt continued. "I'm loyal to his majesty but I can't always control who comes in here for a drink. I'd rather not see you get into any trouble – and I'd rather my inn and my niece stayed out of trouble too."

At these last two additions, Max's expression softened and he gave me a thoughtful look. He jerked his head back towards the tap room. "Is that the general mood of the city then?" he asked.

"No, no, they're just a group of hotheads," she replied. "Most people remain loyal – for now."

I looked at her in surprise.

"It's been a hard few years," she said, with a shrug, "and that always gets people grumbling. But there's no real heat in it yet. Still, it'd be better for everyone if the heir to the throne didn't wander around unprotected. Accidents do happen, after all."

I looked over at Max in concern. I certainly wouldn't let him come with me on any future visits, whatever he thought about it. I wished I hadn't let him bring me this time.

I was glad I had met my aunt and would soon recover my possessions. But it hadn't turned out to be the relaxing afternoon I'd been hoping for. Instead I found myself with several more worries to add to the ones already pressing on my mind.

Chapter 15

When I woke the next morning, I looked around for the tight walls of my alcove in confusion. Instead my eyes fell on my window and the memories of the day before came back in a rush. I got up and went over to rest my head against the glass. I stood there quietly watching the distant waves for several minutes, trying to prepare myself for the day ahead. This was the day the rest of the court would return.

The princesses were already awake when I went through to their bedroom but they seemed entirely uninterested in the arrival of the court. Instead they were full of plans to take me out to see their ponies.

"No promises," I said, "you know that the court is arriving today and I don't know what plans your parents might have made."

Sophie scrunched up her face and Lily sighed in a long, exaggerated way. "Court is stuffy and boring," she complained, "they'll all just be fawning over Max anyway."

"Really?" I asked, in an attempt at nonchalance. "I suppose he's pretty popular with the court."

"Duh!" Both girls gave me a scathing look. "All the girls are just hoping to become princesses, though. Not that being a princess is so great." The last sentence was murmured in a dark undertone.

"Woah!" I said. "Why the sudden doom and gloom?" I climbed onto Lily's bed and patted the cover beside me. "Come up here girls, we need to talk."

The twins exchanged a glance and then both reluctantly climbed up to join me.

"What is going on with you two? I thought you'd be glad to be back in Arcadie. And what's this about not liking being princesses? It seems to me you two have a pretty nice life. You have a family that loves you, so many servants you never have to do any work, you get to study and learn all sorts of things - which most girls don't get to do - and you have lots of toys and even ponies. Seems to me you haven't got much to complain about." I fixed them both with a pointed stare and then sat in silence, waiting.

It was Lily who finally broke, lifting her eyes from the bed to glare at me. "If our family's so loving why do they never spend any time with us?"

I sucked in a breath. I'd been wondering for weeks when we were going to have this conversation but it seemed strange timing for it.

"What do you mean, they never spend time with you? They spent the whole afternoon with you yesterday," I said.

"No they didn't," said Sophie glumly. "They just dropped us off with Nanny."

"Oh girls," I sighed. I opened my arms and both girls crawled into them. We sat in silence on the bed for several minutes, each taking comfort from the presence of the others.

It was Sophie who broke the silence. "And we're not even very good princesses," she said. "I bet if it had been us who were put in that tower it would be totally empty."

"Now that is not true!" I said firmly. "You two are wonderful girls and you're becoming lovely princesses. And I know that your family loves you, even if they're too busy to always show it. In fact, they've all commented to me on how well you're growing up."

Both girls flushed with pleasure. "Really?" asked Lily.

"Really!" I said, even more firmly. "I know that all the formality of court must be boring for you but so is carting water and cooking dinner and babysitting and all the things that other girls have to do. The difference is that you also have lots of nice things. And even more importantly, all those other girls are looking up to you two. If you study hard in your lessons and study even harder at court, one day you'll have the chance to make a difference in their lives - to make a difference in the whole kingdom."

"What is there to study at court?" asked Sophie.

"People, of course," I replied. "I can help you with that but you'll learn the most by just watching hard and paying attention. If you can learn to understand people then you can learn how to rule a kingdom well."

"But we won't be ruling a kingdom," said Lily, "that's Max's job."

"Well, he can't rule alone," I replied. And then I added, "And it might not be this kingdom you end up helping to rule." I didn't think shielding them from the truth was doing them any favours.

Sophie looked at me curiously but then exchanged a glance with Lily and seemed to realise what I meant. Both girls sat in thoughtful silence.

"I've thought of a new game," I said. "To show you both how well you're doing. I noticed there's an empty attic at the top of this tower. I'm making that your very own enchanted tower room. Whenever you get sick of studying people and want some space, you can go up there. No one will be allowed up there except for the two of you. And every day, depending how you go, I'll add something nice or take something away."

"Like the princess in the story!" exclaimed Sophie.

"Exactly like that," I said with a smile. "You'll be astonished at how quickly it fills up. But for now, it's time to get ready for breakfast."

Both girls smiled as they bounced off the bed and raced for the bathroom. I followed more sedately, wishing I had more answers for them. I was sure the king and queen loved their daughters but I wasn't sure why they spent so little time with them. Was this, I wondered, simply one of the burdens of being born a princess?

Breakfast was a rushed affair; everyone seemed conscious of the big day ahead and ate quickly without much conversation. When I saw Max, sitting at the table, I was relieved to note that my heart kept its usual rhythm. The new glow of affection was still there but I had regained my old comfort in his presence. So that was one positive outcome from our shared afternoon. If I could just contrive to keep a little distance between us, perhaps it would be possible to maintain our friendship after all.

I smiled at him across the table and was surprised not to get a smile in return. He looked unhappy and even, if I was honest, sulky and he kept shooting glares at his parents. I gave an internal sigh, the Summer Palace was beautiful but it didn't seem to make any of the royal family happy.

The king and queen were the first to finish and as soon as they were gone Lily addressed Max. "What's the matter with you? You like court."

"I did like court," he replied, "before this whole princess business."

"Oh, that," sighed Lily.

"You never know," said Sophie, "she might be really nice." I couldn't help making a wry smile at this hopeful contribution.

"Yeah, I suppose," sighed Max, "but I thought I'd have time. Father just told me that there was a royal missive from Northhelm waiting for him when we got to Arcadie. Princess Marie has already set off, she'll be arriving in just over a week."

"A week!" exclaimed Lily. "But I thought they promised you could have your hunting trip first?"

"They did. So I'm supposed to be leaving today. Mother and Father have already sent word to Nate and Felix and the others to pack and be ready to leave after lunch."

"Are Nate and Felix already in Arcadie?" asked Lily with a tell-tale blush. I swallowed another smile. I suppose it was inevitable that the girls would have crushes on their big brother's friends.

"Nate's family got here yesterday afternoon and Felix's yesterday evening. They're both still with their parents down in the Noble's Circle but they were planning to move into their rooms in the Palace today. Now I guess they'll move in when we get back."

Lily and Sophie both looked disappointed which made me hope I was hiding my own disappointment better. I had thought I would have more time too. Now Max would be gone for a whole week and then the first princess would arrive. I kept thinking I had prepared myself for the coming blow and then realising that I hadn't.

"I'm sorry, Alyssa," said Max suddenly.

"What? Why?" I asked, startled and momentarily horrified that he had read my thoughts.

"I thought I would be here to introduce you to the other young people at court," he said. "To help ease you in. You don't talk about it much but I know you're worried about the whole rank thing. And now you'll be on your own."

He turned his attention back to his sisters. "You'd better look after her, you two. You know what some of them can be like."

"Don't worry, Max," said Lily, "we will."

"Now you're all being silly," I said with a laugh, "I'm the one who's supposed to be looking after you."

But the laugh was forced. I had forgotten about my coming introduction. And on top of that, the truth behind my words was ringing in my ears. The king was trusting me to look after them all and the first delegation would be arriving in just over a week. For the first time I wished I had never left the forest.

Max explained that the royal family usually ate lunch separately in Arcadie so we said goodbye to him at the door to the breakfast room. I put all my effort into keeping my tone light and inconsequential with the result that he was gone before I'd had a chance to register our farewell. I followed the girls back to their tower with a heavy heart.

My mood only darkened when Gretchen arrived for the girls' lessons. I had been secretly hoping Lily and Sophie would have a different governess here at the palace. She ignored me as usual, but the smug, satisfied expression on her face made me nervous. Gretchen had left the Winter Castle with the first wave of servants and had consequently been in Arcadie for several days already.

I had intended to retreat to my room to gather myself for the afternoon's ordeal but was interrupted by a friendly face.

"Psst!" Mathilde hissed at me from around the door. When I looked over she gestured for me to come out into the hallway. When I appeared she gave me a big hug.

"Welcome to Arcadie!" she said. "What do you think of it so far?"

"It's so big," I said, "and the palace is so beautiful. And the ocean! Do you ever get a day off? Maybe you can take me down to see it?"

Mathilde laughed and started to lead the way down the tower. "You won't need me to go see the ocean. You'll be spending your time with the court and the young nobles are always going on outings."

I sighed. "I'd rather go with you."

"Thanks!" said Mathilde. "But they're not all like Gretchen, you know. In fact, she's not really one of them. She wouldn't be a governess if she was. You'll be fine."

I wasn't entirely convinced by her words but I did feel a little cheered. "Where are we going?" I asked.

"Mrs Pine sent me to get you. Apparently the queen's ordered you a whole summer wardrobe. You're so lucky! The seamstresses here at the palace are incredible. They want your measurements now so they can get started. Mostly they'll just be adjusting pre-made dresses but it'll still take them a few days. The queen wants them to rush one through for you to wear this afternoon, though."

I felt a rush of gratitude towards the queen. She might be a queen but she was still a woman and she understood the confidence boosting properties of a new, well-fitted dress.

The servants at the palace had an entire wing that jutted out towards the stables. It was a hive of activity with servants rushing in every direction and the whole place hummed with energy. I found myself smiling again. Mathilde had been right – life in Arcadie had an extra buzz – maybe the summer wouldn't be as bad as I was imagining.

The rooms set aside for the royal seamstresses seemed even busier than the hallway had been. At least half a dozen women were occupied with fitting, cutting or sewing and several beautiful dresses were pinned onto dressmaker's dummies. I looked around with interest until I was sharply adjured to get out of the way by a young girl who came into the room, her arms overflowing with material.

Mathilde cheerfully told the newcomer to watch who she was talking to and then hustled me over to a middle aged woman who managed to look calm and collected in the midst of the chaos.

"Good morning, Korrine," she said, "I brought her as commanded. Alyssa, this is Korrine - she's in charge of the royal wardrobes and is a veritable wonder with any sort of cloth."

"Thank you, Mathilde," Korrine said with an amused smile. She held out her hand and I shook it respectfully.

"It's nice to meet you, ma'am," I said.

"Please, call me Korrine," she replied, "everyone does." And then, "Annice!" Her voice wasn't loud but it was commanding and the girl who had chastised me earlier popped out of the chaos around us.

"Yes, Korrine," she said, breathlessly.

"I need you to measure Alyssa. Her majesty wants the pale blue court dress adjusted for her by this afternoon."

"This afternoon!?" exclaimed Annice but was quelled by a forbidding look from the older lady.

"Yes, Korrine," she repeated and the next thing I knew I had been efficiently undressed and was being measured. I stood there in my underclothes and looked helplessly across at Mathilde.

"I'll come back and pick you up later," she said with a wicked grin and then sailed out the door with an airy wave.

By the time she came back for me, I was exhausted. Such a quick succession of dresses had been pulled onto me and then whipped off of me again that I retained only a hazy impression of any of them. I was relieved to be rescued and enjoyed the tour that Mathilde gave me on our way back to the princesses' tower.

This tour included the servant's wing and was much more thorough than the speedy one given by the Princesses on the first day. I began to tentatively hope I would be able to find my way around on my own – although I was sure I wouldn't remember the names of the many servants Mathilde introduced me to.

We arrived back at the princesses' tower just as lunch was also arriving. Gretchen was thankfully gone and Lily and Sophie were full of questions about my morning and my new wardrobe. They were exasperated by my inability to describe a single one of the dresses and were only consoled by the arrival of a package from Korrine.

Both girls were delighted by the pale blue court dress inside and refused to get into their own court dresses until they had seen me in mine. They were still too young for V-neck or full length gowns and they oohed and ahhed over my dress for several minutes. It had a tight bodice and wide skirt and was covered in silver embroidery. It was definitely the most beautiful dress I had ever worn, with the exception of Lily and Sophie's Princess Dress, and it gave me the confidence boost I so badly needed.

It also helped that in the rush to get Lily and Sophie dressed and presentable there was no time for me to think about my nerves. The footmen who had arrived to escort us down had to wait for several minutes and consequently rushed us through the palace at a trot.

Before I had time to think, I found myself at the door of the throne room. Lily had explained on the way down that the king usually received courtiers and applicants in the royal receiving room. The throne room was only used for special occasions.

We were given time to catch our breath and then the doors were thrown open and the herald drummed his staff on the floor. "Their Royal Highnesses, the Princess Liliana and the Princess Sophia," he announced. After a brief pause he added, "And Alyssa, the Royal Princess Companion."

Lily and Sophie advanced into the room and down the long red carpet that led to the throne. I followed several steps behind. The throne room was huge and was lined with marble columns. The doors, windows and columns were all decorated with elaborate gilt patterns that matched the golden throne. The king was sitting in the throne and the queen was sitting in a smaller golden chair on his right side.

Both sides of the red carpet were lined with courtiers, the women in bright colours, the men in sober black or dashing, military blue. They sank into curtseys or bows as the princesses passed but I noticed their heads quickly bobbed back up, their curious eyes fixed on me. For a forgetful moment I looked around, hoping to share a reassuring glance with Max. Then I remembered that he was already gone.

When Lily and Sophie reached the bottom of the dais that held the thrones, they sank down into perfect, identical curtsies of their own. Still standing a few steps behind them, I also gave a deep curtsey. I held it as the king rose and descended the few steps to take his daughters' hands. He smiled and pulled them up, kissing them each on the forehead. He then smiled in a friendly way at me, indicating that I could also rise. All three of us went to stand to the right of the dais and the king ascended back to his throne.

I was so relieved to be out of the spotlight that I missed most of the king's official words of welcome to the court. Luckily they were short and seemed to be of no great consequence. As soon as he was finished, some musicians on a balcony began to play gentle background music and servants began to circulate with drinks on platters. The courtiers broke into small huddles and the room was soon full of chatter and laughter.

The largest huddles formed around the king and queen who were now mingling with their guests. I almost laughed when a corresponding group began to form around Lily and Sophie. This group looked almost identical except that it was a good foot shorter than the one around their majesties. The young girls were dressed in a similar fashion to their seniors except that their dresses ended mid-calf and they had high necklines. The young boys were also dressed like the adults, only their height and the constrained looks on their faces setting them apart.

I took a step back and observed from outside the circle. I hadn't expected many children at court, not given Lily and Sophie's dislike of it, and I was surprised to see them surrounded by boys and girls their own age. I wondered why they never talked of any friends.

Only a few minutes observation served to enlighten me. Lily and Sophie never relaxed but maintained the formal masks they wore around strange adults. The other children, however, were trying much too hard. Straining to entertain and engage the princesses. It was clear from their behaviour that they were completing a disagreeable duty. I suspected they had been instructed by their parents to make a royal connection.

Lily and Sophie were polite but not effusive and the children quickly gave up, breaking into smaller groups. I could see that these children had their own complex social structure and that the princesses somehow stood outside it. Slowly, Lily and Sophie inched their way away from the other children and came over to stand next to me.

I looked down at them with slightly raised eyebrows.

"We hate fakeness," said Lily, quietly but fiercely. "None of them wants to be friends with us for us."

"And we don't need them," added Sophie, "we have each other."

"They might not all be so bad," I said. "You should give them a chance."

"We already have," said Lily. "We like you best." She smiled up at me and I couldn't help but smile back.

"Although Georgiana isn't so bad," said Sophie fairly. "And Thomas is alright."

"But not when their parents are watching," said Lily.

"No," sighed Sophie. "Normally they don't make us come here," she explained to me. "Most of the other kids are better when the adults aren't around."

"Fair enough," I said. "I guess all those other children know something about pressure, too."

"I suppose so," said Lily thoughtfully, "that's what you meant earlier, about understanding people, isn't it?"

"That's part of it," I said with a smile. "You should go back in there and talk to them. That's the best way to observe."

The girls exchanged a glance and then nodded their agreement. Slowly they drifted back over and were absorbed into one of the groups. I watched them, proud of their progress and sad to see them robbed of a normal childhood.

My eyes wandered away from the children and I noticed a young woman watching me intently. She was a tall, beautiful brunette and looked like she was in her early twenties. I couldn't read her expression and wondered uneasily if I should go over and talk to her. Something about her bearing, and possibly the exquisite beauty of her dress, made her intimidating. I stood there debating with myself for so long that she turned away. I breathed a cowardly sigh of relief.

"Princess Companion?" The sharp voice behind me made me jump. "Alyssa? You will let me call you Alyssa, I hope."

I turned around and found myself confronting a blonde girl about my own age. Her features were as sharp as her voice but she had a good figure and carried herself as if she was beautiful. After a few moments I found myself tricked into thinking of her that way.

"I'm Lady Marissa Edgewaring," she said and held out her hand as if she expected me to curtsey over it.

I just stared at her in surprise and after a moment she let her hand drop.

While she had been talking a group of other young nobles had congregated behind her. A quick glance around told me that everyone below the age of twenty-one was now standing in this corner of the room. I spared a glance for the princesses and saw that they were still safely ensconced with the other children.

The group in front of me was mostly made up of girls and I was surprised at the gender imbalance until I remembered Max's hunting trip. There were two young men left but neither looked like the hunting type. One, blond haired and boasting incredibly fine features, was more intricately dressed than any of the girls. He looked like he was in his element here, surrounded by a group of girls, many of whom kept throwing him admiring glances. The dark haired boy looked like his complete opposite. I was pretty sure the presence of so many girls was terrifying him and he kept shooting desperate glances at one of them. From the family resemblance, she was clearly his sister. In response to his anguished stare, she took a firm grip on his arm. I wondered how long it would be before he managed to escape our group altogether.

The girls were harder to classify. To begin with, there were more of them, and they stood grouped together in a way that said 'we belong together and you do not'.

"We're so delighted to have you join us," said Lady Marissa with a sweet smile. "But the herald seems to have made a mistake – he didn't announce your full name – and we're all dying to know what family you're from. Aren't we ladies?"

She glanced around the group for support. It was obvious from her tone and expression that she knew perfectly well what my background was.

This reception was so exactly what I'd been expecting that I would have laughed if I hadn't felt so much like crying. I had worked so hard to find my place at the Winter Castle – it was frustrating to have to start all over again now. For a moment I felt angry at Max for going off and leaving me to face these girls alone. Then I remembered that he owed me nothing. This was my fight and if I couldn't succeed on my own I didn't deserve a place here.

"You wouldn't know my parents," I replied, "but you might have heard of my aunt, Corilyn. She runs the Blue Arrow."

"Runs the Blue Arrow?" echoed Lady Marissa in feigned astonishment. "Your aunt runs an inn?"

"Not just an inn," I said with a smile, "the biggest inn in Arcadie." Let them see that I was proud of my aunt, not ashamed. "And it's so nice to receive such a warm welcome," I added.

I looked enquiringly at the girl standing closest to Lady Marissa. She reluctantly introduced herself as Clarisse Winters and the others took the cue and began to introduce themselves too. The peacock boy was called Rivers and the shy one was Allen.

Most of the girls blended together except for a redhead standing at the back of the group. She was so tiny that I hadn't seen her at first but she pushed through to introduce herself as Lady Elizabeth.

"But most people just call me Beth," she said with a tentative smile.

I gave her a big smile back and resolved to find a chance to talk to her without the other girls around.

Unfortunately Beth was the only glimmer of hope I received the whole afternoon. Some of the group wandered away but Lady Marissa stuck by my side and continued to gently interrogate me. All her comments were made with the same sweet smile and fake tone and I found myself biting back my temper more than once.

I was determined not to let her see me crack so I was relieved when Lily caught my eye and gestured that they were ready to leave. I excused myself to the young nobles and the three of us made our escape.

"Well, how did you go?" I asked the girls.

"It was alright," sighed Sophie, "but tiring."

"Do you think we could go up to our tower room now," asked Lily. "The one where no one is allowed to disturb us?"

"Absolutely!" I said with a smile. "And after the efforts you made today, I think some cushions will be magically appearing in your empty tower."

Both girls smiled and Lily began to hint that her favourite colour was blue.

Chapter 16

I encountered Lady Marissa again the next morning on our way down to breakfast.

"Good morning," I said in response to her greeting. "You're here early."

"Here early?" she repeated blankly. Then she gave a little trill of laughter. "Oh Alyssa, you didn't think we all spent the summer with our families did you? Believe me, the winter is quite long enough for that. My family does have a town house in the Nobles' Circle, *of course*. All our families do. Oh, except for your family, I do beg your pardon." She smiled brightly at me. "But most of us young ones would rather stay up at the palace. This is where all the excitement is happening and their majesties are *so* kind about letting us each have a suite of rooms."

I remembered Max's comments about Nate and Felix having rooms at the palace and kicked myself for my forgetfulness. Knowing I would be tripping over Lady Marissa for the next eight months did nothing to improve my mood but I forced a smile anyway.

Before I could think of a suitable reply, Lily piped up.

"You seem familiar," she said and then paused to look at Sophie who squinted in concentration.

"One of the Edgerton girls, I think," she prompted her sister.

"Oh that's right," said Lily, "Lady Marissa, isn't it?" She smiled at her brightly and held out her hand.

Lady Marissa smiled with less enthusiasm than usual and dropped her hand as soon as she had finished her quick curtsey.

"We must be going, though," said Sophie. "Mother and Father are waiting for us. Come on Alyssa." And grabbing my hand she led me away.

I threw a smile and a quick wave over my shoulder at Lady Marissa. As soon as we rounded a corner I gave both girls a quick squeeze.

"Thanks for that," I said, "but I can take care of myself, you know."

"We saw the way she was treating you yesterday," said Lily darkly, "and Max told us to look after you, remember."

"It's very sweet of you but I don't want you two making enemies for my sake."

"But it's not just for your sake, Alyssa," said Lily. "My family chose you, my Father asked you to be Princess Companion. If they disrespect you, they disrespect us. It's not enough just to be liked. We have to be strong too."

I stared at her in considerable surprise. "That sounds very wise," I said. "Where did you learn that?"

Both girls rolled their eyes at me. "We *are* princesses, you know," said Sophie. "We've had a whole lifetime of listening to royal conversations at meals. We do pay attention sometimes."

Lily laughed at my expression and then they both ran ahead into the breakfast room. I was left standing in the hallway, shaking my head in astonishment.

After three days, I was convinced that Lady Marissa spent all her time lying in wait for me. I could barely step out of the princesses' tower without running into her. Sometimes she was alone, sometimes Clarisse or one of the other girls was with her. I concluded she must have begun a sort of guerrilla campaign to get rid of me.

Striding through the palace on the fourth afternoon since the court opening, I was ready to scream. Lady Marissa, Clarisse and two of the other girls had turned up in the large park behind the palace where the princesses and I had our daily ride. Before her appearance, the rides had been a much-appreciated escape from the restrictions of palace life. The necessity of pulling Starfire into a sedate walk and making insincere chitchat had made me want to throw something.

"Princess Companion?" The quiet voice behind me pulled me to a stop.

"What!?" I snapped, wheeling around.

To my surprise it was the tall brunette I had noticed at the court opening.

I flushed. "I'm sorry," I said, "I was expecting someone else. Can I help you?"

I held out my hand in a friendly way and she came over to me and shook it warmly.

"I can imagine who you were expecting," she said with a sympathetic smile. "I'm Lady Helena, Baroness of Lilton by the way."

I looked at her with surprise. So this was Gretchen's sister-in-law.

"I just wanted to apologise to you," she continued.

"Apologise to me, Lady Helena?" I asked. "Whatever for?"

"For Gretchen," she said. "This whole situation with Lady Marissa is her fault. She spread all sorts of stories about you when she got back to Arcadie. She made you sound like an arrogant social-climber who had somehow got her hooks into the royal family." Lady Helena smiled apologetically. "Even I believed her at first. But I've been watching you since you arrived and you don't seem to fit that description to me."

"Gretchen!" I exclaimed, "I should have known."

"She wasn't so bad when we were little," said Lady Helena. "But ever since I married Gregory she's just gotten worse and worse."

I looked enquiringly at her and she explained.

"Our family is barely part of the gentry. It was a very unequal match but we were in love," she smiled reminiscently, "and the nobles have come to accept me. Whatever I was before, I'm a baroness now." She shrugged. "Unfortunately they don't extend the same *entree* to Gretchen. And she just can't accept that."

So she was Gretchen's sister, not sister-in-law. That explained a lot. I had been wondering why a baron's sister was excluded from the nobles' social circle and left to be a governess.

"Whatever Gretchen's done, it's not your fault, Lady Helena," I replied. "In fact, I'm grateful to you for keeping an open mind."

"Please, call me Helena," she replied.

"And please call me Alyssa," I responded.

"Well, Alyssa, I wanted to invite you to a small gathering at my home tonight," said Helena. "There won't be too many of us, and Lady Marissa will not be there," she added with a smile.

"That's very kind," I said. "I'd love to come but it will depend on whether I'm needed for the princesses."

"Oh, just come along whenever they're in bed," said Helena. "Direct the coachman to the Baron of Lilton's town house. They all know where we are."

"Thank you," I said, "I'll definitely be there, then."

It turned out to be as easy to find her townhouse as Helena had indicated. When I had asked the queen for permission to go out in the evening she had insisted that I not only take the entire night off but that I take one of the many carriages kept at the palace for royal excursions. And the coachman had indeed known the directions to the house.

When the carriage pulled into the large circular driveway of Helena's home, I took several steadying breaths. The house was one of the more beautiful I had seen in the Nobles' Circle and was made of a soft red stone. It was surrounded by extensive gardens but I couldn't see any details in the darkness.

I quickly made my way to the front door which was opened by a somber butler. A footman sprang forward at once to take my cloak and the butler then ushered me into a bright sitting room. He announced me and then fell back and I got my first glimpse of the other occupants of the room.

I was instantly glad I had decided to wear the light blue court dress again. The rest of my new wardrobe was still being adjusted and the blue dress was the only nice one I owned. Even so I was the most simply dressed person in the room.

I recognised the exquisite Rivers and Lady Elizabeth, who once again pressed me to call her Beth, but the others were unknown to me. Helena introduced me to them, starting with her husband Gregory, Baron of Lilton. He was some years older than her, in his late twenties or early thirties and I realised that all the other guests were older than the young nobles I had met at the court opening.

Fortunately for me, they all seemed more inclined to follow Helena's lead than Lady Marissa's and treated me with friendly ease. After only a few minutes I began to relax and to turn my attention to the conversation being led by Gregory. He was discussing some of the issues facing the kingdom and I noticed that both the failed harvests and the bandits were hot topics. Their comments made me think of the drunken men in the Blue Arrow and I listened to their various suggestions with interest. After half an hour, I was even participating and making suggestions of my own. It felt like I was back in the library at the Winter Castle, discussing foreign relations with the king, except that I knew almost nothing about farming or keeping the peace. I resolved to get back to my studies as soon as possible.

When refreshments were brought in and the conversation broke up, Rivers wandered over to me. Thankfully, I was now so comfortable that I was able to answer his exaggerated compliments with a laugh.

"You really can't be serious," I said. "My hair has as much copper in it as gold."

"Pure gold, I absolutely insist," he said seriously, and I laughed again. "Beth, come and back me up. I'm assuring our newcomer that she is the most gorgeous vision of femininity that I have ever encountered. Such green eyes! Such golden hair! Such wondrous grace!"

Beth skipped over to us but rolled her eyes at him. "Rivers, you are eternally ridiculous. I'm sure you were telling me only yesterday that a serving girl you met in a tavern was 'the most gorgeous vision of femininity you ever encountered'. You really need to get some new lines."

She smiled up at me, inviting me to share her friendly disdain.

"I can see Alyssa has already worked out she shouldn't believe a word you say."

"Alas," sighed Rivers, "no one appreciates me."

"You know better than to come to one of Helena's gatherings looking for appreciation. You want Clarisse and Mildred for that," said Beth scornfully.

"Ah, but I want appreciation and intelligence," said Rivers.

Beth laughed. "I'm afraid that's a combination you're not likely to find anywhere."

Rivers reached forward to whack her but she danced out of his reach.

"You see how maligned I am, Alyssa," said Rivers mournfully, "I'm off to find the divine Helena. Perhaps she will treat me with more kindness."

And with an airy wave, he drifted away.

I watched him go in mild astonishment. "Is he always like that?" I asked Beth.

"Absolutely," she replied. "But it's all a game to him. He likes to admire women and he likes to be admired by them even more. There's no real harm in him, though."

"I was a little surprised to see him here," I said tentatively.

"Oh, he's much more intelligent than you'd expect," she replied. "You just have to get past his vanity. Helena only ever invites the good ones. Which means you mustn't be anything like Gretchen said."

"I hope not," I said with a rueful smile.

"You must be having a horrible time with Marissa."

"Yes, she's driving me a little crazy," I admitted.

"She's just jealous," said Beth, "she was hoping you'd be a hag and you're not. Gretchen said you'd somehow hoodwinked the entire royal family, including Prince Maximilian. Marissa's had her sights set on him since she was twelve."

I felt a rush of anger, tinged with a little jealousy of my own, and quickly stamped it down.

"Hasn't she heard?" I asked. "She has much worse competition than me – Princess Marie will be arriving in a few days."

"Of course she has. The whole castle's buzzing about it," said Beth. "She's been telling anyone who'll listen that she thinks a foreign alliance is a foolish idea." Beth laughed. "She doesn't seem to realise everyone can see straight through her. If you keep ignoring her, she'll lose interest in you soon enough. Especially once there's royal competition for her to hate."

"Does Max like her?" I asked, curious.

"*Max*, hey??" said Beth with raised eyebrows and a smile.

I couldn't prevent a small blush. "It was all very informal at the Winter Castle," I explained hurriedly.

"If you say so," she said, still grinning. "And no, I never got the impression that the prince likes Marissa much. He usually treats all us girls the same – he's always very careful not to raise any expectations – but I've sometimes noticed him going out of his way to avoid her. Not that she would ever believe that, of course."

We shared a laugh (mine one of secret relief) and then she asked me if I'd heard anything about Princess Marie. I had heard almost nothing but we settled down for a very enjoyable session of wild speculation anyway. By the end of the evening I felt sure that I had at least two friends amongst the nobility – three if you counted Rivers, but I wasn't sure I should really count Rivers.

Chapter 17

The next morning I woke up thinking about the various conversations from the night before. I wished I could discuss them with Max but he wasn't due back for another two days. Instead, I rolled out of bed and hurried Lily and Sophie down to breakfast. I had decided that it was time I visited Aunt Corilyn again.

A short time later I was mounted on Starfire and riding into the city, a letter addressed to my parents tucked inside my cloak. I didn't usually ride Starfire until the afternoon and she was excited and fidgety at the change in routine. It took all my concentration to direct her through the busy traffic but I relished her high energy. She was a beautiful horse and had the smoothest gait. I pressed an impulsive kiss on the top of her head before dismounting. Three friends after all – no one who saw Starfire could doubt her nobility.

When I entered the Blue Arrow I was spotted by the same serving maid who had greeted us last time. She recognised me instantly and waved me through the tap room. I found my aunt in a small office off the main hallway and apologised for interrupting her. She brushed my apologies aside and called for tea and toast.

We spent a comfortable hour exchanging family news and she extracted a promise that I would come for weekly visits.

"Your mother thought you'd be safe here under my eye or she never would have let you come to Arcadie," she said. "Now, I figure you'll be safe enough up there at the castle but your mother will still be expecting regular reports."

I agreed with pleasure and promised to come next week to meet my cousin.

"He's been out of town on business for the inn," explained my aunt, "but he'll be back any day now and he's right curious to meet you."

I was just as curious to meet him. I had never met my cousin, Harrison, but he had always been held up to my brothers as the ideal son. They had dreaded the arrival of one of Aunt Corilyn's letters because it was sure to produce days of lamenting from my mother.

"Why can't you be courteous, like your cousin Harrison?"

"Why can't you help out your mother without being asked – my sister only has one son but she barely has to lift a finger."

"Stop that roughhousing at once – Harrison never roughhouses!"

I had always found the whole thing rather amusing and was delighted to have the opportunity to meet this paragon of virtue.

I was still thinking of my aunt and cousin when I dropped Starfire back at the palace stables but a message from one of the grooms sent my thoughts in another direction.

"A message came down from the palace," he said, "Korrine wants to see you as soon as you're back."

My wardrobe! I almost skipped with excitement and headed straight for the seamstress' rooms. Korrine wasn't there when I arrived but Annice appeared out of nowhere and deposited a large number of packages at my feet.

"Here's your wardrobe," she said. "If anything doesn't fit right, send it back to us." I could tell from her expression that she didn't expect to receive anything back.

"Thank you," I said enthusiastically and then, as she disappeared again, "but wait…"

I looked down at the large pile in dismay. The other seamstresses were all absorbed in their work and ignored me.

With a sigh, I crouched down and eased my hands beneath the bundle. Groaning, I stood up, my vision obscured by the huge pile of material in my arms. With some difficulty I managed to maneuver through the doorway and start down the hallway.

I was amazed at how heavy a pile of material could be and several times considered abandoning it. I kept dropping parcels off the top and having to stop to retrieve them and rebalance my load. Because my vision was obscured I also kept running into things. My thighs seemed to be at the perfect height to catch table corners and I could already feel a couple of bruises developing. Several people passed by and looked at me curiously but they all hurried on, busy with their own tasks.

Grumbling under my breath I took a shortcut through one of the many sitting rooms. I had only made it a few steps into the room before a familiar voice said, "Alyssa?"

I felt a rush of joy, quickly followed by relief. "You're back early," I said and waited to be relieved of my load.

Nothing happened.

"Max?" I said with confusion and attempted to peer around all the parcels in my arms. "You *can* see I'm struggling here, right?"

"Oh, sorry," he said and this time the parcels were lifted away. I gave a massive sigh of relief and swung my throbbing arms.

"Thanks, they were killing me! What are you doing back already…" my voice trailed away as I realised we weren't alone in the room.

Lady Marissa and Clarisse were staring at me with a look of horrified shock. Beth, standing beside two unfamiliar young men, showed a milder expression of surprise. The young men, who I recognised from Max's descriptions, looked amused and appreciative.

I followed all their eyes and regarded the heir to the throne, laden down with my parcels.

"What is wrong with you?" hissed Lady Marissa. "He's the *prince*, not a footman."

I grimaced at my mistake and stepped forward to take back the parcels.

"Sorry, Max," I said, "I wasn't thinking."

There was another hiss from Lady Marissa at my use of Max's name.

Max just laughed. "Don't be silly, Alyssa. I have arms that work as well as the next person's. And rather better than yours."

He grinned at me affectionately to show he meant no offense.

"I'll just put them here for now." He dumped the parcels onto a chair.

"They *were* heavy, though," he said. "What were you doing carting them around on your own. You're lucky you didn't run into anything."

"Oh, I did," I said with a wry smile, "several things in fact."

"Ridiculous!" he exclaimed, turning towards his two friends with a grin.

Before he could introduce either of them, the one on the right spoke.

"I'm Nate," he said. "And you are obviously the Alyssa about whom we've heard so much." He gave me an extravagant bow.

"But Max," said the other, reprovingly, "you never told us she was so lovely. I can see you were trying to keep her all to yourself!"

He elbowed Nate out of the way and held out his hand. When I put mine into it, he bowed and kissed it.

I quickly snatched my hand back, but smiled at them both. There was admiration in their eyes, certainly, but also a mischievous glint that told me they were taking delight in roasting Max. I was happy to take their words in the light-hearted way they were obviously meant.

"You must be Felix," I said. "I've also heard a lot about you. And I must say, the word 'lovely' was never mentioned in connection with you, either."

Both boys grinned at this sally.

They looked much as I had imagined them. Tall and straight with athletic figures and open, friendly faces. Their colouring was so similar they could easily be mistaken for brothers. Both had brown hair and brown eyes and lightly tanned skin. They were more charming than handsome but there was no denying that they were attractive young men. I suspected Lily and Sophie weren't the only girls at court with crushes on them.

I looked at the wary glance that Beth was throwing between Nate and me and my assumption hardened to certainty. I threw her what I hoped was a reassuring smile.

A glance in Lady Marissa's direction told me that her anger was starting to overpower her shock. I couldn't help a small feeling of triumph but decided that retreat was the wisest course.

"I really do need to get these parcels up to the princesses' tower," I said and took a step towards the chair where the parcels had been dumped.

"I'll help you, of course," said Max quickly and put a hand on my arm to hold me back.

I felt a rush of butterflies at his touch and looked down at the ground, scared of what the others might see in my face.

But Felix and Nate seemed oblivious to any underlying currents. They both rushed forward, protesting that they would carry my parcels.

Max stepped back with a smile and let them fight it out. I felt a momentary pang at his swift surrender but it melted away when he sent me a conspiratorial smile.

"Lead the way, Fair Alyssa," said Nate.

Both boys looked at me expectantly, their arms full of parcels. I gestured for them to precede me from the room. Max followed us, offering a polite bow in farewell to the girls left standing in the sitting room.

I stepped around Felix and Nate so I could lead them in the right direction.

Max joined me.

"See, boys," he said. "This is why I'm the one who's going to be ruling the kingdom someday. I've got the brains. If you hadn't been in such a rush to claim the parcels, either of you could have been the one with an arm free. Then you would be escorting the 'Fair Alyssa' instead of me."

He offered me his arm with an exaggerated bow and I took it, laughing.

"You never answered my question," I said as we walked towards the tower. "Why are you back so early?"

"Well, he claimed it was so we could all have a few days to settle in before Princess Marie arrives," cut in Nate.

"But he seemed unsettled while we were away and eager to be back. We can see now he had a very compelling reason to hurry home," said Felix mischievously.

When I glanced back at him he winked.

I felt flattered by their teasing but also sad. They had no idea how much I wished their words were true.

"Ignore them," said Max loftily. And then, in a quiet voice, "How have you settled in? Has everything been going well with the court?"

"I think we've settled in pretty well," I said. "You were completely right about your sisters' ponies, by the way. They love them."

"Ah," chimed in Felix, "old Comet and Charger. Many is the slow, placid trot we've taken beside those little firebrands."

I laughed. "They are getting a bit old," I said. "But the twins still love them, so don't you dare say a word against them in the girls' hearing."

"I assure you, my lady," said Felix solemnly. "I am not so foolhardy with my life."

I smiled over my shoulder. "I'm not a 'my lady', you know. Please call me Alyssa. Both of you."

They assented with enthusiasm and I was surprised when I turned back to see a rather grim expression on Max's face.

He didn't say much more for the rest of the walk and only stayed to give his sisters a quick greeting before rushing his friends away.

I watched them go with some confusion and was only called back to attention by the twins. They were eager to know what I thought of Felix and Nate and asked me lots of questions, punctuated by giggles.

In the end I was forced to distract them with all the parcels the boys had delivered.

My new wardrobe consisted of an astonishing number of dresses – from walking gowns and riding habits to court dresses and even ball gowns.

My astonishment faded over the next few days, though, as the castle busied itself for the arrival of Princess Marie. It seemed that the foreign delegations would receive an official greeting in the throne room and then be entertained with a dizzying succession of parties, concerts, routs and excursions culminating in a grand ball on their last night. I liked parties but I had a feeling it was going to be a long summer.

As glad as I was that Max had returned early, I didn't have any opportunity to talk to him about the conversations at Helena's party. He was kept busy preparing for the delegation's arrival, and Lady Marissa's new life goal seemed to be making sure we never had a moment alone. We couldn't so much as run into each other in the corridor without her appearing from nowhere.

I wouldn't have seen Max at all if it wasn't for breakfasts and dinners and the new Northhelm etiquette classes the king was putting us all through. Lily and Sophie's regular morning lessons had been put on hold and the four of us spent those hours with the royal Master of Protocol, learning about Northhelm customs. Apparently Princess Marie would be joining us for family meals and, if the Master of Protocol was to be believed, the honour of Arcadia rested on our shoulders.

On the day the princess was due to arrive, the king gave us a lecture over breakfast.

"You all know the purpose of these visits," he said. "Princess Marie may be part of our family one day. I want you all to make her feel at home here. And even if we don't end up making an alliance with Northhelm, this is an opportunity to strengthen our ties with them." He looked at us all sternly and we nodded our understanding.

"All right then," said the king briskly, "Lily and Sophie, you're back to your normal lessons this morning. You won't be coming down to the docks to greet the royal ship. You can meet Princess Marie at the reception tonight."

Both girls groaned and opened their mouths to argue but he silenced them with a stern look.

"Max, you need to go get dressed for the official welcome. Alyssa, I'd like to see you in my office for a minute."

Max looked between his father and me in surprise. "What do you want to see Alyssa for?" he asked.

"That's between me and Alyssa," replied his father. Max looked like he wanted to argue but he received the same stern look the king had given the twins.

We all stood up to go our various ways and the queen went over to Max who was still looking rebellious. She put her hand on his shoulder and led him out of the room, speaking quietly into his ear.

King Henry hadn't mentioned his request for me to act as spy since that last night in the Winter Castle. I had begun to wonder if he had changed his mind and had felt relieved. Now all my dread came rushing back. I wished I were braver – less afraid of pain and trouble and more worthy of the task he had assigned me.

I had never seen the king's office before and I was impressed by its size and magnificence. Like his study at the castle, the furniture was made from dark oak. But this room boasted gold decorations and dwarfed the other in size. Even his desk was at least twice as large. In fact, it seemed much larger than was practically useful and I suspected its purpose was to intimidate guests. I wished it didn't work so well on me.

To my relief the king didn't sit down behind the desk. Instead he used a key from his pocket to open one of the drawers. From the drawer he drew a second, larger key.

"What I am about to show you is a state secret," he said seriously. "I am trusting you never to reveal it to anyone."

"Yes, your majesty," I said, nodding my head nervously.

The king crossed over to one of the bookshelves and showed me a small lever hidden behind some of the books. He pulled it and the bookshelf swung away from the wall, revealing a small door with a large keyhole. Fitting his key into the keyhole, the king opened the door.

"This palace is very old," he said, "and this room is one of its oldest secrets. It has been here since before the time of my grandfather's grandfather's grandfather. It can only be opened with this key."

I nodded again and wondered fearfully what would be revealed behind the door. But when the king bowed his head to fit through the doorway and gestured for me to follow him, I found myself in a small empty room. I looked around with surprise.

The king laughed at my expression. "It's not *what* is in the room that matters," he said, "but *who*."

My confused expression didn't change so the king gestured me over to the wall next to the doorway. He pointed out a series of small holes at various heights. The holes were grouped in pairs and the king demonstrated their purpose by peering through a pair of holes at his eyelevel.

In wonder, I put my own eyes up to a pair of holes lower down on the wall. I could now see clearly through into the king's office although my view was mostly taken up with the back of the bookshelf.

"When the door is shut and the bookshelf returned to its normal position," explained the king," you will be able to see into the room clearly."

"But what is the purpose of this room?" I asked in confusion. "It seems like it's made to spy on you."

"And so it is," he replied, "which is why it's secret and its entrance is guarded so closely. No-one can run a kingdom alone and always make the right decisions. No one man can always see and judge correctly. And yet often people insist on audiences with the king alone. At such times, I can place my most trusted advisors in this room. They can observe what is happening and afterwards give me their advice.

"My grandfather used to put guards in here whenever he met with a certain powerful but treacherous earl. The earl always insisted on meeting with the king alone and one day he became enraged during one of their meetings. He overpowered my grandfather and began to smother him. The king was unable to call for help but his captain of the guard was watching from this room. He leapt out and fought the earl, killing him and saving the king."

"Fortunately I have never needed to post guards in this room until now. The head of each delegation will meet with me here to discuss potential treaty terms. To include guards at such a meeting would be an insult to the delegation. Yet with an unknown enemy working against me, I cannot risk being unprotected. I will post several guards in this room and I would like you to be in here as well. After each meeting you will tell me your impression of the delegation."

"Me, your majesty?" I squeaked.

"You," he said with a smile. "I have already told you that I trust your instincts. You should trust them, too."

As we left the secret room I pondered his words. His confidence only made me doubt myself. I had always trusted my instincts about people before, but the fate of a kingdom had never been riding on them. And not just a kingdom but the lives of people I had come to love. It all seemed too much.

Chapter 18

The princesses were engaged in their lessons when the delegation from Northhelm arrived. Since I was not needed to accompany them, I wasn't invited down to the wharf to greet the royal party. Instead I wondered around the palace, unable to settle.

Finally I decided to visit the Blue Arrow. It hadn't been a full week since my last visit but I needed to get my mind off my fears. Hopefully my cousin would already be there.

I changed into one of my new riding habits and took a moment to admire myself in the mirror. The gown was a deep, unaccented green and the simple lines showed off my figure while conveying a sense of understated wealth. I knew that the gown belonged to my role and not to the real me but I couldn't help being glad my cousin would see me looking so fine. I would show him that my family were not uneducated savages beside his shining magnificence.

Starfire seemed to have accepted the idea of morning rides and proved more settled than on our previous excursion. I was glad because the palace yard was more than ordinarily busy. Lily, Sophie and I might not have been invited to meet the princess' ship but it looked like at least half the court was going. They were accompanied by a large squad of guards looking smart in their dress uniforms.

I edged Starfire around the milling guards and had nearly reached the outer gate when a hand grabbed her bridle and a sharp voice commanded, "Stop!"

To my surprise I saw that the hand belonged to Max.

"What are you doing?" I asked, baffled by his behaviour and stung by the peremptory tone of his voice.

He acted as if he hadn't heard me.

"Where do you think you're going?" he demanded imperiously.

I had never seen him behave in such a manner, not even with the most humble of his servants. All the pressures and uncertainties of the last few days had been building inside me and now something snapped.

"Release Starfire at once!" I demanded angrily.

Frowning into the face of the prince, I realised that his anger matched mine.

"Where are you going?" he insisted forcefully, once again ignoring my words.

"Into the city to visit my aunt!" I declared hotly. "Not that it's any business of yours! Your sisters are safely with their governess and my mornings are my own time. As for the horse, you yourself gave me permission to ride Starfire."

I glared down at him, unable to understand his sudden anger.

"Where are your guards?" he demanded, his voice rougher than I had ever heard it before.

"Guards!?" I gasped in shock. "I'm not a prisoner, *your highness.*" I wrenched Starfire out of his grip and turned her head towards the gate. He lunged forward and grabbed her again, preventing my escape.

"Of course you're not a prisoner," he snapped, irritated. Some of my tension transferred through to my mount and Starfire began to sidle and throw up her head. Max was distracted for a moment, tightening his hold on the horse.

I realised this was our first real fight. It was nothing like our debates all those evenings in the library. Our time at the Winter Palace now felt distant, as if years had passed instead of weeks.

"You heard what your aunt said," Max continued once he had Starfire back under control. "She said we shouldn't be

189

wandering around the city without guards. Don't tell me you've been going down to visit her alone while I wasn't here!"

"I knew I shouldn't have gone away." This last comment was muttered under his breath and I wasn't sure I'd heard it correctly.

Some of my anger faded when I realised he was only concerned about my safety. I still felt irritated at his controlling behaviour, though.

"I do remember what she said, Max," I replied. "She said that *you* shouldn't be wandering around the city without guards. She didn't say anything about me."

"But what if those men find you," said Max, his voice sounding a little desperate. "What if they decide to make an example out of *you*?"

"They won't," I said. "They know who I am at the inn – the servants wouldn't let anything happen to me. And I defy anyone to catch me when I'm up on Starfire." I patted the mare's neck. "If anyone tried to accost me in the street she would get me safely home. I trust her."

Max didn't say anything this time but he maintained his grip on Starfire.

"Really, Max," I said, my voice softening. "This is me we're talking about. I'm sure I'm more afraid of me getting attacked than you are."

"I doubt that," he muttered under his breath.

"I wouldn't go if I wasn't sure I was safe," I finished.

Max finally let go and stepped back.

"I'm sorry," he said, "you're right. You can do what you like with your free time. I guess I forget sometimes that you're not really part of the family."

His words startled me and before I could think of an appropriate response he had slapped Starfire on her rump, spurring her towards the gate.

I twisted in my seat to wave goodbye. He was standing watching me go but he didn't wave back.

For the first time I barely noticed the sights and sounds of the city. I guided Starfire through the streets but I did it automatically without really seeing what was in front of me. My mind was too busy processing what had just happened. Why had Max acted so strangely and what had he meant by the odd things he had said?

By the time I turned in to the Blue Arrow I'd concluded that Max viewed me as another sister. I had always appreciated the protective affection he showed towards his actual sisters and I tried to be glad that he'd extended it to include me. After all, sister was the closest relationship I could hope to have with him. It was much closer than a woodcutter's daughter had any right to expect with a prince.

At least, I thought grimly, it's a great deal more than he seems to feel for Lady Marissa.

"Alyssa?" the polite enquiry broke through my reverie. I focused on the young man in front of me. He wasn't dressed like one of the grooms and I didn't recognise him. He was good-looking but in a friendly, next-door-neighbour sort of way.

He was looking at me appreciatively and in some surprise and when I nodded acknowledgement of my identity he helped me to dismount. A groom came running to take Starfire and I gave the young man a closer scrutiny.

He was significantly taller than me, but slim rather than athletic. He had blonde hair and green eyes that looked vaguely familiar. He seemed to find my confused examination amusing and stood silently waiting for me to finish.

"Harrison?" I gasped, suddenly realising why his green eyes seemed so familiar. They were the exact colour of my own.

"Yes, little cousin," he said with a grin, "it's me. And it's lovely to finally meet you."

He held out his hand to shake mine but I pulled him into a tight embrace instead. He stiffened for a moment and then hugged me back enthusiastically.

"Somehow you're nothing like I imagined," I said when I finally emerged from his arms and we started towards the inn.

"Really?" he asked with a laugh. "What did you imagine? I must say you're just as intimidating as I imagined you."

"Me, intimidating?" It was my turn to laugh. "I guess I imagined you would be stunningly handsome and incredibly proper."

"Thanks for the compliment!" he said wryly.

"No, no!" I protested. "I think you're much better than I imagined. Much more approachable, anyway, which is better in my opinion."

"Well, thanks. I think," he said. "Although I can't imagine how you got that impression. I thought I was generally acknowledged to be the unsatisfactory runt of the family."

"Runt of the family?" I gasped in astonishment. "More like a paragon of virtue!"

"A paragon of virtue?" he asked, confused. We had passed through the tap room now and into a private sitting room that belonged to Harrison and his mother. "How can you say so when you spent most of your life with your brothers?"

"My brothers?" I asked, crinkling my forehead in amazement.

"Yes, you know, the four tall, strong, handsome, intelligent, talented boys who share your blood. The ones I could never live up to."

I stared at him for a minute and then collapsed into an armchair, laughing so hard that tears leaked out of my eyes. Harrison joined in after a moment but it seemed more out of sympathy than real amusement.

"Those four boys do not exist," I said firmly, once I could speak again. "I do have four brothers but they're perfectly ordinary, I assure you. And they've always felt inferior to their good-looking, courteous, considerate, charming cousin."

Understanding sparked in Harrison's eyes and he gave a bark of real laughter. When my aunt came into the room half an hour later we were happily ensconced on the sofa, busily comparing our actual childhoods with the glowing letter portraits painted by our mothers.

"Really, Mother!" said Harrison. "If you begged me to show you the tiniest bit of consideration once, you must have begged me a thousand times. How could you write such whoppers to your sister?"

"Well," said Aunt Corilyn, looking between us in dismay, "she had four sons, and all so well-behaved!"

"Well-behaved?" I gasped. "Surely, you know your own sister. Did you really believe her sons could be so very well-behaved?"

"Well," repeated Aunt Corilyn with a sly smile, "I guess I might have realised a thing or two. But then it seemed to me that Harrison could do with some good role models. What with his father being gone and all."

Harrison pulled a cushion from behind his back and threw it at her. "And here I was quaking in my boots at the thought of meeting one of my beautiful, talented cousins. Not that your beauty was exaggerated, Alyssa."

I laughed and waved his flattery away. "Believe me," I said, "I get enough empty compliments at court. I don't suppose you've had a young noble called Rivers in your inn?"

"Rivers!" exclaimed my aunt. "We have to lock all the pretty serving girls away whenever he comes in. Otherwise we have them mooning and sighing and unfit for work for a week."

"And let that be a lesson to you, cousin," said Harrison with a grin. "There's no reason to get a big head from Rivers' compliments."

"Oh, it's not just Rivers," I said airily, "there's also Felix and Nate and Max."

"Max?" My cousin looked at me sharply. "You mean Prince Maximillian?"

I nodded and looked away, embarrassed by my name dropping. "Well, I guess the prince doesn't exactly pay me compliments," I admitted. "But the rest of them are positively outrageous. It's a relief to escape down here occasionally. So don't you start it up!"

Harrison smiled and solemnly promised not to pay me any fulsome compliments.

I allowed myself to be talked into staying for lunch and the time went so quickly that I suddenly realised I was overdue back at the palace.

"Oh no!" I cried. "The girls will be waiting for me and it's the worst possible day for them to get up to any mischief!"

Harrison called for a groom to fetch Starfire and then asked if he could accompany me back to the palace. "Just to see that you arrive safely," he assured me.

I agreed to his escort, thinking in the back of my mind that it would please Max.

As it turned out this hope was completely unfounded.

When we arrived at the palace we found the yard blocked by the Northhelm delegation and the many Arcadian welcomers. I said a quick goodbye to Harrison and scanned the delegation for Princess Marie.

I finally found her just as she was entering the palace, deep in conversation with Queen Eleanor. All I got was a glimpse of bright gold curls. Max, however, was in full view. He was standing at the top of the stairs, about to enter the palace, and he was glaring at me across the courtyard.

I sighed and turned Starfire for the stables. The grooms were busy in the confusion of the royal arrival and I had to lead Starfire right up to her stall before someone came to take her. By the time I entered the palace, Max was gone. I climbed the stairs to the princesses' tower wondering whether he was still angry with me after all or whether something was wrong with Princess Marie.

"Where have you been?" demanded Lily as soon as I appeared in the doorway of their playroom.

"We tried to get a look at Princess Marie through the window but it wasn't at the right angle," said Sophie. "And we didn't dare leave the suite without you. Father would have killed us if he'd seen us."

Both girls looked at me reproachfully and I felt even more guilty.

"I'm so sorry," I said. "I was visiting my aunt and I met my cousin for the first time. I just lost track of time."

"Your cousin?" asked Sophie curiously. "What was she like?"

"It's a he actually," I said with a smile. "And he was very nice. Maybe I'll get the chance to introduce you to him someday."

"We don't have any cousins," said Lily. "At least no real cousins."

"We have some step-cousins," Sophie explained. "But we never see Mother's step-sisters so we don't know them."

"I never met any cousins until today, either," I said.

This confession seemed to soften the girls and I was able to win my way back to favour by offering to let them pick out my dress for the royal reception that night. There was one sticky moment when I was forced to admit that all I had seen of Princess Marie was the back of her head but luckily Korrine and Annice arrived at just that moment and diverted the twins' attention.

The seamstress had come in person to deliver the dresses that the twins would wear to the reception. Since the queen had agreed that just this once the girls might wear full length dresses, Korrine had made two new gowns for them. The dresses were made of soft cream silk and were identical except for the colour of the ribbons used to accent the dresses. Lily had chosen pale blue and Sophie pale gold.

The two girls were speechless at the effect they created, standing side by side in their new dresses and I began to compose some new stories about the evils of vanity. I figured it would be a good idea to have a few in reserve.

The last reception had been for the royal family so we'd entered through the main doors of the throne room. This time the reception was for Princess Marie so she would be the one to make the grand entrance. The royal family gathered in a small antechamber that opened onto the back of the dais instead.

We were the last to arrive and the girls ran over to their parents, eager to be admired in their new dresses. Max took the opportunity to pull me aside.

"Who was that?" he demanded quietly, looking grim.

"Who was what?" I asked, genuinely confused.

"Riding with you before," he clarified, in a low growl.

"What is wrong with you," I whisper-yelled. "That was my cousin, Harrison. I thought you said you didn't want me riding alone?"

"Your cousin?" He looked surprised. "I didn't know you had a cousin in Arcadie."

"Well, I do," I snapped.

"Fond of you is he, this cousin of yours?" asked Max, watching me closely.

"I only just met him today," I said, "but he was very nice. He didn't seem to want me riding alone either."

"I'll bet he didn't," said Max, turning away.

I stared after him in frustration. *What a hypocrite!* I thought. He can play the role of protective older brother but my actual cousin can't do the same thing. I wondered if he suspected Harrison of trying to take advantage of my connection with the royal family. That was rich considering how my aunt had rescued us that day at the Blue Arrow. *I think my family has shown their loyalty*, I thought, grinding my teeth.

I was about to start after Max to give him a piece of my mind, when the door opened and the herald announced the royal family of Arcadia. I was forced to paste a smile on my face and follow them into the throne room.

The king and queen took their seats and their children stood behind them, Max to the left of the king and the twins to the right of the queen. I stood at the bottom of the dais, on the twins' other side. The court curtseyed and bowed and then rose just in time for the great doors to be thrown open. Another herald announced the various members of the Northhelm delegation and about twenty people filed into the room. They proceeded down the red carpet and bowed or curtseyed before the dais. They then took their places to the side with the Arcadian court.

The last one to be announced was Casimir, Count of Weston. I remembered from my etiquette lessons that he was the delegation head. After he had made his bow, the herald stamped his staff several times and announced Her Royal Highness the Princess Marie Christina Adrienne Camille of Northhelm.

I held my breath as a tall girl swept into the room. She was wearing the largest dress I had ever seen but her height made it look regal. It was a pale gold that admirably set off her bright gold curls. From a distance she looked much as I had expected although perhaps a little taller. But as she got closer I realised with surprise that she wasn't beautiful.

She wasn't ugly, either, but her features were too irregular for beauty and her eyes, though blue, were a pale colour that seemed to fade as you looked at them. My surprise was followed by a momentary surge of satisfaction but I felt instantly ashamed of my spitefulness. Was it court, I wondered, that was making me so shallow? I had never thought physical beauty of any great importance before.

As she progressed down the room, the court swept into deep curtseys and bows but I also heard the faintest hiss of surprised whispers. I guessed I wasn't the only one surprised by her appearance. Princesses were usually famed for their beauty after all.

I felt a stirring of pity for the princess. She must have spent her whole life being compared to the typical princess – petite and beautiful. But she carried herself with confidence and elegance, standing straight despite her height. Watching her sweeping towards me, the pity disappeared and was replaced with admiration.

I felt suddenly that she was someone I would like to have for a friend. I wondered if this was the kind of instinct the king would want to know about.

When she reached the foot of the dais, the princess swept into a graceful curtsey. Neither too deep nor too shallow, it conveyed the exact level of respect due from a princess to a king. My admiration grew. I remembered that Northhelm was a strong kingdom with a formidable military and that they had recently made an advantageous trade agreement with Lanover. Reluctantly I found myself thinking that this would be a good alliance for Arcadia.

Princess Marie rose and spoke in a strong voice, expressing her thanks for our hospitality. The king gave a brief speech in return, welcoming her to our kingdom. Then the music began and the food started to circulate.

Queen Eleanor ushered her daughters forward to be introduced to Princess Marie and I lingered behind them. When the girls had finished gushing over her dress, the queen looked around for me and gestured for me to come forward and be introduced. I bobbed a quick curtsey and smiled respectfully. We exchanged standard words of greeting and then I was happy to fall back, replaced by an eager member of court.

While I had been talking to Princess Marie, Lily and Sophie had been swamped by the other young girls who were eager to hear their impressions of the visiting princess. I looked around for a friendly face of my own and saw Max. When he saw me looking his way, he detached himself from his conversation with Count Casimir and came towards me.

He was no longer glaring at me but I still felt angry at his unjust assumptions about my cousin. So I turned my back on him and went over to join Beth who I had just seen deep in conversation with Helena and Rivers. When I reached their group I risked a quick glance back at Max. He was standing watching me with an expression on his face so close to anguish that I felt guilty immediately. And then I felt more anger at him for making me feel guilty. *What had I done wrong?* I reasoned. *Nothing.*

Still, it was hard to concentrate on the conversation in front of me and I found myself giving answers to my friends' questions about the princess at random. When I next risked a glance at Max he was talking to Princess Marie and I realised with savage satisfaction that she was half an inch taller than him. When I asked myself why that should give me such satisfaction I was unable to come up with an answer.

When Felix and Nate came to join our group I greeted them with delight. A casual movement on my part left Beth and Nate standing side by side and she flashed me a timid, grateful smile. I smiled back before turning my attention to the sallies of Rivers and Felix. Playing off one another, the boys' comments grew more and more outrageous. I laughed and flirted with both of them, determined to relax and enjoy myself for one evening.

Twice I saw Max watching us from across the room. Both times I turned away to flirt even more determinedly with Felix. He was delighted to oblige me, but he reignited my guilt by expressing pity for Max, stuck with the boring dignitaries while we were all having such a delightful time.

Chapter 19

By the time the party broke up I had a headache and was desperate for my bed. Lily and Sophie had gone to bed some time ago, escorted to their rooms and tucked in by Nanny, but the queen had told me to stay with the other young people. She clearly thought she was being kind, though I secretly wished I could have escaped with the twins.

I had said goodbye to the others and was making my way up towards the tower when a familiar voice called for me to wait. I stopped with reluctance, the last thing I wanted now was another fight.

"Alyssa," said Max, sounding breathless and looking hesitant. "I'm really sorry about earlier."

"Which time?" I snapped, instantly regretting my tone.

"Both times," he said quickly. "I'm glad your family is looking after you and I'm sorry I said anything. Not that it's an excuse, but I guess this whole princess thing is getting to me more than I like to admit."

I suddenly felt sorry for abandoning him at the reception. "Thanks for the apology," I said. "Sorry for running away from you before."

His expression softened and for a moment I thought he was going to take my hand. But he didn't and the moment passed.

"That's alright," he said. "By the way, you can sleep in tomorrow. They'll deliver breakfast to our rooms. And Father said he wants to see you in his office after breakfast. He said to make sure you were there before ten."

I nodded, my remorse intensified. I had been so focused on my own drama that I had completely forgotten the king's request to observe the delegation. Other than the princess, I couldn't even recall a single face. I wondered what I would tell him.

"Don't worry," joked Max, who must have read something of my distress in my face, "I'm sure you're not in trouble."

I smiled back, forgetting my concerns for a moment. It had been a while since we had shared a friendly moment like this. No wonder I had been in such a bad mood. I had forgotten how much I had come to rely on his companionship.

Something of this must have shown in my face, too, because Max smiled and tucked my hand into his arm. We walked to the princesses' bedroom together and chatted the whole way, laughing at some of the stranger elements of Northhelm protocol and cheerfully picking Felix's character to shreds. But we carefully avoided any mention of Princess Marie.

When we reached the door, Max took my hand and squeezed it.

"Friends again?" he asked.

"Friends," I agreed, with a smile that felt both lighter and heavier than before.

The next morning I arrived at the king's office at half past nine. I was hoping punctuality would help cover some of my negligence from the night before. To my relief there were already several guards in the room when I arrived and the king didn't ask me any questions about the delegation. Instead he explained that Count Casimir would be arriving for their closed door meeting at ten. He then introduced me to Markus, the captain of his guard.

Markus was a tall, broad man who projected a reassuring aura of strength. He shook my hand and congratulated me on saving the prince from Claud. I stammered and blushed and tried to assure him that it had been the prince who had saved me. He just smiled knowingly and I subsided, even more embarrassed.

"I've asked young Alyssa to watch from the hidden room with you, Markus," explained the king. "I need her instincts. If she tells you she senses trouble, you listen to her."

"Yes, sir," agreed Markus.

I avoided both of their gazes, unable to imagine myself giving any sort of direction to this man.

"Now I assume you've warned your men it would be treason to mention this little exercise to anyone?" asked the king.

"Yes, sir," repeated Markus. "I have picked my most discreet and trustworthy men."

"Good, good," said the king, "I knew I could rely on you, Markus."

He pulled the key to the hidden room out of his pocket and stepped forward to work the concealed lever. He then opened the door and we filed inside, leaving him alone in his office.

The room seemed very small now that I was sharing it with three men and I tried to take up as little room as possible. The two guards stood at the back of the room, leaving the wall with the eye holes to Markus and me. I positioned myself in front of two eye holes and looked into the room. Sure enough, I could see clearly through the back of the bookshelf. The king was sitting at his desk reviewing reports.

"I wonder if they can hear us out there," I whispered.

"Given we can hear them, I think it would be best if we stayed as quiet as possible," said Markus slowly. I gulped and nodded. The last thing I wanted was to cause an international incident.

The outer office door swung open with a creak and I quickly put my eyes back up against the wall. But it was Queen Eleanor and not the count who entered the room.

"I've just spoken with Princess Marie," said the queen. "She said she had a very restful night." For some reason the queen looked disappointed by this news. "Apparently she gets mildly seasick and she said last night was the best sleep she's had in weeks."

There was a moment of silence. "It's such a pity," burst out the queen, "I like her. But maybe it's not surprising, she's not exactly a typical princess." The king gave her a warning look and then glanced back towards the bookcase that was hiding our presence. The queen put her hand in front of her mouth and looked embarrassed.

"I'll come back later, then," she said and left the room.

I was looking at the back of the king's head so I couldn't see his expression. I turned to Markus in confusion and saw that he was standing back with the other guards. He had obviously chosen not to spy on the king and queen's conversation and I instantly felt ashamed.

But my curiosity lingered in spite of my shame. If the queen liked Princess Marie, why was she so disappointed that she had had a good night's sleep? It seemed very strange. Fifteen minutes worth of pondering brought no answers. But it did bring the arrival of Count Casimir.

This time Markus joined me at the eye holes and we remained there, silent spectators of the meeting. The king and the count talked for over an hour, discussing trade and some proposed joint military activities.

After fifteen minutes I grew bored and after half an hour my feet were aching. I began to subtly move my weight from side to side in an attempt to ease my feet. All three soldiers stood motionless and showed no signs of pain. I knew that soldiers were trained to stand to attention for long periods of time and I had always thought it was a pointless exercise. Now I could see I was wrong – there was a use for it after all.

When the count finally left, the king swung open the bookshelf and let us out into his office. He thanked the soldiers who saluted and left the room. I started to follow them but the king gestured for me to stay.

"What did you think of the count?" he asked after the office door had closed behind the soldiers.

"He seemed genuine, your majesty" I said. "I didn't see any hint of duplicity – and no weird feelings in my spine." I smiled tentatively and was relieved when the king smiled back.

"That's good to know," he said. "I like the count – he seems like a straight dealer. But keep your eye on the rest of the delegation whenever you have the chance. You never know."

I nodded my agreement and the king sighed.

"It would be nice to have an alliance with Northhelm," he said wistfully. "It's a pity things didn't work out with Princess Marie and Eleanor." He sighed again and I tried to look interested but not too curious. The king didn't take the bait and I left without any idea what had gone wrong between the princess and the queen.

Time seemed to fly by after that. Each day we accompanied the delegation on some outing and each evening we had another party. Some were smaller and some were larger but I could always count on Nate and Felix for company and often Beth and Helena were included as well.

I lingered near the delegation as much as possible and listened to their conversations but observed nothing suspicious. Princess Marie joined the royal family for breakfast and dinner each day and I continued to be impressed by her intelligence and good sense. My initial nerves subsided and I began to feel certain that whoever our enemy was, it wasn't Northhelm. With that fear gone I began to actually enjoy myself on some of the excursions.

I couldn't help but be delighted, for instance, with our trip to a sandy beach just outside the city. It was only the young people on that outing and I even dipped my toes into the ocean. It was shockingly cold, and Lady Marissa complained loudly at my 'racy' behaviour, but I didn't care.

Princess Marie said she had never felt Arcadian waters and joined me. When I threw her a grateful look she smiled and whispered that she had a Lady Marissa in Northhelm too. We chased the waves back and forth together for a few minutes and I felt certain now that if circumstances had been different we could have been friends.

But circumstances were not different. I was a woodcutter's daughter and she was a foreign princess. And if that was not enough, each day she spent in Arcadie made it more obvious that she would be an excellent wife for Max. It raised an insuperable barrier between us.

I began to think about leaving the palace. Once Arcadia was allied with Northhelm the kingdom would be safe. Our unknown enemy wouldn't dare strike against our combined strength. Whenever I could I slipped away to the Blue Arrow and I began to hint to Harrison that I might be looking for a job soon.

"Are you unhappy at the palace?" he asked.

"Yes!" I said and then, quickly, "No!"

I shrugged, embarrassed. "It's complicated."

The day before, I had sought refuge in the palace library and found Max and Princess Marie there. They had been discussing the Northhelm-Lanover treaty and invited me to join them. I mumbled an excuse and fled, my heart burning.

"Don't worry, Alyssa," said Harrison, "we'll always have a place for you here."

I smiled at him gratefully. But I was beginning to suspect that life with the royal family had ruined me.

Could I ever be happy at the Blue Arrow now?

Chapter 20

The final ball for Princess Marie arrived much too quickly. There was plenty of buzz around the palace and even some betting in the servant's wing over whether or not an engagement would be announced at the ball. Most people seemed to think it likely.

I briefly considered telling Lily and Sophie that I was too ill to attend. But I couldn't bear to lie to them. They liked Princess Marie and had been making a lot of effort over the last few weeks. Their tower room was starting to look quite cosy.

The girls didn't seem to mind my inattention. They were perfectly happy to have a life-sized doll to dress up as they pleased – directing the maid on how to arrange my hair and even lending me some jewelry to wear. They seemed to take my pleasure in the ball for granted.

And when I looked at myself in the mirror I did feel a small stirring of interest. It was my first ball and I looked almost as magnificent in silver satin and chiffon as I had looked in any of my childhood fantasies.

As we approached the ballroom, the strains of the orchestra grew louder and I found my feet tapping in time to the music. The twins had been teaching me to dance for the last week and in spite of myself I was eager to try out the steps I had learnt.

Entering the ballroom felt like entering a fairy tale. Lined with gilt-edged mirrors, the room appeared even bigger than it actually was, filled with a never ending sea of twirling dancers.

Anything that wasn't a mirror was covered in flowers and the room smelt delicious. A long refreshment table lined one wall and scattered chairs covered other walls but I could barely pull my eyes away from the dancers to notice these details. The twins told me they were going to find Georgiana and I nodded absentmindedly, not even turning to watch them disappear into the crowd.

"Want to join them?" asked an amused voice.

I started from my reverie and saw that Felix was gesturing at the dancers. "I've never actually done it before," I admitted. "Lily and Sophie have been teaching me but now that I'm here I'm realising it's not quite the same!"

"In that case I insist on having the honour of your very first dance," said Felix. "I promise I won't let you trip. All you need for a successful dance is a strong male lead. Isn't that right, Nate?"

Nate, with Beth on his arm, had walked up while we were talking.

"In that case she'd better wait until the next dance when I'll be free to show her how it's done," said Nate with a grin. Felix gasped in mock outrage and called on us girls to defend him.

"It's not as scary as it looks – truly!" said Beth, ignoring Felix.

I smiled at her gratefully and agreed to make the attempt.

"If I humiliate myself I'm relying on the three of you to remain my friends!" I warned jokingly.

"You can count on us," declared Nate nobly but then added, "but I won't promise not to laugh," which rather spoiled the effect.

As a new song started up, Beth smiled in delight. "A waltz!" she exclaimed and in another moment she was gone, swept onto the dance floor in Nate's arms.

I watched them go with some concern. The waltz seemed very intimate and I had never quite understood the twins' instructions. How, for instance, did the couple know to turn the same way? I was still stressing about this not-so-minor detail when I felt an arm slip around my waist.

"Don't worry, Alyssa, I'm an excellent dancer," grinned Felix and suddenly we, too, were swept into the dance. I gripped his hand tightly and looked down at my feet, determined not to step on him.

"It *is* customary to look at your partner while you dance," said Felix, "or at least to stare over their shoulder." When I looked up, he added, "I think you'll find it's actually easier if you try not to think about your feet."

I doubted this could be true but as the dance progressed I was surprised to find that he was right. His firm grip steered me around the room and I realised with delight that I wasn't disgracing myself at all. It helped that Felix was both a charming dancer and an amusing conversationalist. He kept me distracted and even forbore to comment the one time I did step on his foot.

While I danced I could forget about the coming announcement and my subsequent departure from the palace. It was quickly apparent that, like the palace itself, a ball lived up to its fairy tale reputation.

After Felix, I danced with Nate, then Rivers and then Felix again. Whenever I caught a glimpse of Max, twirling across the dance floor with another girl in his arms, I couldn't quite suppress a pang of longing. But with iron self-control I was able to prevent myself from watching for him and thus reduced these pangs to the three or four times that we passed on the dance floor. Felix caught the direction of my look on one of these occasions and laughed.

"Max had better watch out," he said, "he's going to lose his reputation as the best dancer at court if he keeps watching us instead of his steps. Maybe he knows it's just a matter of time until the court recognises my superior grace and style."

To demonstrate this claim, Felix picked me up by the waist and spun me around in time to the music. When my feet were safely back on the ground, I risked another quick glance at Max and was surprised to see a sour expression on his face. Apparently he didn't approve of Felix's attempts to upstage him.

After a short break for refreshments, I even danced with Allen. This time I was the one doing the distracting and by the end of the dance I almost had him talking fluently and looking at my face instead of his shoes. He was getting warmed up on an exposition on one of my favourite authors when the arrival of the prince at his elbow reduced him back to stammering half-sentences.

"Will you dance with me, Alyssa?" Max asked and I shivered at the look in his eyes. The old intensity was back, completely replacing the light friendliness he had maintained since the welcome reception.

I nodded, suddenly shy myself, and felt a thrill when the orchestra struck up another waltz. He took my hand in his and put his other hand around my waist. As we swept into the dance I forgot all about concentrating on my feet. The rest of the ballroom seemed to fade away compared to the warmth of Max's embrace. It felt nothing like being held by Felix.

Neither of us said anything and I wondered if Max also felt the intensity of the moment. I was afraid that my emotions were transparent and that he could read my heart in my eyes.

I wished the song would keep playing forever but instead it ended. When the music stopped I felt as if I were waking from a particularly vivid dream. It took me a moment to remember where I was and what was going on. But when reality returned it did so with a crash.

The king had begun his farewell speech to Princess Marie and I looked at Max in anguish. My total absorption in the dance had pushed the dreaded announcement from my mind. I waited for him to leave my side and go to the king. He didn't move.

"Shouldn't you be over there with your father and the princess?" I asked.

Max shook his head but said nothing, his gaze fixed on his father. I stared at him in wonder and felt a bubble of hope fill my stomach.

The king finished his speech and no engagement was mentioned. The princess followed with a speech that was gracious and friendly and again there was no mention of an engagement. Toasts were made and then the king and queen withdrew – leaving the younger members of court to continue dancing.

"But... I don't understand?" I said to Max.

"Mother didn't feel she was the right one," said Max quietly. "The next delegation comes in only a month, though, so it's only a small reprieve." He broke off and looked across the ballroom.

I followed his eyes and everywhere I looked I saw small knots of people discussing the lack of engagement in whispers. Several members of court had begun to move in our direction but Felix and Nate appeared from nowhere to flank Max like guards. The people who had been coming towards us suddenly swerved off in different directions.

On the far side of the ballroom I saw that the Northhelm delegation had surrounded Princess Marie in a similar manner. I wondered if she felt disappointed about returning home unengaged or if she felt the same relief Max seemed to feel. It was impossible to tell her feelings from her expression or bearing. I was once again impressed – she was born to be a diplomat in more ways than one.

I suddenly wanted to speak to her without the engagement lurking in my mind. I left the boys to their conversation and made my way around the dance floor to where she stood. She greeted my approach with a smile which was a relief.

"I'm sorry you're going home tomorrow," I said.

"I am sorry, also," she said in her strong voice. "While I miss my home there is a light-heartedness here which I like. Northhelm is a good kingdom but we are rather serious." She paused for a moment. "Not that I would replace virtue with fun," she assured me, "but Arcadia has shown me there can be room for both."

"Your friends Felix and Nate are examples of this," she said with a smile. "And your prince."

I wondered again how she felt about remaining unengaged.

Seemingly in answer to my thoughts she said, "Northhelm would have welcomed the alliance with Arcadia. And your Maximilian is both handsome and kind. But…" She paused for so long I thought she intended to keep her reservations a secret.

"But I am glad as well," she finally said with a warm smile. "I feel that we could be friends, Alyssa, and I do not steal my friends' men. Do you think we could write to one another, when I return home?"

"I…I… yes, of course," I stuttered, too shocked to think of a more coherent answer. Princess Marie seemed to find my response amusing because she gave a low chuckle.

"You must thank him for me, by the way. His parting words to me were kind. I will certainly treasure his gift. Although we are not to be allied through marriage, I hope that it will be a sign of unity between our kingdoms."

I looked at her enquiringly, struggling to concentrate on what she was saying after her previous words.

"He gave me a book," she explained, "on the similarities and differences between Arcadian and Northhelm customs and traditions. It is a very pretty book and he included a very gracious inscription in the front." She laughed again quietly. "It is perhaps fortunate that I am more familiar with its contents than he is."

I grimaced at her words, wondering how Max had transgressed in the matter of Northhelm customs. But my concern didn't last long before it was swallowed by the other emotions swirling through me.

"I will be very interested to see how it all plays out," she said. "You must be sure to write me."

She then wished me a warm goodnight and swept her delegation out of the ballroom.

Helena descended on me as soon as they were gone and I was forced to put my thoughts aside and to focus on the rest of the ball.

But that night as I lay in bed I considered her words from every angle. It was flattering that she wanted to be friends. But her comments about Max and me were frightening.

For one thing, it was terrifying to think that my feelings were on such open display that she had seen them after only two weeks. And, for another, the idea that Max belonged to me was an intoxication I could not afford to allow myself.

I tossed and turned for hours and was glad that I had the ball as a convenient excuse for the shadows under my eyes the next morning.

Chapter 21

My efforts at resisting intoxication turned out to be futile. Marie's words, combined with the departure of the foreign delegation, induced such a heady release that I forgot all about the other delegations. Instead I threw myself headlong into the activities of the court.

The rate of entertainments slowed slightly from the mad frenzy of the previous two weeks but our days were still full of activities, outings and parties. I accompanied Lily and Sophie on many afternoon excursions, including some that were put on solely for the entertainment of the noble children.

I was delighted to see the twins' friendship with Georgiana growing and even more delighted to see them take their place amongst the children. Watching the princesses at work, I had little doubt that they would be queening it over their own miniature court before long. Once or twice Lily saw me watching them and gave me a wink that reminded me of Sophie's words from weeks ago. *We* are *princesses, you know,* she had said. Whatever amazement I felt then had completely faded away. There could be no doubt now that their birthright included more than just golden hair and piercing blue eyes.

In the evenings I went to parties without the twins. I was becoming comfortable amongst the nobles and while my inner circle of friends didn't change, I had a growing circle of friendly acquaintances. Lady Marissa had given me a temporary ceasefire so she could obsess over Princess Marie. While the ceasefire was over now, it had given me the chance to prove myself to everyone except her closest circle.

With Felix, Nate and Beth by my side I could laugh at Lady Marissa's snide comments and offensive slights. And when Max was around she ignored me completely. For this I had him to thank. He had responded to her insults with such chilling severity that she no longer dared to attack me in his presence.

Unfortunately, she usually made up for this restraint the next time I saw her. And while I laughed it off at the time, I spent many nights muttering scathing rejoinders into my pillow. Goose feathers might have offered a less satisfying target than Lady Marissa herself, but they still afforded me some relief.

Whenever I felt tempted to utter one of these retorts to her face, I reminded myself that although the nobles accepted me, I wasn't really one of them. While I showed restraint, the other nobles were supportive. If I showed up one of their own, it was hard to know how they would react. I couldn't afford to make any more enemies than I already had.

The next time Helena invited me to one of her parties, I asked permission to bring along some friends. When I turned up with Max I could almost feel the restraint his presence brought and wondered if I had done the wrong thing. I fretted that it would be years before I truly understood all the social dynamics of court.

But before half the evening had gone, the conversations had resumed their usual lively tone. Max showed himself to be eager to learn and willing to engage in debate without taking offense. The nobles that the baron and baroness gathered around them couldn't help but respond. I felt proud that I had been the one to show them a new side to their prince.

Felix and Nate had also decided to tag along which gave me some qualms. But after that first evening I felt guilty for having doubted their ability to hold intelligent, serious conversations. All three of them quickly became regulars at the Lilton Manor.

For four weeks I threw myself into unchecked merriment and there was very little to mar my happiness. Once again I allowed myself to pretend that this life, and more importantly Max, were mine to keep. The court seemed to have accepted me as some sort of less royal member of the royal family and no one even looked surprised anymore when they heard me calling the prince 'Max' or heard us laughing over some in-joke.

There were only two things that concerned me during those halcyon days. One was the growing coldness between Max and Felix. Both boys retained their usual attitudes towards Nate and me but towards each other they began to behave with icy politeness. Anyone meeting them for the first time would conclude that they barely tolerated one another. I begged each of them in turn to tell me what was wrong but they would only shrug and change the subject.

The other discomfort was a nagging sense of guilt that I was neglecting my actual family in pursuit of my adopted one. My visits to the Blue Arrow had stopped and several times Harrison had come to the palace to ask for me, only to be told I was out on some excursion of pleasure.

Inevitably, reality returned with a jolt. It happened when King Henry announced at breakfast that our protocol lessons would be resuming the next morning, this time with a focus on Lanoverian customs.

Max asked me if I wanted to join him in the library for a little pre-reading but the sudden reminder of the approaching delegation made it too painful to be around him. Instead I decided to ride down to the Blue Arrow.

As I rode through the streets I felt more and more stupid. If my thoughtless selfishness had hurt my aunt and cousin I had no one to blame but myself. I flushed with embarrassment at what my parents would think if my aunt wrote to them and described my behaviour.

And worst of all, my selfishness had been without purpose. I was sure that I would now be feeling a great deal more satisfied and a great deal less heartbroken if I had thought of something other than my own heedless pleasure in the last four weeks.

By the time I turned into the yard of the Blue Arrow I was prepared to accept any level of rejection from my aunt and cousin with humility.

"Alyssa!" Harrison's enthusiastic hug was the last thing I expected but I received it with pleasure.

"I'm so sorry it's been so long," I apologised into his chest, "and I'm sorry I didn't come see you after you came up to visit me."

"That's fine, Alyssa. Everybody's saying the court hasn't been this busy for years. I only wanted to check that you were alright anyway."

His kindness broke me down more thoroughly than recriminations and I began to cry.

Harrison ushered me into his sitting room and a moment later his mother appeared. I was handed off to her with relief (both on my part and my cousin's) and she turned out to be nearly as comforting as my own mother would have been.

When I was finally able to dry my eyes, I apologised – both for my absence and my tears. "Don't be foolish," said Aunt Corilyn, patting my hand.

"It's just that I know better," I said, "I don't know what I was thinking. I guess I just got caught up in the whirl of it all."

"Small wonder," replied my aunt. "I don't forget, even if you do, that you're only seventeen. Wisdom comes with age, my dear, and you'll have it soon enough. Which reminds me – it's your eighteenth birthday in a week. Harrison and I were wondering if you'd like to come have a quiet dinner with us – although we'll understand if you'd rather celebrate with your friends up at the palace."

"No," I shook my head, "I would love to have dinner with you. Birthdays are for family." *And I can always have lunch with my friends*, I thought.

My aunt smiled warmly and began to enquire about what dishes I would like. We were interrupted by a serving maid who bobbed a polite curtsey and then launched into an apologetic recital.

"The Turners in the second room have asked for their lunch on a tray. When Martha went up she found that they're sick too. The doctor was still here seeing the Hawthorns but now some of the other guests are talking about checking out early."

My aunt heaved herself to her feet with a sigh. "Ah well," she said, "the last thing we need is a fever outbreak at the inn so it might be for the best if they took themselves off. I'll come and talk to them." She turned back to me. "And best you be taking yourself off, too, Alyssa. We'll see you on your birthday unless I send word telling you to stay away."

I embraced her and returned to the palace, buoyed by the easy forgiveness of my family. The good cry had also helped and I was able to meet Max at dinner with my usual calm.

Lanover protocol turned out to be much more complex than that of either Northhelm or Arcadia and with only three days until the arrival of the Lanoverian delegation, the four of us were pushed hard. We each had to learn a different series of genuflections and formal greetings based on our own rank and the rank of each of the delegation members. Their table manners were also much more formal than our own and we spent hours practicing the correct way to eat everything from soup to pudding.

After the first hour of lessons each morning, a dull ache began behind my temples and it only got worse as the day progressed. The endless curtsies left me feeling dizzy and my sleep no longer felt refreshing. I found myself desperately wanting this royal visit to be over – regardless of the outcome. I wasn't sure my mind or body could take this strain for long.

Princess Celeste was also coming by sea and once again Lily, Sophie and I were excluded from the dockside welcome. This time I stayed at the palace with the twins, revising our etiquette lessons. I would have sneaked the girls down to watch the royal arrival through one of the first floor windows but the king had expressly forbidden it.

"I won't have you girls peeking and spying," he had warned, "it isn't dignified." The restriction seemed unnecessarily harsh to me but Lily and Sophie were used to being told their desired behaviour was unbefitting a princess.

By the time the maids arrived to help with our dresses and hair for the welcome reception, my headache was back and throbbing even worse than on the previous days. Finally it got so bad I couldn't bear it any longer. I wondered if Max would think less of me and then remembered that he already knew about my sensitivity to pain.

"I'm sorry girls," I told the princesses, "I have a terrible headache – it's making me feel quite sick. I'm not going to be able to come down with you."

"Don't be silly!" said Lily, her voice more shrill than usual. "Of course, you're coming. You wouldn't abandon us now!" Sophie came over and slipped her hand into mine.

"Please?" she asked, raising beseeching eyes to my face.

I remembered telling Max that I could be brave when needed. This wasn't the sort of situation I had had in mind but I couldn't resist their pleading faces.

"Alright," I said softly, pressing a hand to my forehead, "I'll come."

I hardly noticed our preparations or the walk down to the antechamber – all my energy was focused on not giving way to the pain. When we entered the room, Max came straight over to me.

"Are you alright, Alyssa?" he asked softly, concern in his voice. "You look pale."

I smiled with an effort. "It's just a headache," I replied. "I'll be fine." I was pretty sure this was a lie but it was one I was telling myself, hoping to make it true.

We were announced like the last time and then the Lanoverian delegation was announced. Only the style of their dress had distinguished the members of the Northhelm delegation from Arcadians. The Lanoverians, however, had a much more golden skin tone. I remembered from my geography lessons that, unlike Northhelm, Lanover was located to the south and included a large archipelago of islands. The delegation was slightly smaller than the Northhelm one had been but the members were more richly dressed.

I was starting to feel dizzy by the time they had all filed in and was relieved to hear the herald bang his staff in preparation for the entrance of the Princess.

"Her Royal Highness the Princess Celeste Victoria Agnese Alessandra of Lanover," he announced. A girl swept into the room and down the red carpet. She was wearing a stunning deep blue silk dress. It was tightly fitted with a trumpet skirt that flared out from mid-thigh into a long train. Her skin was golden and her dark chestnut hair was piled elegantly on her head, showing off the deep golden highlights.

I blinked several times and tried to focus. As she got closer I was forced to conclude that I was not hallucinating – Princess Celeste truly was the most beautiful girl I had ever seen. I couldn't tear my eyes away from her perfect, symmetrical face and heard nothing of the king's welcome speech. Only the sound of the orchestra starting up jerked me from my daze.

My head was pounding worse than ever and the dizziness was also getting stronger. I tried to step forward but found my limbs were no longer responding to my commands. I was sure I was experiencing a nightmare as I watched Max step forward to greet Princess Celeste, undisguised admiration on his face.

I felt sick. Literally. "Lily," I said softly, but when I turned the girls were gone. I looked across to where they were being introduced to the princess. I licked my lips and tried to call to someone but found I had lost my voice. A loud ringing in my ears was slowly drowning out the music and the royals in front of me disappeared, obscured by yellow clouds that were filling my vision.

Waves of heat rushed up and down my body and I felt a sudden, urgent need to lie down on the ground.

"Max?" I managed to call but only softly and then I felt my body crumple and everything went dark.

Chapter 22

My awareness of the throbbing in my head returned slowly.

I didn't even try to open my eyes so it took me several more moments to realise that I was being carried in someone's arms. I moved my head slightly, searching for a more comfortable position and heard Max's voice say my name.

I forced my eyes to open and discovered that he was carrying me up the stairs towards the princesses' tower. I stirred feebly in protest but stopped when it brought on another rush of dizziness. Like it or not I wasn't going to be able to walk on my own.

"I'm sorry to be such a bother," I whispered and then added, "Princess Celeste…" before trailing off.

"Don't even think about it," said Max, sounding almost angry. "Why didn't you say you were sick?"

I looked up into his eyes and was touched by the worry I read in them. "Did I hit my head when I fell?" I asked, thinking that might explain the increased pain.

"No," said Max shortly, "I caught you."

"Oh," I said, digesting this. "Thank you."

"You don't need to thank me, Alyssa," he said softly. "I would never let you be hurt if I could help it."

I smiled weakly at his words and then wished the pain would subside so I could enjoy the experience of being carried in Max's arms.

If I was honest it was something I had imagined on more than one occasion but it was hard to find pleasure in anything when my head hurt so badly. I opened my mouth to say something but forgot what it was. Instead I fell back into darkness.

When I next woke I was lying in my bed. I didn't know how much time had passed but I was roused by the sound of someone crying.

"It's all my fault," sobbed Lily. "She said she was sick but I made her go to the reception anyway."

"Don't be silly," I said but my voice was so quiet that no one heard. "Don't be silly," I tried again, louder.

This time the sobs and the murmured voices quieted and Lily ran up to my bedside.

"Alyssa! Alyssa!" she cried. "Are you alright? I'm so sorry! Please don't die."

I laughed weakly. "I'm not going to die, foolish child. I'm just a little unwell. Don't cry." For some reason this just made Lily cry harder.

Nanny came into the room and put her arm around her shoulders. "There, there, pet," she said, pulling Lily away. "You come away and let Alyssa have some rest and quiet." She threw me a concerned look as they both exited the room.

"What's going on?" I asked the two adults who were left in the room. I had never seen them before but recognised from their uniforms that they were a doctor and a nurse.

"I'm afraid you're rather ill, Lady Alyssa," said the doctor.

"I'm not a lady," I said, inconsequentially.

"Yes, well, lady or not, you've got a very high fever. I'm afraid we're going to have to move you. The risk of infection, you see…" He glanced towards the princesses' room.

"Lily and Sophie!" I gasped. "Yes, you should move me at once."

The doctor and nurse seemed relieved to find me so amenable and began to talk through the logistics in quiet voices. At first I tried to follow the conversation but my mind wasn't working properly. Somewhere between phrases I drifted back into unconsciousness.

For a long, unmeasured time I drifted between dreams. Sometimes I could feel soft hands on my head or cool water in my mouth and often I heard familiar voices. But these blended together with the familiar voices I heard in my dreams and I couldn't distinguish between what was real and what was fantasy.

At one point I crawled from family member to family member, begging for forgiveness. I wasn't sure what I had done wrong but sensed that it was something terrible. One by one they turned away from me, their expressions cold and merciless.

At other times I felt my mother's arms around me as she crooned a lullaby. Once I dreamed that I was back in my parent's cottage, healthy with my family around me. *At last*, I thought, *I'm home. And this time it isn't a dream. I'm really here.* When I woke, I felt tears sliding down my cheeks. It had been a dream after all.

A voice called my name and I struggled to turn my head but I was already slipping back into another dream. For endless hours I chased through the castle, searching for something I couldn't find. Sometimes my friends were just ahead of me, taunting or encouraging me onwards by turns, other times I was alone. Sometimes Lily and Sophie were behind me, begging me to stop but I ignored them.

Every time I threw open a new door I found a new party. The guests varied but Max and Princess Celeste were always there. Each time I found them, they were standing closer together until finally I found them embracing. I came to a stop, my searching over, and stared.

Slowly my horror was replaced with a sense of certainty. *Look at them*, I thought, *the perfect couple*.

Once again I felt my body crumple but this time I was falling upwards, into consciousness. I opened my eyes to see a familiar face bending over me.

"Mathilde?" I asked, my voice rough from lack of use. "What…? Where am I?"

"Alyssa!" Mathilde exclaimed. "Welcome back to the land of the living."

"Where am I?" I repeated.

"You're in one of the quarantine wards of the hospital suite." I looked around and saw that I was lying on a thin bed in a small, plain room. "You've been feverish for five days but the fever broke this morning."

"Five days?" I said feebly. "But what are you doing here?"

"I've been nursing you," she said cheerfully, bringing over several more pillows and helping me to sit up slowly. Once she had propped me up she held a glass of sweet liquid to my mouth. I screwed up my face but she made me drink it.

"I don't understand?" I said, finding it hard to follow a train of thought. "Why have you been nursing me?"

"I volunteered," she explained. "You needed someone in constant attendance and everyone knows that we're friends. The actual nurses and doctors helped as well of course."

"I don't know what to say," I said. "Other than thank you."

"You don't need to say anything," she said. "In fact, I think you've done me a favour. The head nurse said I did an excellent job and hinted that she'd accept me if I wanted to start an apprenticeship. Nursing is a big step up from being a housemaid!"

I smiled at her happy plans for the future but I didn't forget my own guilt. It hadn't only been my family I had abandoned in the last couple of months. I couldn't even remember the last time I had spoken to Mathilde and yet, here she was, risking infection herself to care for me.

I reached up one weak hand and gripped her arm. "Thank you," I said again, meeting her eyes steadily.

"You're welcome, Alyssa," she said, equally seriously. "And now, you need to get back to sleep." She removed the pillows and carefully lowered my head back down.

"More sleep?" I asked, aware of how weak I was but feeling fractious.

"Don't worry," she reassured me, "this sleep should be different. Fewer dreams."

"Dreams?" I looked up at her sharply. "Did I talk during my sleep the last few days?"

"You moaned about all sorts of things," she said, "mostly your family. And you spent a lot of time searching for something."

I could read the prevarication in her eyes and groaned.

"Don't worry," she repeated, "no one heard much but me and I won't say anything."

Flat in the bed again, I sunk back into sleep – if only to escape from my embarrassment.

When I woke up again I could tell that many hours had passed. I felt significantly stronger than I had the first time which gave me hope that I was truly recovering.

Mathilde was still in the room but this time Lily and Sophie were with her. The two girls stood side by side looking at me with such identical expressions of concern that I managed a short laugh.

"You really are better!" cried Sophie, smiling in response to my laugh.

"This is the first time they let us see you," said Lily quietly. "We thought you were going to die." Her eyes looked tired and sad so I took her hand.

"Well I didn't die," I said with a smile. "And I hope you're not still blaming yourself. This would have happened whether or not I went down to the reception."

She nodded and smiled but the seriousness lurked behind the smile.

"I'm glad they wouldn't let you come," I added, "I would hate for you to get sick because of me. I suppose I'm not contagious anymore." I looked at Mathilde for confirmation and she nodded.

"All your friends wanted to come see you but they wouldn't let anyone in," said Sophie. "Not even your cousin when he came to ask after you. He said that it was your birthday and they'd been expecting you down at the Blue Arrow. You didn't tell us it was your birthday!"

I had completely forgotten about my birthday and now realised with a pang that I had turned eighteen with only my fever dreams for company. I felt another pang when I realised that Aunt Corilyn and Harrison must have had a birthday dinner waiting for me. I wished I had woken up in time to send them a message.

"They wouldn't let your cousin come in to see you," said Lily quietly, "but when Max heard it was your birthday he stormed down here. He said that he was the prince and they couldn't tell him what to do."

She looked at me steadily but for once I couldn't read what was in her eyes. I looked over towards Mathilde and she nodded.

"He forced his way in here over our protests," she confirmed. "He sat with you all night and in the morning your fever broke. That was two nights ago now, though. He visited during the day yesterday when he heard you'd woken up but you were already sleeping again and he didn't want to disturb you."

I blushed and turned my face away. "It's so lovely to see you girls," I said, "but I'm very tired and I think I need to sleep again now. Come visit me tomorrow?"

Both girls agreed that they would and allowed Mathilde to usher them out of the room. I knew I was being cowardly but I needed time to process their words.

Unfortunately all I managed to do was conjure up a picture of Max's face before my words came true and I drifted back into sleep.

The next day I managed to stay awake all day and received a visit from not only the twins but also Felix, Nate, Beth, Helena, Max and even Harrison. Mathilde kept each visit short but she said she didn't have the heart to refuse any of them.

"They've been so worried," she explained.

A letter even arrived from Princess Marie saying she had heard I was sick and hoped I was now recovering. It was the third letter I had received from her since her departure and I was touched by her concern.

Each of my visitors brought me flowers so my room no longer looked bare. Mathilde hadn't said anything more about my feverish ravings but she silently arranged the flowers so that it was Max's bouquet of pink roses that sat on the small table beside my head.

I also said nothing but I tried to communicate my gratitude with my eyes.

Each day I slept less and less and I quickly grew bored. My friends visited when they could but the court was once again caught up in the whirl of a visiting delegation and they had little free time.

The hours of the day dragged by and I found it almost impossible to keep my mind from dwelling on the Lanoverian delegation. If I wasn't picturing Princess Celeste smiling up at Max with her perfect lips and sparkling eyes, I was worrying over her possible duplicity. I wondered if the king had had his intelligence chief hide in the little room with Markus while he had his meeting with the delegation head.

Mathilde could see that I was fretting myself back into a fever so she brought me books from the library. The books were a welcome distraction but I couldn't read for too long without getting a headache so Mathilde spent hours reading to me or chatting to me about her family and her life in Arcadie. I learnt more about Mathilde during that second week of the Lanoverian visit than I had in the whole three months at the Winter Castle.

Mathilde had obviously recovered from Claud's treachery and I noticed that one of the young intern doctors seemed to be regarding her with interest. He didn't speak much himself but Mathilde told me that he was here on a medical exchange.

From her comments about him I gathered that she returned his interest but she said much less about Aldric than she had said about Claud. Occasionally I would gently tease her and she seemed pleased that I had noticed his interest but she refrained from the giggling that had punctuated her infatuation with Claud. It made me a little sad but it also made me realise we were growing up.

For myself I was starting to view the world differently. My understanding of people had always been good but I was now learning to value them in a deeper way. I realised that I had been using my insight to benefit myself and I resolved to be less self-absorbed in the future.

Of course, these lofty ideals had a tendency to fly out the window when I was bored and tired and sore from lying so long in bed. I was lucky that Mathilde was such a cheerful nurse.

The final night of Princess Celeste's stay arrived at last and was attended by the requisite ball. I was still much too weak to attend but Lily and Sophie came to visit me on their way to the ballroom.

"Have you grown?" I asked them, a furrow in my brow. "You look older somehow." Both girls smiled proudly and Sophie said she thought they might have grown a little since winter.

"Well, something's changed," I said, although I wasn't actually sure if it was a physical change.

Mathilde and I said nothing to each other about Max or Princess Celeste as we talked over the ball and the possible dresses at length. But I noticed she kept making excuses to leave the room. She returned from her third such excursion with a smile.

"The king made his speech," she said. "There was no engagement announcement." I couldn't keep back the smile that spread across my own face and for a moment we just grinned at each other.

"Have you heard what Princess Celeste was wearing?" I asked finally and we launched into a discussion of her various outfits. I was now perfectly willing to marvel over her incredible beauty and to discuss which of the courtiers had fallen madly in love with her.

"She's the most stunning princess I ever imagined," agreed Mathilde. "But you know," and she dropped her voice to a whisper, "they say her head is completely empty."

"Really?" I asked, not even bothering to hide my delight.

"Completely empty!" confirmed Mathilde. "Dumb as a doorpost, in fact."

And we both laughed and laughed, for no other reason than that we were young and alive and no one had ever called us dumb as a doorpost.

Chapter 23

"Well this is cosy!" said Max, surveying the comfortable sitting room. I was reclining in a large armchair and was surrounded by small tables bearing cups of tea, pieces of fruit, bouquets of flowers and several piles of books.

"Your mother has been so kind," I agreed. I had been released from the hospital suite a couple of days after the ball and I now spent my days in the queen's personal sitting room.

"It's been delightful to have the company," said Queen Eleanor from her desk in the corner of the room.

"Well your gain is the court's loss, mother," said Max.

"That's very impressive!" I said admiringly. "Have you been taking lessons from Rivers?"

"I thought it was quite a good one, actually," said Max, laughing and dropping down into one of the other armchairs.

"That's why I need you around, Alyssa, you keep me from getting on my dignity."

We sat in friendly silence for a couple of minutes and then Max sighed. "Everything feels a bit flat now," he said.

"Oh really?" I asked. "Missing the beautiful Princess Celeste?" My tone was teasing but inside I felt tense.

"Celeste?" asked Max with genuine surprise. "Hardly! I think Rivers is missing her, though." He grinned reminiscently. "He finally found a woman as beautiful as he thinks he is himself and he doesn't seem to be recovering from the experience."

"Yes I know," I said with my own rueful grin, "I was treated to a full twenty minutes on her charms yesterday. I fully expect that I'll emerge from my sick room only to discover that he's packed up and moved to Lanover."

"You've been getting a lot of visitors have you?" asked Max in a would-be idle tone. "I suppose Felix comes a lot – and Nate, of course," he added when he saw the curious look his mother was giving him.

"Oh yes, the boys have been lovely," I said. "They brought these flowers and Helena brought the fruit. And Beth sits with me for at least half an hour each day. I feel very fortunate in my friends."

"And your family?" he asked, even more nonchalantly.

"Harrison's been up to visit three times," I replied, "and my aunt has even been up once. She asked after you."

With Queen Eleanor in the room I couldn't elaborate but Max seemed to understand what I was trying to say. He gave me a curt nod and I smiled in relief.

We chatted idly for a few more minutes and then Max abruptly rose to leave.

"I'll see you both at dinner," he said and strode out of the room.

"Goodness," said the queen mildly, "I don't know what's gotten into Max lately."

"Alyssa! Alyssa!" cried Sophie, bouncing into the room. "Harry says you'd better get better quick because Starfire is pining away without you."

"That's very kind of him," I said, "but do you want to try that sentence again?" Sophie just rolled her eyes at me so Lily spoke up from behind her. "Harry hopes that you're feeling better soon, Alyssa, Starfire is missing your daily rides."

"Nicely put, Lily," I congratulated her. She smiled but Sophie just sighed and plopped down on the floor.

"But that's not what he said," complained Sophie.

"I know," I said with a sympathetic smile, "and I know it's horribly boring, but the truth is people don't like to hear a princess talking the same way a groom does."

"That's silly!" announced Sophie after a moment's thought.

"Yes, it is a little silly," I agreed. "But we've talked about this before. Being a princess isn't just who you are – it's also your job. You're a diplomat whether you're talking to a foreign delegation or to your own subjects. And it's the job of diplomats to find the best and least offensive way of saying things."

"But you don't get offended whatever we say," Sophie pointed out.

"No, I don't – thank goodness!" I said. "But we have to practice it in here so that it becomes second nature to you out there." I waved towards the door.

"Fine," sighed Sophie. "I'll do it better next time. And if I promise to try harder can we not lose something from our tower?"

My instinct was to agree but I stopped myself. I was pretty sure my illness was making me soft and I had seen the damage done by the indulgence of the princesses' previous caretakers.

"Just something small," I said instead. "Maybe that nice lamp I let you have last week. And not for what you said," I added, "for the eye roll. Neither princesses nor diplomats roll their eyes."

"But you roll your eyes sometimes," said Lily with a cheeky twinkle.

"Yes," I said with dignity, "but I am fortunate enough to be neither a princess nor a diplomat."

A small noise, like a quickly stifled chuckle, reminded me that we had an audience. I wondered once again what the queen thought of the way I taught the princesses. The girls came to the sitting room every day after their afternoon ride and the queen had never so much as commented on one of my lessons.

"Will you tell us a story, Alyssa?" asked Sophie.

"I'm feeling a bit tired this afternoon," I replied. "I had a lot of visitors this morning. Why don't you play with your tower instead?"

The girls' doll tower had been moved down to the sitting room several weeks ago.

"I don't feel like the doll tower today," said Lily. "Let's play charades."

"Alright," I said, "but you and Sophie aren't allowed to be on the same team – I'm sure you cheat somehow. The two of you can take turns doing the charades. I'll guess for you and your mother can guess for Sophie."

"Would you, mother?" asked Lily, turning hopefully towards the queen.

I knew I was taking a risk because the queen had refused to join in the girls' games on all the previous afternoons. Lily and Sophie had given up asking. But I was determined to get to the bottom of the mystery behind their relationship.

For the first few days it had made me mad to hear the queen's refusals and to see the rejection in the girls' eyes. But then I'd started to surreptitiously observe the queen. She might refuse to join them but once they were engrossed in their activity she would watch them. And hunger was the best word I could find to describe the look in her eyes.

"Of course she will," I said briskly before she could reply. "You can't play charades with less than four people."

"Thank you, mother!" cried Sophie, running over to embrace the queen.

The look of surprise on Eleanor's face softened. "Certainly I'll play, if you wish it," she said.

"Thank you, mother," echoed Lily but with a tone of reserve.

"Bring me some paper and a pen," I requested. "And a hat to put the words into." The two girls scurried to obey and called out silly suggestions as they did. The queen laughed, which only spurred the girls on to make more outrageous suggestions. Soon we were all laughing and I felt a warm glow of satisfaction. I was convinced that it was possible to remove whatever barrier stood between the queen and her daughters.

"Tell me, Woodcutter's Daughter," said the queen the next morning. "How do you come to know so much about being a princess?"

I had been reading a new letter from Princess Marie and it took me a moment to formulate an answer. "By observation, I suppose," I replied. "I read a great many books at the Winter Castle and I've been watching the court for weeks now. And from watching you, of course."

"Me?" asked the queen, confusing me with the surprise in her tone.

"Well, you're not a princess now, of course," I said, "but you used to be one."

"Not really," she said quietly. "I was a merchant's daughter, you know. I was never raised to be a princess."

"Of course," I said quietly, "I think everyone in Arcadia knows your story."

"Do they?" she said, her voice vibrating with some deep emotion I couldn't identify.

I looked at her in wonder, my confusion growing – where was this coming from?

I said nothing, unsure of myself, and after a moment she continued in a calmer voice. "Sometimes I think no one knows my real story. Henry has certainly never understood."

"The king?" I asked, tentatively.

"I used to call him Harry back then, when I first knew him," she said. "He was so handsome – not as handsome as Max, of course, but so charming."

She smiled, but it was a sad smile.

"You met him at that famous series of balls," I prompted. "And after the third ball, you left your shoe behind and he used it to find you. It must have felt like a dream."

"It was," she nodded. "Exactly like a dream. My life before the ball was so bleak and then he came..." She seemed to be searching for words.

"Love at first sight," I supplied.

"No!" she said sharply. "There's no such thing as love at first sight."

I recoiled from the sharp edge to her words – it felt like sacrilege to hear her, of all people, speak this way.

"But... are you saying you don't love King Henry?" I asked, my words the faintest whisper. "Are you saying it was all a lie?"

"No, no, I'm sure it was real," she said, her words low and fast. "I loved him then. He was just a boy but I was so young myself. And I love him now," her voice got lower still, "in spite of everything. I can't help myself."

"Then it was true love," I said, relieved but confused.

"Then why doesn't the kingdom prosper?" asked the queen, tears trembling behind her words. "His father died so soon after we were married and things have gotten worse since then. Now we have the problems with the harvests. And the attacks. My poor godmother did everything she could but I couldn't make him love me. I wasn't good enough."

There were actual tears running down her cheeks now and I was aghast. The calm, collected queen I thought I knew was gone. In her place was a distraught woman on the verge of falling apart. I didn't know what to do.

After several moments of silence, I stood up and took her my handkerchief. "I'm sure King Henry loves you," I said. But I felt the inadequacy of my words even as I spoke them. The queen said nothing.

I thought about what she had shared. It was true that the kingdom wasn't prospering. It was also true that a kingdom ruled by love was a place of peace and prosperity. That's why godmothers worked so hard to ensure true love for princes and princesses. Everyone knew that.

But I found her claim that she wasn't good enough hard to believe. She was as beautiful, gracious and kind hearted as all the stories claimed she was.

"What happened?" I asked at last.

"The problem with love at first sight," she said, "is that it isn't really love. Infatuation, perhaps, but not love. We were married so quickly. Harry didn't really know me. No one at court knew me." She seemed to have slipped into the past as she spoke and I wondered if she even remembered I was there.

"He knew that I was a merchant's daughter, I admitted as much at the final ball. And he knew that my step-family mistreated me, he could see that when he came searching. But he didn't know that I had lived most of my life as a servant. He expected me to know something about trade, economics, even diplomacy. Even if I only knew what I picked up at the dinner table. But I was never included at meals, not even the family ones, and certainly not at dinner parties. I knew nothing – nothing!"

"The first few weeks after we were married I was so happy." Another tear slid down her cheek. "And then I began to see what a bad choice I was, how completely ill-equipped for court.

And then suddenly I was queen but what did I know of ruling a kingdom? The best I could do for Harry was to stay out of the way. And I was proud – I can admit that now – I didn't want him to know how ignorant I was. I tried asking questions but the answers only made me more confused. As if they were in a language I didn't understand. I gave up after a while."

"Sometimes, in those early years, I thought I hated him. He had promised to rescue me from all my suffering but here I was, suffering still. And somehow those few short weeks of happiness and hope made the loneliness harder to bear. I couldn't bring myself to tell him how I felt – I told myself I shouldn't have to. He should have seen how unhappy I was."

"Sometimes I still blame him for not seeing it. And then I remember that he saw my inadequacy instead. Can I blame him for that when I was so very inadequate?"

Eleanor looked up at this question and saw me watching her. She tried to paste a smile onto her face but it wouldn't stick. "So you can see," she said, "why I have nothing to teach my daughters on how to be a princess."

I stared at her in horror.

She was so much older than me, and a queen as well! It had never occurred to me that she could be so broken or her thinking so warped. I felt an almost physical pain at having my illusions shattered. I groped around for words but came up empty.

I wanted to cry at the sorrow in her life but even more at the unnecessary pain she had brought into her daughters' lives. Was it always like this? I wondered. The pain passed down from generation to generation.

"Is this why you never spend time with Lily and Sophie?" I asked at last.

"My daughters will have a better chance of growing up to be true princesses without my interference," she said sadly.

"Your majesty – Eleanor – Ella," I said, kneeling down and gripping her hand. "Your daughters desperately love you," I said. "Your absence hurts them. You saw how they were yesterday, when you joined in charades. Do you want them to feel the same loneliness you've felt all these years?"

A deep shudder went through her and she began to cry again. "You see," she said, "you see how inadequate I am. I need mothering advice from a teenager."

It was hard to think of an answer to this.

"Don't think of it as mothering advice," I offered. "Just think of it as an outsider's perspective – it's always easier for an outsider to look at things objectively."

My handkerchief was completely soaked now and the queen pulled out her own. "I don't know why I even told you all this. You're practically a child yourself," she said.

I also wasn't sure why she had told me, unless it was the forced intimacy that comes from sharing a room all day every day for weeks.

"It sounds to me like you've needed someone to talk to for a very long time," I said softly. "And it also seems like you need someone to tell you that you are a kind, gracious and wise queen."

Eleanor looked up in surprise at my final comment.

"I don't know what you were twenty years ago," I continued, "but you've certainly grown into your role. Now you just need to tell yourself that every morning and every night for the next twenty years and maybe you'll start to believe it."

This suggestion earned a watery chuckle so I felt safe to go back to my own seat.

While Eleanor's need had been desperate I had been able to put my own emotions aside. Now that she was somewhat stable, I could feel my composure starting to crack. I sat in my chair with my face turned to the wall and let the silent tears run down my face.

Chapter 24

"Her Royal Highness the Princess Ava Charlotte Anika Beatrix of Rangmere," announced the herald.

I stifled a feeling of resentment that Princess Ava had arrived the day after Aldric had finally cleared me to return to my usual activities. The Rangmeren delegation had come on horseback and had arrived earlier than expected. I had been out riding with the princesses and so was once again seeing the princess for the first time at the welcome reception.

I had seen their horses, however, and had been very impressed by them. Starfire had been less impressed to find a strange horse in the stall next to hers but Harry had promised her some oats if she behaved.

Princess Ava entered and all thoughts of horses fell away.

Here, I thought, is the princess from my childhood tales.

Princess Ava was petite but not tiny and her figure was exquisite. Her features were refined – small nose, blue eyes, high cheekbones – and her golden hair fell in tight curls. Her complexion was roses and cream and the overall effect was one of the most traditional beauty.

Princess Celeste was more beautiful, I thought a little resentfully.

But if the queen is looking for a true princess, whispered a voice in the back of my mind, surely this is what she had in mind. I imagine Lily and Sophie will look something like this when they're grown.

Princess Ava had reached the front of the dais and now made a graceful curtsey. The king addressed his welcome speech and she made her reply. Her voice was light and musical but something about the dulcet tones made a shiver run down my back.

I jolted to attention at the sensation and looked at her more closely. I saw nothing but the same beauty I had already noticed. There was nothing in her words or appearance to justify the feeling of mistrust.

After a few more moments of observation I was forced to admit to myself that I was no longer an unbiased observer. Rangmere was a large, strong kingdom and I didn't want its relations with Arcadia to be tainted because I was jealous of its princess. I resolved not to say anything unless I heard or saw something duplicitous.

I scanned the rest of the delegation for signs of villainy but they looked like any other group of officials and courtiers. I laughed at myself. Even in fairy tales villains didn't always look villainous.

When it was my turn to greet Princess Ava I gave a deep curtsey and looked straight into her eyes. Her beauty was disarming and again I doubted myself. But the longer I held her gaze, the more I sensed something lurking behind the blue of her eyes. They had a coldness I had never sensed from Lily, Sophie or Max.

I stuck close to the Rangmerens throughout the evening but heard nothing suspicious. Princess Ava was courteous and gentle and seemed to be a perfect princess. It was clear that she was making a favourable impression on the court.

I caught a glimpse of Lady Marissa seething in one corner and felt a surprising rush of affection for her. There was something reassuring about knowing she would always react exactly as I expected her to. And it was nice to know that someone other than myself was displeased with the new princess.

Of course, I could find no actual fault with Princess Ava. Or at least not until we all met at breakfast the next morning.

"How did you sleep, Princess Ava?" asked the queen.

"Please, just Ava," said the princess graciously. "And since you asked, I have to admit that my sleep was a little disturbed. There seemed to be a small lump in my bed."

"A small lump!" said the queen, glancing at the king. "I'm so sorry. I'll have that looked into immediately."

I froze in the act of buttering my toast and barely restrained myself from glaring at the princess. Complaining about the bed on her first night! How rude!

Of course, I knew that my annoyance partially stemmed from my suddenly remembered negligence. I had completely forgotten to tell Mrs Pine about the spring poking through the mattress and if it was still there that meant poor Marie must have suffered through it for two weeks.

At least she was polite enough not to complain about it, I thought. Although I had to admit to myself that a quiet word to Mrs Pine through a maid would not have been amiss. I might be polite but I didn't approve of needless suffering!

When we rose from the breakfast table King Henry gave me a significant look. I let the others move ahead and then took the corridor leading to the king's office. King Henry was waiting for me around the first corner.

"Secretary Leopold will be meeting with me in twenty minutes," he explained as we walked. "I'm sorry you missed the meeting with the head of the Lanoverian delegation. I would have enjoyed hearing your perspective on the Duchess of Sessily. She was an incredibly astute woman." He chuckled reminiscently. "Now that I've met her I'm sure you're right, by the way."

"Right, your majesty?"

"About the Northhelm/Lanover trade treaty. Apparently she was responsible for negotiating the treaty and, given that, I'm convinced Lanover got exactly what they wanted out of it."

I glanced up and down the corridor but we were alone. "Did she seem suspicious, your majesty?"

"No, no, I'm convinced Lanover has nothing to do with our… Claud problem."

"Oh." For a moment I debated telling him about my reaction to Princess Ava but reached the same conclusion as before. A bad feeling wasn't enough.

A brief hope that the meeting with the delegation head would give some sort of credence to my instincts quickly died. Secretary Leopold gave no hint of duplicity whatsoever. The man didn't even seem particularly intelligent and I was surprised that a powerful kingdom like Rangmere would send such an unimpressive delegation head.

Perhaps they don't really want an alliance, I thought hopefully.

"I hear you like to hunt, your highness," said Princess Ava with a look of innocent interest. "Perhaps you could tell me about the hunting here in Arcadia. I have always enjoyed hearing my brother's stories of the chase."

"Please, call me Max," said Max before launching into one of his favourite hunting tales.

I turned my back on them and made a retching motion at Nate, Felix and Beth. They all smiled sympathetically and Felix shook with silent laughter. Neither Princess Ava nor Max seemed to notice.

"You know he had to tell her to call him Max," said Nate in a quiet undertone. "She's told the whole family to call her Ava."

"She's just so… so…" I couldn't think of the right word and gave up.

"She seems nice enough," whispered Beth, with a look of hopeful concern on her face. "Maybe she really is interested in hunting stories."

I stared at her with raised eyebrows.

"Well, it's possible!" she said defensively.

"No girl is ever actually interested in hunting stories," I said with certainty. "Or any other story about a male's prowess. And let that be a lesson to you, boys," I added for Nate and Felix's benefit.

"Well maybe she's just trying to be nice," tried Beth.

"I'll excuse all the comments you've made so far because you're the sweetest person in the kingdom," I replied. "I think you actually believe that rubbish. As for me – I don't believe a word of it. There's something about Princess Ava that I just don't like."

Both Nate and Felix looked thoughtful at my words. They seemed to be uncertain about the new princess. Neither got the same sense of mistrust that I did but neither of them really liked her either.

Maybe we were the most wary because we were the closest to Max. And so far Princess Ava's pursuit of him had been determined indeed. Whether or not Rangmere wanted an alliance, Princess Ava certainly did. And she seemed to know an awful lot about how to make herself pleasant to a prince like Max.

In fact she seemed to know an awful lot about how to make herself pleasant to everyone. Queen Eleanor was entirely delighted by her and the twins were almost equally impressed. It was a little hard for me to refute this impression since Ava acted like the ideal princess at all times. And as much as I hated the idea, Ava might one day be the girls' sister. It would be cruel of me to try to turn them against her.

After two days, only Lady Marissa and I seemed to hold the princess in aversion and after a week even Lady Marissa started to soften. I began to seek refuge in the library more and more often.

I had finally found a nook that felt cosy in the midst of the giant room. It was located on one of the mezzanine balconies and was tucked between the end of one of the bookshelves and a wall. Someone had squeezed a little armchair in there and if you sat in it, you could just see out the bottom of one of the tall windows.

During Princess Ava's visit, I discovered that the spot had an added charm. Once I was in the chair it was almost impossible to spot me unless you came up to the balcony and walked all the way to the window. I didn't always admit to myself that I was hiding from the Princess Ava mania of the court but the effect was achieved anyway.

"Haven't you had enough of sitting around and reading?" asked Max, the one person who knew about my preferred chair. My heart leapt at the sight of him and the grey day took on some colour.

"I just needed a break."

"Don't think your increasing absences aren't noticed," said Max lightly, sitting down on the floor at my feet. I felt a warm glow at the knowledge that he had noticed my absence and come to find me. Perhaps he was less enamoured with Princess Ava than I had thought. I decided to try the truth.

"I just don't like her."

"Who? Princess Ava?" He sounded more thoughtful than surprised which I took to be a good sign.

"Yes, I can't put my finger on why exactly but…"

"I think I know what you mean," Max said after a moment's reflection. "She never puts a foot wrong. And somehow it comes across as a little… calculated. Mother likes her, though." He looked up at me and I couldn't read the expression in his eyes. "She's been hinting pretty broadly that Princess Ava is the one."

This wasn't exactly surprising news but it still made my head spin. "And what about you?" I asked tentatively. "Do you think she's the one?"

"I don't know. Something about the whole thing just feels a little off. My whole world has been stable for years and years and now ever since these princess visits were suggested everything has been falling apart. First there was Claud and then those men at the Blue Arrow. I confronted Father about what they said, by the way, and it's all true, except for the part about him not doing anything – he's been trying to fix it, of course.

"And Mother's been a bit odd about the whole thing from the beginning but she's been acting even more strangely for the past week or so. Everyone seems to agree that my kingdom needs me but I find myself wondering what exactly it needs me to do."

I nodded slowly. The queen had certainly not been herself for the last few days and I felt guilty that I knew why and was unable to tell Max. Although she hadn't said so, I was completely certain that the queen expected her minor break down to be treated in confidence.

"Maybe you should talk to your father," I suggested. "He must have a reason to think that an alliance is the answer."

"I guess that's the only thing I can do," sighed Max. "He gave me my grandfather's diary, you know. He thought it might help me understand what it means to rule. But Grandfather seems to have used the diary as an outlet for his frustrations rather than as a record of his actions. So I'm learning a lot about the problems that plagued him but not much about how he solved them."

"Your father might have some answers to that as well."

"You know, I think you're right," said Max with decision. "And I'm going to ask him about Mother. I came into the room the other day and I could have sworn they were arguing. And they never argue! Thanks Alyssa, you've been really helpful."

Once again I was overwhelmed by the intensity of Max's full attention. I felt enveloped by his blue eyes and the feeling was as unsettling in the Summer Palace as it had been in the Winter Castle. I longed to reach out and run my fingers through his hair.

Instead I knotted my fingers tightly in my lap and refused to leave the library with him. Clearly I needed more time away from him before I slipped up and embarrassed us both.

After Max left I considered his words. If Max was going to speak to the king then I wanted to be sure the king had every possible bit of information. What was it the king had said to me back at the Winter Castle? *You feel anything strange in any part of your anatomy and I want to know about it.*

I decided I would tell him about the shivery feeling in my spine when I looked at Princess Ava and leave it up to him to decide what to make of it. Having made the decision, I leapt to my feet resolved on instant action.

Luckily the king was in his office when I knocked. He was surprised to see me but not unwelcoming and I quickly explained the reason for my visit.

"Interesting," he said, sitting back in his chair and regarding me thoughtfully. "So you're saying Princess Ava gives you the same feeling Claud did? The one that said he couldn't be trusted."

I nodded.

"But you didn't have any concerns after my meeting with Secretary Leopold."

"No, your majesty, it's only the princess."

"Well," he said again and then was silent for several minutes. I began to shift in my seat uncomfortably.

"I've always been considered something of an astute man," said the king, breaking the silence at last, "and I can't help but wonder if your personal feelings might have something to do with this." He didn't elaborate but continued to regard me.

I felt myself flush and then pale. I had been afraid my jealousy was affecting my intuition but I hadn't expected the king to think the same thing. I felt completely foolish and was unable to think of anything to say.

"Rangmere is a strong kingdom – they would make a powerful ally," he said gently. "I'm afraid I need actual evidence of double dealing before I could discount them."

I nodded, mortified, and stood up, anxious to get out of the room.

"I'm glad you came to me though, Alyssa. It's what I asked you to do after all. And I'll talk to my Intelligence Chief."

"Thank you," I said relieved he was willing to consider my concerns but still anxious to be gone.

When I pushed open the door I rushed straight into Max who had to grab my arms to stop me from falling. I flushed again. Apparently I couldn't escape looking like a fool this evening.

"Alyssa!" said Max in surprise. "I just came to talk to my father." He gave me a significant look. "Will you wait for me?" He gestured at the corridor outside the office.

"Of course," I managed.

Outside in the corridor I paced up and down trying to calm the roiling in my stomach brought on by my humiliation. There was no shame in loving someone like Max, I told myself. And therefore no shame in having my feelings known by the king. After all, I had never sought to use or entrap Max in any way.

Somehow my stomach wasn't convinced by this logic and I barely had time to get myself under control before Max came back out. "He was just heading off to a meeting," Max explained, "but he said to come back in an hour. So I think I'll head down to that musical soiree in the yellow drawing room. Mother made me promise I'd at least look in on it. Will you come with me?"

I shook my head because his mention of the queen had given me an idea. It was terrifying and enticing and I needed to think it through. Shrugging, Max left me alone.

Did I dare? I wondered. Did I dare?

Chapter 25

Ten minutes later I was walking into the queen's sitting room and over to her desk. She was clearly dressed for the soiree and I was glad I had caught her in time.

"Your majesty – Ella," I said intentionally and she looked up, attention caught. "Do you still have a key to the king's desk?"

She nodded slowly and looked at me warily. I plunged on recklessly.

"Right now the king is off at a meeting. His office is empty. But in forty-five minutes Max will be meeting with him in his office. And Max told me that he means to ask his father about you. If you really want to know what the king thinks of you this is your chance. I think you're wrong, I think he loves you. And I think this might be the only way you believe that." I took a deep breath and hoped the queen wouldn't call in her guards to arrest me for treason.

You wanted to fix the queen, I told myself to bolster my courage, well this might be your only chance.

"Are you suggesting that I take the key to the hidden room out of my husband's desk and spy on his conversation with my son?"

I nodded, some of my certainty evaporating. When she put it like that it sounded bad.

"I'll do it," she said suddenly, "I have a right to know what my own family thinks of me after all."

The frenzied light in her eyes dissolved my remaining certainty. "You know, now that I think about it," I said uneasily, "it doesn't seem like such a good idea."

The queen turned on me and grabbed my arm. "Good idea or not, we're doing it." She began to drag me from the room.

"We?" I squeaked.

"We," she confirmed grimly.

Oh no, oh no, oh no, I thought as we reached the king's office. The queen didn't bother to knock but pulled a large key from her pocket. Pulling open the door, she rushed us both inside and locked it again behind us. With a smaller key she unlocked the king's desk and removed the key to the hidden room.

The bookcase rumbled as it slid open but the queen didn't hesitate. Opening the door, she gestured for me to enter first.

"How are we going to close the bookcase?" I asked, torn between curiosity and hope that the queen would agree to abandon the whole plan.

"There's another lever inside," said the queen, showing me the hidden lever that mirrored the one in the bookcase. When she pulled it, the bookcase rumbled shut.

"Now we wait," she said calmly and sat elegantly on the floor. I stared at her in wonder, unsure just what I had unleashed.

"Are you sure," I began but was cut off.

"I think it's best if we remain silent. Henry may return at any time." I nodded dumbly and sat beside her.

Sitting in silence on the hard floor with nothing to look at and nothing to do made the minutes drag. Despite my uncomfortable position I had nearly dozed off by the time we heard the outer office door open. Two people were entering the room.

Pressing our eyes to the wall we were able to observe the king and Max. King Henry didn't cross around to his usual seat but took a seat next to his son. The angle of their seats allowed us to see both of their faces in profile.

"You wanted to speak to me?" opened the king.

"Yes. I just want to understand why it's so important that I marry a foreign princess."

The king sighed. "This is partially my fault. I keep forgetting how old you are. I should have started to include you in the governance of the kingdom before now. After all, it will be your burden to bear soon enough."

"I want to help you, Father, but is it really necessary for me to get married? I'm not that old!"

The king sighed again. "It's the alliance we need. The harvest failures have been increasing steadily for the last few years and bandits are more active than they've ever been before. The people aren't happy."

"I've been reading Grandfather's diary." The king said nothing so Max went on. "From what he's written, the kingdom was having the same troubles back when you were a young man. From a restless populace, I mean. Nothing's been done about it in all these years and nothing terrible has happened. Why do we have to do something now?"

"But something was done about it."

"Really? There was nothing in the diary."

"Are you sure? I imagine my father would have written something about my marriage to your mother. He had rather strong views on the subject, as I recall."

"Your marriage? Well, yes, he wrote about that, of course. But what does that have to do with it?"

"Your mother was a commoner before I married her. A merchant's daughter. It was the first time an heir to the throne had married a commoner in three hundred years. It was a good compromise – it calmed things down. The people felt she would be their voice, I suppose."

"And the nobles? What did they think about a commoner queen? They can't have liked it."

"I don't know if they liked it exactly but it was a love match. With a godmother involved and everything. Nobody dared speak out against true love. After all, the whole kingdom is supposed to benefit from our happily ever after." The king sighed.

"But I still don't understand," said Max. "What went wrong? It doesn't seem to have worked, everything is worse than before."

"It's your mother that's the problem." I could just see the king's face from where I was standing and he looked somehow older than he had at the start of the conversation. And even more tired than usual.

I glanced at the queen beside me. There was just enough light for me to see a silent tear run down her cheek.

"As I said, you're not a child anymore. You have a right to know how things really stand between your mother and me. She's the one insisting on these foreign princesses, it was her idea that we seek an alliance through marriage. She's obsessed with finding a 'true princess' for you. I've tried reasoning with her but she won't listen. She even yelled at me last time I brought it up."

"Yelled? Mother?"

"The first time in twenty years of marriage. I used to wish she would yell and scream and throw things in the first few years. Anything other than her constant cold withdrawal. But when it actually happened it was horrible."

"So you just gave in to her? This is my future, father! Your kingdom!"

"You don't understand, I used to promise her I would support any request she made. I tried to implement policies I thought she would like – like making sure every villager had the opportunity to learn to read and write – but she never got involved. I pleaded with her to express an opinion in council

256

meetings, to take an active role in governing. But she refused. And the more I asked, the more she withdrew. And now, for the first time, she's made a request. I can't say no."

"So you still love her then?"

I held my breath. This was it. The reason we were standing here, spying in this unconscionable way.

"Love her?" the king's voice had dropped so low I had to strain to hear it. "Can you love someone who's not really there?"

An icy feeling swept over me and I didn't dare look at the queen beside me.

"Not really there? What are you talking about? Mother almost never leaves the palace."

Max's confusion seemed to remind the king that he was speaking to his son and he made a visible effort to appear more cheerful.

"I meant emotionally. But, of course, I still love your mother. It's why I can't refuse her now. Not when it means so much to her."

Max was silent, digesting all these revelations. I found myself wondering if the king was telling the truth or just appeasing his son. Did Harry still love Ella? Or more importantly, did Henry love Eleanor?

"Besides," said the king, "at least I learn from my mistakes. Letting some local girl marry into a crown is only a short-term fix. But a strong alliance with Northhelm or Rangmere will give the people something to think about. With their armies they can help me keep any rebels in line."

"Rebels?" Max sounded alarmed. "Are things that bad?"

"Not yet but they could get there."

"I see," said Max quietly, "so it has to be Marie or Ava then?"

257

"No, Celeste would also be acceptable. We wouldn't have invited her otherwise. Lanover doesn't have much of an army but Celeste will come with a steady flow of gold. Gold that could help us build up our own force."

"I need some time to think about this."

"Of course, of course. Take a few days."

"A few days?" Max looked alarmed.

"Or a few weeks, we can afford a few weeks. But the sooner the situation is stabilised the better." He paused and seemed to be debating whether to continue.

"Your mother's awfully keen on Ava. But I've told her it's your decision, I can give you that much." At least he wasn't endorsing Ava himself. Some part of him must have believed my warning.

"So this is how it has to be," said Max quietly.

"I'm sorry Max but I won't bend on this."

Max looked at his father sadly and then nodded once. He stood up to go and the king stood up as well. He held out his hand and Max took it hesitantly.

"I'm proud of you, son," said the king. "I know I can trust you to do your duty."

A look of understanding passed between the two men and then Max left the room.

Silently I twisted and slid down the wall so I was sitting with my back against it. I hid my face in my knees. I still hadn't looked at the queen.

The king had said he loved her just as I had hoped but even I hadn't been convinced. And he had blamed her for everything – the state of the kingdom, forcing Max into a political marriage. It was much worse than I had expected.

Finally I couldn't put it off any longer. I looked up.

The queen was standing against the far wall, a stricken look on her face. She wasn't crying but her dead expression was more terrible than tears.

I stood up and went over to her. "I'm so sorry," I whispered. "I never should have suggested this. But he said he still loves you. You have to tell him what you told me. He just doesn't understand – he doesn't know you were trying to help him the only way you knew how."

"No!" whispered the queen on an exhaled breath. "It's just what I always thought. He blames everything on me. Why should I have to explain myself to him?"

She strode proudly over to the door. My eyes widened with horror.

"Ella, no," I cried in the loudest whisper I dared use but she pulled the hidden lever anyway.

I heard the king's startled exclamation as the bookshelf swung forward behind him. Eleanor flung open the hidden door and stood, framed in the doorway, facing her husband.

For a long moment there was silence. I held my breath.

"So, Henry, you blame me for the woes that befall our kingdom." The queen's voice was icy. "Then I will take responsibility for fixing them. Max will marry Ava. She has proven herself – it must be her."

She finally moved out of the doorway, sweeping around the desk and pulling open the office door. As she moved I was able to see the king. He had obviously risen hurriedly from his desk and he was standing now, gripping the wood behind him for support. His face was pale.

I scurried after the queen, keeping my eyes on the ground and trying to make myself as small as possible but the king's eyes fixed on me anyway.

"Alyssa!" he said and his voice was terrible. I had never heard it sound so harsh. I froze. "Shut the door." Though these words were quieter, the tone was no less frightening. I moved slowly forward and gripped the door.

I looked out, hoping the queen would turn around and rescue me but she had already rushed from sight. I could only assume she was so shrouded in her own drama she had forgotten all about me. I shut the door and turned around.

I took several steps towards one of the chairs but then stopped. The blaze of anger from the king's eyes held me in place.

"I trusted you!" he said, his words cold and strong. "I invited you into my home and my family. I put my daughters into your care. I even entrusted you with one of my most closely guarded secrets." He gestured towards the open door behind him.

"And now I find that you have betrayed me!"

"No!" I protested. "I didn't... I mean I..." I stopped unable to think of anything to say.

"Oh?" said the king. "Am I supposed to assume that it was my wife's idea to hide away and listen to my private conversations? It would be the first time in twenty years!"

I didn't even try to defend myself this time because he was right. I was trembling all over and struggling to breathe. One stupid decision and I had destroyed everything I had worked for – all the trust I had built.

"For the past few months I have been looking all around me with suspicion," continued the king, "waiting for the next act of treachery. I didn't expect it to come from you."

"Guards!" he suddenly called in a loud voice, not taking his eyes off me. "Guards!"

"I can assure you," he said, "I won't give you the opportunity to do it again."

260

My pain and shame were joined by horror. How could everything have collapsed so quickly? I wondered what my friends would think when they heard I had been – what? Thrown into the dungeon? Exiled from the kingdom?

What would Lily and Sophie think? What would Max think?

When the door banged open and the guards entered the room I was trembling so hard I was visibly shaking.

Chapter 26

The two guards looked between me and the king. "Arrest her," said the king authoritatively.

The guards didn't hesitate despite the confusion on their faces. The more senior one grabbed me by the arms and pulled me towards him. He twisted my wrists so they were both behind my back and he could hold them in one of his hands. I winced in pain at the rough treatment.

"Take her to the dungeons."

"Yes, sir."

"Your majesty," I cried, realising this might be my last chance to plead my case.

"Don't speak to me," snapped the king before I could go any further, "guards, take her away."

The guard who was holding my wrists pushed me ahead of him so that I stumbled out of the door and down the corridor. The other guard walked behind us. I was pushed down another corridor and then another. We passed several servants who watched us go by with wide eyes.

Finally we turned down a corridor I didn't recognise. I assumed this must be the way to the dungeon – I had never been there before so couldn't be sure.

Before we arrived at any cells, another guard approached us and called for us to stop. He surveyed the three of us with even more interest than the servants.

"You seem to have made a mistake, Jonas," he said with a harsh laugh. "I could have sworn this is one of the courtiers you've managed to pick up."

"Just following orders," said my captor curtly.

"Orders, is it?" said the new man, circling me with a predatory gleam. He rested one hand lightly on my elbow. "I can take her from here."

For the first time I tasted real fear in the back of my mouth. Swallowing hard I drew myself up to my full height and put on the most commanding expression I could manage. "Don't touch me," I snapped.

My retort made the new guard laugh but the original two looked at each other apprehensively and Jonas tightened his grip on my wrists. It hurt a little but I could tell that wasn't his intention so I forgave him for the pain. If anything, his grip was reassuring to me.

"Don't give us any trouble, Matthias," he said. "You've already been reported for fighting twice and if you start any more trouble you won't like the consequences. The sergeant runs a tight ship, you know that."

"Aye, I know that. I was warned Arcadia was a boring kingdom," replied Matthias and for the first time I noticed his slight accent. "But I'm not doing any harm, am I, dear?" He grinned at me and ran his hand up my arm to my shoulder.

I jerked away from him but his hand followed me. I shuddered. Dimly I heard racing footsteps and wondered who was receiving reinforcements.

"Get your hands off her," snapped a familiar voice and I nearly collapsed with relief.

The guards, however, seemed too startled to respond.

When Max came into my view his face was blazing with anger. "I said, get your hands off her," he snarled.

Jonas released me and stepped back beside his companion. But Matthias stayed where he was, his eyes narrowed. And then suddenly he was gone too, sent sprawling by a sharp blow from Max's fist.

Max stood over him, both his hands clenched while the original guards watched them both with wide eyes. I stood frozen, shocked. The whole interaction had taken barely more than a second.

"Jonas," said Max, his voice harder than I had ever heard it. "Arrest this man immediately."

The second guard moved towards Matthias but Jonas stood his ground. "We have orders from the king, your highness. About her," he pointed at me.

"I will deal with my father," said Max, "do as I say at once."

This time both guards moved forward and together they raised Matthias to his feet.

"You might be in control for now," said Matthias, cursing and spitting at Max's feet, "but you won't be for long. Just you wait and see who has the last laugh." He began to chuckle as the guards dragged him away and I thought he sounded a little mad.

The situation had changed so quickly that my head was still reeling. I stared at Max, thinking dumbly that he had never looked so handsome to me. I had certainly never been so glad to see him.

"Are you alright?" he asked me with concern, sweeping me into his arms. "One of the servants told me they saw you being dragged down here. I didn't think it could be true."

"I'm glad you came," I said, my voice muffled against his chest. I could feel his heart racing at a pace almost as feverish as my own.

"But why?" he asked. "What happened? I don't understand. I was with my father only a few minutes ago."

I shook my head, unsure how to explain and ashamed to admit that I had eavesdropped on his conversation.

"We're going to see him right now," said Max. "I have to tell him about that guard anyway. The man sounded quite mad. It may have been empty threats but there's always the possibility he's working for Claud's employer."

I shuddered and Max tightened his hold on me.

"Are you alright?" he repeated and this time I nodded.

He released me and took one of my hands. We walked in silence and Max kept throwing me concerned looks.

When we reached the office he pushed the door open without knocking. The king looked up from his desk, startled by our sudden appearance. His eyes bounced between us.

"Father," said Max, his voice hard again. "Why did Jonas arrest Alyssa? He said it was at your orders but I find that hard to believe."

"It was. She betrayed us."

"Betrayed us?" To my relief Max only tightened his grip on my hand. "I don't believe you."

"It's true. She was in the hidden room watching our conversation earlier."

"In the hidden room?" Max looked down at me in bewilderment. "But why?"

"I didn't mean any harm," I said. "It was the queen, she told me some things and I thought, if she could only hear the truth from you two –"

"My mother was in there too?" exclaimed Max.

I nodded miserably. He looked at me silently for a moment.

"You knew I was going to meet with my father and even what I planned to talk about – I told you myself. And you thought my mother needed to hear it? Why?"

"I can't tell you," I said quietly. "She told me some things in confidence. But you should ask her to tell you herself – both of you should," I added glancing at the king.

"But I *can* say that I meant it for the best and I'm very, very sorry. Please believe me." I was looking rather desperately at Max, expecting to see him turn away from me at any moment.

But his firm grip on my hand remained. He faced his father. "If she says she didn't mean any harm and she's sorry then I believe her. I certainly won't allow you to throw her in the dungeon!"

"Won't you?" asked the king, regarding us both thoughtfully. "Perhaps I was a little hasty." I almost melted at the reprieve – until he continued.

"But if you want to keep her out of the dungeon then you'll have to help mend the damage she's done between your mother and I. I will pardon Alyssa if you will promise to marry Princess Ava. I'll announce it at the ball tomorrow night."

I gasped but the king ignored me. He held Max's gaze.

"Your mother is determined that you marry Princess Ava and she will serve our purpose as well as any other. She's beautiful and charming, I'm sure she'll make a suitable wife."

"But, your majesty," I cried and the king finally looked at me.

"Unless you have some actual evidence against the princess I don't want to hear a single word against her," he said and I subsided.

Max looked between me and the king several times and then sighed. "Alright," he said. "I'll do it, you can make the announcement tomorrow night."

As he spoke Max seemed to shrink and I wondered if this night could get any worse.

The king seemed to have noticed the change in Max's bearing as well. "You'll see, son," he said softly, "this will all work out for the best."

Max just shook his head and pulled me towards the door. Just before we reached it he stopped and turned back to his

266

father. "I nearly forgot. I've had a guard thrown into the dungeons. I think you should have the Intelligence Chief interview him. Jonas can explain the situation." Without waiting for a response he swept me out of the room.

Once more we walked down the corridors in silence, hands tightly clenched. Twice Max opened his mouth as if he was going to speak and then shut it again. I followed him blindly, my shock merely compounded.

He led me up several staircases and then out onto a balcony. Night had fallen but there was enough light coming from the moon and spilling out through the double doors to illuminate us. Sometime during the last few weeks summer had arrived and the air was balmy despite the late hour.

"This is my favourite balcony," said Max. "I'm surprised I haven't brought you here before. I guess we've had parties every night. And then you were sick…"

I walked up to the elegant stone balustrade and looked out into the night. The balcony was on the back of the building and overlooked the large park where the court went to ride. I could imagine the beautiful view during the day.

"I'm sorry," I started to say but Max cut me off with a gesture.

"No," he said. "I think this was inevitable. You just hurried it along a little."

"Thank you," I said softly, "for rescuing me."

"When I saw him touching you like that –" he broke off and then continued softly, "I wanted to kill him."

Turning he strode the short length of the balcony and back to my side. He looked down into my face and I could see him wrestling with some inner turmoil.

"I don't care anymore," he said, his voice deep and rough with emotion. "I'm sick of fighting it."

"Fighting what?" I asked, confused but breathless from the intense emotion in his eyes.

"This," he said and took the final step forward.

Suddenly his arms were around me, pressing me close against him and for a moment he held me there, looking down into my face. Then his head moved downwards and mine moved upwards and we were kissing.

It was everything I had imagined and nothing like I had imagined at the same time. I suddenly knew with absolute certainty that I never wanted to kiss any other man. Max was it for me – would always be it.

One of my hands moved upwards into his soft, thick hair and he tightened his grip in response. I was suspended in time, the moment endless – until suddenly it was over. Max let me go and fell back a step, panting.

We stared at each other.

"This changes nothing, of course," he said sadly. "It doesn't matter if I love you, I'm still the prince. Tomorrow night I'll be engaged to Ava and I don't know how I'll bear to even look at you after that. It will be too painful."

All the warmth seemed to drain instantly from my body and I felt my flushed cheeks paling. I couldn't seem to focus. He loved me? The wonder of it made it hard to think.

But he was right, of course, and I had always known it. It didn't matter how we felt – we couldn't be together. I wished I hadn't let him kiss me. I wasn't sure I could bear the empty, bleak look that had replaced the passion in Max's eyes. Not on top of my own pain.

He turned away and I did nothing to stop him. What was there to say? For a moment he turned back and reached out a hand towards me. But then he let it drop and left the balcony with heavy steps.

I stayed where I was and slowly the minutes turned into an hour. I was so absorbed in the wonder of my own blindness I didn't even notice the passing time.

I relived every tiny hint Max had dropped. Every warm look, every outburst of jealousy. I had been so sure that Max thought of me as a sister.

Suddenly I remembered Felix. How horrible to think that I was what had come between them! I decided to talk to Felix about it. I wasn't sure what I would say but I would think of something.

The minutes continued to creep by. After I had examined every moment, every conversation, I realised there was something else, buried underneath. I began to worry at it, pressing down until the emotion sprang fully into life. Anger.

Max had said he loved me but what good was love if it didn't motivate you to action? If he loved me so much, why wouldn't he fight for me? He was so certain we could never be together. But he had never even tried.

I embraced the anger. It was invigorating. But slowly the deep lethargy of my sorrow returned. Of course I wanted him to fight for me but at the same time I loved him for who he was. He wouldn't be Max without his sense of duty to his kingdom.

I sank back into listlessness.

Many more minutes passed.

It must be very late, I thought. I was sure I wouldn't be able to sleep tonight but Lily and Sophie would worry if they found my bed unslept in. Mechanically I turned away from the balcony.

Chapter 27

I hadn't been paying attention when Max had led me to the balcony so it took me a moment to orient myself. I was near the guest wing and I realised with grim humour that Princess Ava was sleeping just down the hall. I wondered if her mattress had been replaced and then shook myself. What did I care about a mattress when my whole world was collapsing?

Slowly I moved down the hallway. After a moment I heard whispered voices and realised I wasn't the only one awake. I couldn't bear to face anyone or answer any questions so I drew back into a niche in the wall. The space was filled by a statue on a pedestal and I slipped behind it. Two figures passed me. They came from further down the guest hallway and they stopped not far from my hiding place, facing an intersection of passageways.

"Take the left branch and follow it all the way to the end. There's a door that will let you out into the yard." I started in surprise, almost banging my head on one of the outstretched arms of the statue. It was Princess Ava.

I drew back further into the shadows and held my breath, straining to hear above my now rapidly beating heart. The voice was familiar but also different. It was still musical but it was no longer sweet. Instead it was hard and cold.

This is my chance! I thought exultantly. She's clearly talking to one of her own people and thinks they're alone. The engagement hasn't been announced yet - if I can overhear something to convince the king, I can still save Max.

"You were a fool to come into the palace in the first place," Ava continued, "and I don't suffer fools gladly."

"I'm sorry, my lady," said her companion. "But one of my men in the palace was taken into custody. There's a chance your position will be compromised."

"I heard you the first time," snapped Ava. "But the people here are soft. They are blinded by kindness. They won't break him."

"I trust you are right. He's not the brightest of my men but he knows how I repay traitors," said the man in a voice nearly as cold as the princess's own.

Something about the timbre of his voice stirred a memory. I strained to bring it to the surface but it hovered just out of reach.

"I'm always right, Joran," said Ava. "The ball is tomorrow night and I confidently expect an engagement to be announced. You shouldn't be in Arcadie at all – there's a chance someone might recognise you and I won't have my plans overset. You should return to the forest at once."

Her mention of the forest brought the memory rushing back. I recognised the man's voice because this was the second time I had inadvertently spied on one of his secret assignations. The princess was talking to Claud's employer.

I hadn't thought it possible but my heartbeat sped up. My excitement was now tinged with fear and I pressed my body more firmly against the wall.

"Once our engagement is announced I'll send Secretary Leopold back to Rangmere. He'll have played his part by then and I can't bear having the fool around me."

"A fool, maybe, but one who inspires trust," commented Joran.

"I know that," retorted Ava, "why do you think I brought him? After that botched business at the Winter Castle King Henry has been suspicious."

I could tell from her tone of recrimination that she blamed Joran for Claud's discovery and capture.

"Set some of your men to watch the road. When you see Leopold pass by, you'll know it's time to bring your men into Arcadie. Have them in full livery. They'll have to pose as my ceremonial guard until after the wedding."

"And the rest of the men, the ones waiting at the border?"

"They can stay there for now. There'll be plenty of time to bring them in after I'm married."

Men in the forest? Men at the border? It was even worse than I had feared. She talked as if Rangmere was planning a complete annexation of Arcadia. *Those bandit attacks!* I thought. *They must have been the work of this man and his troops in the forest.*

A sharp spasm stabbed through my calf. I squeezed my eyes shut and fought against the pain. My tense stillness had brought on the cramp but I didn't dare move and hardly dared to breathe I was so afraid of being discovered.

Gritting my teeth, I forced my muscles to relax, one by one. But my body had no sooner relaxed than I tensed again, startled by the sound of a door further down the guest corridor.

Both Ava and her companion started also and the man cursed under his breath.

"You stay here," he said quietly. "I'm going to check it out."

"No, you fool, come back," hissed the princess. "I've already told you – you could ruin everything if you're seen. It's almost certainly one of my staff. I'll take care of it."

Joran had already passed my hiding place on his way back down the corridor but at her words he turned around. And as he turned, his glance raked across the niche where I was hiding. He swore more loudly this time and pounced forward.

I screamed but it came out without volume because I had been holding my breath. I tried to run but the statue blocked my escape and Joran caught my arm. I tried to pull away but he yanked me back hard and I fell, hitting my head on the statue.

Dazed, I struggled to get to my feet but Joran was already standing over me. He dragged me up and out into the corridor. I drew in a breath to scream and he quickly pulled me against his body. With one hand he held me around the waist, my back against his stomach and with the other he covered my mouth.

I fought hard, kicking back against his legs and pulling against the hand covering my mouth but my efforts made no impact. My head was still ringing from the blow it had received and my kicks had no force.

"It seems we have a spy, your highness," said Joran calmly. "Shall I dispose of her?"

I struggled harder but with no better result.

"No," said Ava sharply, "I recognise her. This is the Princess Companion. Now what are you doing here, Alyssa?" she asked, her voice dropping into a sickening parody of her usual sweet tones.

"She must have heard everything," objected Joran.

"I'm not suggesting we let her go," said Ava, the coldness back in her tone. "But the royal family all seem to have an attachment to her. I won't have her harmed – I suspect she'll be very valuable in days to come."

Joran grunted a question and Ava sighed. "To keep the king and my darling husband-to-be in line, of course. I suspect young Max will do anything I command if I threaten Alyssa."

I could hear the pleasure in her voice and was nearly sick.

"The ball is less than twenty-four hours away. Tie her up, gag her and stash her in my closet. My own servants tend to my rooms so no one will find her there. I can recover her after the announcement. A day without food or water won't harm her beyond repair. And once the announcement has been made there'll be nothing she can do. If Arcadia tries to draw back from a public alliance, it will be grounds for a declaration of war. We can drop the whole charade completely."

She shrugged. "Father would rather I married into the throne legitimately, but I'm not sure I want to be saddled with the tiresome prince. Either way we get Arcadia."

"Your father won't be happy if the marriage doesn't go ahead," warned Joran.

"I don't care," snapped Ava. "I'm handing him Arcadia on a silver platter, he should be grateful. And you had better remember where your loyalty lies, Joran. I will be the one to rule in Arcadie, not my father. And I'll remember my friends – and my enemies."

"You know my loyalty, my lady."

"Yes," she said, her voice softening. "You are a most loyal lieutenant. So trust in me just a little bit longer. Everything will be done according to international law. The other kingdoms will have no grounds for interference."

I was crying now, the tears running down Joran's hand. He ignored them as completely as he ignored my pounding feet and scrabbling hands. Realising his distraction, I pulled my right arm forward and drove my elbow back into his stomach hard.

He groaned and loosened his grip and I tore myself free. I turned to run and once again filled my lungs, preparing to scream. But Joran turned, quick as a cat, and tackled me to the ground. His weight landed on my back hard. I lay there, winded, my mind panicking as my body struggled to breathe.

By the time I had managed to suck in a breath, Joran had rolled me over and stuffed a piece of material into my mouth. He quickly tied it in place with another strip of material, all while he sat on top of me, pinning me in place. Once my mouth was secure he pulled me back to my feet and forced me down the corridor, my hands twisted behind my back.

Ava stalked in front of us, on the lookout for any more nighttime wanderers. I desperately hoped someone else would stumble upon us but no one appeared. When she reached her own suite, Ava opened the door and gestured for Joran to push me in ahead of her.

Ava's suite looked like a larger version of the Princess Room at the Winter Castle, everywhere I looked was red velvet and when they marched me through to the bedroom I saw an almost identical bed. Joran produced a rope from somewhere and quickly cut a short section that he used to tie my hands and feet together. I tensed my muscles and spread my hands as far apart as I dared but he yanked the rope tightly so it did little good.

Once I was securely bound, Joran picked me up, cradling me like a child and deposited me in the large wardrobe.

"You can kick against the wall all you like," said Ava, her sweet voice back. "The next room over belongs to the captain of my guard. And Hans is even more loyal to me than Joran. No one will hear you and no one is coming to rescue you. You might as well save your strength." And she closed the door, shutting me into darkness.

Chapter 28

For a long moment I just lay on the floor, letting my eyes adjust. There was a line of light around the door and I focused on that, fighting back both panic and bile. Eventually my mind calmed and my eyes adjusted.

I took in long, deep breaths through my nose and took stock of my situation. The rag in my mouth tasted vile and was already sticky and disgusting from my saliva but it didn't hurt exactly. My head, however, was still throbbing from the blow against the statue.

I strained to pull my hands free from their binding but the knots didn't even loosen. My wrists were soon throbbing from the effort and I gave it up. With my wrists and ankles already sore, I dreaded the hours ahead. I suspected that I would soon find it impossible to concentrate on anything other than the pain. With this in mind, I wriggled around, trying to find the most comfortable position.

Once I had settled again I looked around the wardrobe. It was large and deep and I was sure I could maneuver into a standing position. Once I was standing I could open the wardrobe door. That would let me out into Ava's bedroom. I wondered if I had the strength to attack her while she slept. If I found something heavy, I could hit her over the head.

As appealing as this thought was, I rejected it. If I accidentally killed her it would provide Rangmere with a perfect excuse for war.

The more I thought about it, the more I realised I had no chance of escaping while Ava remained in the suite. I would have to wait until she left. And once I was out of the wardrobe I would have to find some way to free my hands and escape the room. The prospect was daunting but not hopeless.

My mind wandered to Lily and Sophie. What would they do when they woke up in the morning and I wasn't in my bed? What would Max do when I didn't turn up for breakfast?

King Henry and Max might think I ran away after the events of the evening. King Henry might even be glad of it. But I was sure Max would go down to the Blue Arrow to see if I was there. Then my family would be worrying about me too. Tears leaked out of my eyes and ran down the side of my face. I tried to blink them away but eventually gave up and rubbed my face against one of the dresses hanging next to me instead.

And when they didn't find me, would they search, I wondered? I didn't hold out much hope of a rescue. There was no reason for anyone to suppose I was locked in Princess Ava's wardrobe.

Slowly but surely my heartbeat returned to its usual rhythm. I found my thoughts slipping in and out of focus. It had been a long and tiring day and my fear had exhausted me. Despite my uncomfortable position and my uncertain future I drifted into an uneasy sleep.

I woke the next morning to a sharp pain in my head, shoulders and hips, and an even sharper pain in my wrists and ankles. For a moment I panicked as I tried unsuccessfully to spit out the wad in my mouth and breathe freely. But memory quickly flooded in and I took steadying breaths through my nose.

I found some alleviation for my aches and pains by moving into a new position but the throbbing soon returned. I could hear movement and voices from the suite and I listened
closely, waiting for the rooms to go silent.

Hours passed.

The light around the door was much brighter now but every time I decided that the coast was clear I would hear some new sound. I grew both impatient and bored.

The irony of the situation wasn't lost on me. I was tied up in a wardrobe, the fate of the kingdom hanging on my ability to get free, and I was bored. The pain occupied my mind for most of the morning but I gradually began to lose feeling in my hands and feet. I suspected this numbness was a bad thing but chose to be grateful for the reprieve from pain.

I judged it to be late morning when I heard footsteps approach the wardrobe. The door was flung open and I squinted, my eyes burning as the light rushed in around me. After a moment I was able to make out Princess Ava's silhouette. She glanced down at me and then back at her dresses.

"What do you think, Alyssa?" she asked playfully. "Which dress should I wear to the ball tonight? It's an important decision, you know. I just had confirmation from Secretary Leopold – I'll be getting engaged tonight."

I muttered a rude retort that my gag turned into indistinct mumbling.

"I think you're right," said Ava, sweetly. "The blue one does look best with my eyes." She selected a gown and turned away. Then, as if arrested by a sudden thought, she swung back around.

"And just in case you were wondering, I've told the royal family not to expect to see me today. I'll be staying in my rooms, resting in preparation for the big night. It's been a busy two weeks; they were very understanding."

She smiled down at me and closed the wardrobe doors. I kicked out against the wood in frustration but quickly gave up when the rope began to chafe my ankles. If Ava was staying in her rooms until the ball, that wouldn't leave me much time to free myself. I had been relying on having an entire day to work out how to get free.

My stomach rumbled but I refused to let any tears squeeze out. My throat was already dry and I didn't want to lose any more moisture.

The hours wore on. My escape plans grew crazier and crazier and eventually I gave up thinking of escape at all. Instead I just lay there and thought of all my friends preparing for the ball. Each time I felt tears threatening I remembered the feel of Max's arms around me and warmth of his lips pressed tight against mine.

Eventually I heard an increased flurry of sound and motion followed by the sound of a closing door and silence. I pushed myself up into a sitting position and pressed my ear against the door. Silence.

I didn't have time to wait around so I rolled over onto my knees and pushed myself to my feet. I banged my head against the wardrobe doors in the process but no one came to investigate. I took this as a good sign.

Pushing with my shoulders, I popped one of the doors open and jumped forward into the room.

A lamp and several candles had been left burning and there was still some daylight coming in around the curtains. To my delight the bedroom door had been left open. I slowly jumped across the room, pausing to rest against the bed. When I reached the outer door to the suite, I turned around and tried to open the door with my bound hands. It was locked.

I tried banging against the door but the wood was thick and I could tell the sound wasn't carrying very far. So I stopped and surveyed the two rooms instead.

I had heard the triumph in Ava's voice when she taunted me in the wardrobe. If she was so confident in her victory, she might have gotten sloppy. I just needed something to cut my hands free.

Since I could only move by making short, awkward jumps, it took me a while to circumnavigate the sitting room. And my search yielded no results. My feet, legs and back were now aching but I continued into the bedroom.

With a cry of delight my eyes fell on a hand mirror sitting on the dressing table. Jumping over to the table, I turned around and felt along the surface until I could grasp the edge of the mirror. With satisfaction, I turned it over and smacked the surface hard against the desk. There was a loud crack. I smiled.

More carefully now I felt around with my fingers. Finding a large sliver of mirror, I angled my hands and sawed at the rope. It was slow work and twice my fingers slipped and I cut myself on the mirror shard. The resulting blood only made the job harder and I felt so faint I had to lower myself to the ground.

But eventually the rope weakened enough for me to pull apart the remaining fibers. My hands fell free and I cried out with relief and pain. The numb feeling was gone and the tingling pain that flooded my arms and hands almost made me faint. I reached up and undid my gag, spitting the material out of my mouth. Then I rested my head against the floor and massaged my hands together.

After a long moment, I sat up and began to work on the ropes binding my feet. At first I tried to pull apart the knots but I quickly gave that up and went back to sawing at the rope with the mirror edge. At last my feet were also free. I kicked off my shoes and massaged my feet and ankles until they were ready to bear my weight again. Slowly I stood up.

Opening one of the drawers, I pulled out some handkerchiefs which I used to bind my injured hands. I had left streaks of blood in several places around the room and I thought idly that they matched the room's colour theme.

I couldn't resist returning to the outer door and attempting to open it again but it remained sturdily locked. I then proceeded to tear the room apart looking for a hidden key. I figured Mrs Pine or one of the housemaids might have stashed a spare somewhere unbeknownst to Ava. I found some water and a few biscuits which I immediately demolished but after twenty minutes I was forced to concede defeat. I sat on one of the sofas and regarded the wreckage of the two rooms. The princess would not be happy when she returned and I was glad of it.

With no other options left, I went to examine the windows. Both rooms were lined with windows but the sitting room had large double door windows that gave out onto a balcony. These doors were secured with a simple latch and were easily opened. Unfortunately, the princesses' suite was on the second floor and it was much too far for me to jump.

Her room had a view over the park and I looked out hopefully but it was too late for any riders or gardeners to be out. I leaned over the edge and saw that there was another balcony directly below the one I stood on. I considered the distance and then went back into the room.

I went straight to the wardrobe, remembering that Ava had thrown the remaining length of rope in after me. Opening the doors again made me shudder but the rope was right where I expected it to be.

Returning to the balcony I tied one end around the balustrade and then pulled back on it with all my weight. It held. I smiled, glad for once that I was a woodcutter's daughter and not a courtier. I threw the remaining length over the edge and prepared to descend.

Bunching up my skirts, I straddled the balustrade and lowered myself down until I was able to grab onto the rope. Once I let go of the balcony my descent was more slide than climb and I barely managed to catch my feet on the balcony below. Balancing on the railing, I took a moment to catch my breath.

The handkerchiefs wrapped around my hands had saved them from rope burn but the cuts beneath were stinging fiercely. After several deep breaths I continued my descent, sliding down until my feet hit the ground.

I left the rope dangling there and took several unsteady steps. Now that I was outside I could hear the faint sounds of the orchestra. Some of the windows in the ballroom were obviously open.

I made it to one of the side doors and into the palace but I hadn't made it far towards the ballroom when I caught sight of myself in a large mirror. I was streaked with dirt and blood and my dress was torn. My hair was hanging around my face and I suspected that few people at court would even recognise me. There was no way the guards and servants would let me into the ballroom looking like this.

Turning towards the princesses' tower instead, I began to run. I couldn't manage much more than a shuffling jog but I kept it up all the way to the tower. I dashed into the bathroom, ripping off my clothes as I went, and completed the fastest wash of my life.

Wrapped in a large towel, I ran into my room. I had been planning to pull on the first dress I could find but I was pulled up short in front of my bed. The most stunning ball gown I had ever seen was laid across it.

It was made of white silk and had a tight, boned bodice. The bodice was strapless and would leave my neck and shoulders daringly bare. The skirt flared out from the hips and would lightly brush the ground as I walked. The bodice was covered in thick, ruched green chiffon while the skirt was covered in a single sheer layer. This layer was gathered together under a white rose over the right hip.

Moving closer I saw a small piece of parchment pinned to the dress. Pulling it free I read: *To Alyssa, from Korrine.* After the horror of my last day and night this kindness and the sheer beauty of the dress almost brought tears to my eyes. I scrambled into it, somehow managing the lacing myself. Noticing my bandaged hands, I pulled on some white gloves.

Looking in the mirror I saw an impossible transformation. I felt as if my very own godmother had come and transformed me for the ball. "Thank you, Korrine," I whispered.

When I reached the ballroom doors I didn't pause but stepped straight through. I didn't even realise the music had stopped until I stood at the top of the stairs, surveying the room.

My steps and even the silken swish of my skirts sounded loud in the expectant hush. The noise was soon amplified by the swishing of many other dresses as hundreds of heads swiveled towards me. The sound of indrawn breaths was audible across the large room. I couldn't have arranged a more dramatic entrance if I had tried.

Max was standing across the room next to his parents and Princess Ava. The horrified expression on the face of the princess told me clearly that I had arrived just before the big announcement.

It's not too late! I thought exultantly and my heart buoyed with hope as I caught Max's eyes from across the room. He was looking at me with shock and joy and I felt like my love must be visible to everyone present.

I descended the few steps into the room, careful not to tread on my skirt. By the time I arrived at the bottom, Max was there, grabbing my hands. *He must have run across the ballroom*, I thought, irrelevantly.

"Where have you been," he asked, pressing my hands against his heart.

"Max," I said urgently. "You can't get engaged to Princess Ava. She's the one behind the bandit attacks. She plans to move her troops into Arcadie before you're even married. I heard her talking to the man from the woods. The one with Claud. They caught me and locked me in her room. I only just escaped."

"Locked you in her room?" exclaimed Max, outrage in his voice and eyes.

"That doesn't matter now," I said, grasping the front of his jacket. "You have to stop the king from making the announcement."

We both swiveled to face the king just as Princess Ava stepped away from him. She had obviously been urging him to go on with the announcement and as Max opened his mouth to call to his father, the king said, "It is with pleasure that I announce the engagement of my son, Prince Maximilian, to Princess Ava of Rangmere."

"No!" I cried but my voice was drowned out by a round of applause. All around the ballroom I could see swiveling heads as the guests looked from the king and Princess Ava to me and Max, standing by the door clutching each other.

I saw Princess Ava turn and say something to one of her entourage. The man gestured at two Rangmeren guards who detached themselves from the wall and came towards me. Pulling away from Max, I ran from the room.

Part 3

The Engagement

The Princess

Shock. Anger. Fear. Triumph. The emotions flashing across her face were invisible to the crowd. Her father could have read them but he was far away in Rangmere. He had taught her well.

To come so close and have victory snatched away would have been more than she could bear. But the king had made the announcement. The engagement was official.

Still, her triumph was tainted by anger. To be so upstaged in her moment of victory was intolerable. Even now she could hear the hissing whispers and see the gazes that should have been fixed on her, fixed instead on the girl in green. The Princess Companion. The woodcutter's daughter. How had she escaped?

And she had done much more than just escape. Ava's father had trained his daughter to understand the power of crucial moments – the key minute during which you could control an entire room or sway an essential opinion. And in that crucial moment, as the music had died away, *she* had appeared in the doorway. She had stood there, poised on the top step and had surveyed the room. Ava had understood what she was looking for – had understood the intense emotions transfiguring her expression. But the rest of the room had merely seen a girl, dressed like a princess, made beautiful by the blaze of some internal light.

Ava maintained the sweet smile she had spent so long perfecting but behind it she was clenching her teeth. She had savoured the anticipation of this moment for so long. Sure, she would have been alone in her victory but she preferred it that way. Had always preferred it that way.

And now this woodcutter's daughter had stolen her moment. Ava knew with an unerring certainty that the momentum of the night had shifted. Whatever happened now, this ball belonged to the girl in green. The girl who was even now being held in the arms of a prince – Ava's prince.

Suddenly Ava couldn't bear it. Always she had stood in the shadows. First it was her brother and then his beautiful Lanoverian bride. And now, when she was to have finally stood alone she found herself eclipsed again.

Throwing caution to the winds she turned to the man standing next to her. Hans had been with her for a long time. One word was enough for him to understand her wishes. And his guards were so well trained that a single gesture was all that was needed to pass on the command.

The princess didn't care what sort of stir it made. Didn't care if it was wise. She only wanted to take back some control of the moment.

But Alyssa was watching her and saw the command that was silently sent and received. Instant understanding flooded her face.

I've underestimated her, thought Ava. *Father will be displeased.* The thought was as sharp as a stinging blow across the face.

Alyssa pulled herself out of Maximilian's arms and fled from the room. The guards quickened their pace but the prince was now blocking the door.

Ava wondered how she could keep on smiling when inside she felt so tense. She was too far away to hear the exchange at the doorway but she could see it the moment her guards capitulated. Inside she began to scream and her scream rose up, loud and long.

On the outside her smile remained undisturbed.

Such a pretty, sweet girl, thought an elderly courtier, *really a very beautiful princess.* Smiling placidly, he turned towards the buffet.

The Prince

Every moment that I stood in a ballroom instead of looking for Alyssa chafed at me. My father thought she had run for it, afraid of being arrested again and my mother thought she was bound to turn up somewhere. This vague non-interest was almost worse than my father's suspicions.

I thought she must have run away, too, but not out of fear of arrest. My own words kept haunting me. *I don't know how I'll bear to even look at you after that. It will be too painful.*

She hadn't made it to the Blue Arrow, I'd checked there immediately after breakfast. I kept picturing her lying somewhere, hurt or worse. The thought that she might have fled to save me pain burned my heart. I knew Harrison was scouring the city for her but what could one man do? I gritted my teeth, angry at my father's refusal to turn out the guard. It was all I could do not to pace up and down in front of my guests.

Father was still insisting on making the engagement announcement and I just wished he would hurry up and get it over with. He'd made me promise to stay until then but as soon as he made it I was returning to the search. The music finally sank into silence and I looked expectantly at my father.

But instead of an announcement, I heard a collective gasp and the sound of rustling silk. I turned towards the entrance and there she was! Alyssa!

She looked more beautiful than I had ever seen her – the most beautiful girl in the world. The green of her dress made her eyes blaze and brought out the red in her hair and she looked more like a princess than the one standing beside me. The shock and joy of seeing her, unharmed, hit me so hard it burned as strongly as the pain had done a moment ago.

The strength of it reminded me of the first moment I had seen her.

There had been a terrible storm outside and I had been coming along the gallery when the footman responded to the frantic banging on the door. I had drawn back into the shadows, happy to leave it to the servants to deal with whatever drama was about to unfold. The girl who had stumbled across the threshold then looked nothing like the girl standing in the ballroom now. She had been dripping wet and utterly bedraggled.

And yet, despite that, something in me had responded to her. Utterly unwillingly I had felt myself drawn to her. Seeing her shivering had awoken my chivalrous instinct and it had taken all my strength of will not to run down the stairs and wrap her in my own cloak.

Ironically enough it was the strength of those feelings that had enabled me to hold back. I had grown up on enough tales of love at first sight to recognise the symptoms and I fought against it with everything I had. I would not allow my emotions to be manipulated by some godmother to fit the confines of a story.

And last night, when I had finally given in, I had thought of myself as weak – no longer able to fight the prescribed attraction. But seeing her across the room, miraculously returned to me, was like a blow. The feelings flooding me now were so much stronger and deeper than the attraction of that first night. They made those feeble stirrings seem like the whispers of shadows.

What an injustice I had done her when I had doubted my love! For months now she had been earning my regard with her kindness and intelligence. How could I have thought my feelings forced on me?

Without thought or volition I found myself running across the ballroom. I needed to touch her, to assure myself that she was real and whole. I couldn't wait another second.

I reached her at last and the clasp of her hands felt like a homecoming. Overcome with emotion I pressed them against my heart.

"Where have you been?"

"Max, you can't get engaged to Princess Ava!" Reality came rushing back. Caught up in the strength of my emotions I had forgotten my impending engagement. "She's the one behind the bandit attacks. She plans to move her troops into Arcadie before you're even married. I heard her talking to the man from the woods. The one with Claud. They caught me and locked me in her room. I only just escaped."

"Locked you in her room?" I exclaimed. It was too much to take in at once so my mind caught at this final statement. I was filled with rage that anyone would dare hurt this girl I loved so much.

"That doesn't matter now," she said as her hands moved in mine, grasping the front of my jacket and holding onto me as if she were depending on my strength. I liked the feeling.

"You have to stop the king from making the announcement." Once again reality pulled me from the enjoyment of my newly acknowledged feelings.

I opened my mouth to call to my father, to tell him to wait, but he was already speaking. "It is with pleasure that I announce the engagement of my son, Prince Maximilian, to Princess Ava of Rangmere."

My mouth snapped closed, my head ringing with shock. It was done. I was engaged. What exquisite irony! That I should be forced into an arranged marriage just as I finally understood my true feelings.

I looked down at Alyssa but she wasn't looking at me. Her gaze was fixed on something beyond my shoulder. Suddenly, without a word, she let go of my jacket and pulled away from me. I reached for her but she was already gone.

Racing up the steps two at a time, I looked over my shoulder to see what she had been staring at. Two Rangmeren guards were threading their way through the courtiers, racing for the open doorway. I stopped my headlong flight and blocked their path.

"Stand down," I said when they reached me and my voice was pure steel.

"We don't answer to you," said one of them insolently.

"You're in my palace and I said to *stand down!*" I was almost blinded by rage at the thought that the princess would try to have Alyssa arrested in the middle of my ballroom. Part of me hoped the men would ignore me. A brawl would allow me to expunge some of my whirling emotions. But the men gave way, returning to their original posts with expressions of resignation.

I wanted to confront Ava but Alyssa was my first priority. I ran out of the ballroom to find an empty corridor. I went straight to the princesses' tower and searched each room without success. As I ran back down the stairs, I wondered where to look next. Would she have run for the stables? Should I check to see if Starfire was still in her stall?

Twice on my way to the stables I passed Rangmeren guards moving through the palace with determined expressions. It dawned on me that I wasn't the only one looking for Alyssa. My urgent need to find her intensified but my steps slowed. The palace was a big place and the situation was becomingly increasingly tangled. I needed to confront the source of the problem. I turned back towards the ballroom.

Chapter 29

I didn't even think about where I was going, I just ran. But when I pushed through the library doors I wasn't surprised. The library had been my unacknowledged hiding place for nearly two weeks. I curled into my chair, green and white material spilling over in every direction. Something must have slowed the guards down because they hadn't exited the ballroom in time to see where I went. I was confident that no one had seen me enter the room and it seemed unlikely that they would find me here.

Slowly my heartbeat steadied to its normal rhythm. I felt spent, depleted by the seesaw of my emotions. The cuts on my hands throbbed and I noticed that blood had leaked through the handkerchiefs to stain my gloves. The pain only reminded me that I had failed. After everything I had gone through to get free I had been too late. Arcadia was lost.

I wondered idly at the selfishness of the human heart. Despite my horror and sadness at the loss of my kingdom, I felt more pain at the loss of Max. But I was too tired even to cry. I cradled my head in my arms and let the darkness engulf me.

I didn't realise I had fallen asleep until I woke up. I fell out of the chair, stiff and sore in almost every muscle from my strange sleeping position and the after-effects of my incarceration. It wasn't long past dawn but the huge room was flooded with light.

I peered carefully into the room below but I was alone. Relieved, I stood and stretched. I was still wearing the ball gown but it was now wrinkled and crushed. I was desperately hungry and thirsty but I didn't dare leave the library. I had no idea what was happening in the rest of the palace and wondered if Ava had already sent Secretary Leopold home. If so, the rest of her troops might arrive at any moment. I thought of Matthias and shivered.

Pacing up and down the balcony, I noticed that someone had left a jug of water and a couple of glasses on one of the small tables. Eagerly I gulped the water straight from the jug. It tasted stale but delicious at the same time.

Feeling slightly refreshed I looked at the bookshelves. I had originally chosen my spot because it was next to the section on international relations. The books had felt like old friends, reminders of the happy days in the library at the Winter Castle. Now I realised that if I was trapped here I might as well put my time to good use.

Ignoring the titles I had already read, I pulled off every book on international law I could find. Piling the books next to my chair I began to read.

Twice I heard the library door open and heard quiet voices moving through the library. I hunched in my seat, keeping my head lowered, and the footsteps soon retreated. The third time the footsteps headed straight for the balcony and I tensed, raising the book I was holding like a weapon.

But it was Max who appeared and I ran to him with a quiet cry of delight. He pulled me into a quick embrace and I melted against him. A small shudder ran through his body and then he stepped back quickly.

He looked as bad as I felt, his face worn with fatigue and stress. But there was also a new and unfamiliar light in his eyes as they rested on me. It made me tremble and for a moment I forgot my tiredness and fear.

"I was hoping you would find me," I said, almost shyly.

"I'm sorry I took so long. Ava's had her guards searching for you and I didn't want to lead them here. I've tried talking to my father but he won't listen." He ran a frustrated hand through his hair. "He seems to think you planned your disappearance and dramatic entrance at the ball. That you were trying to disrupt the engagement. I told him that Ava was keeping you prisoner but he wouldn't believe me. By the time I convinced him to at least search her rooms there was no sign that you'd ever been there."

I raised my eyebrows. "That's impressive – I made a pretty big mess of the place. And of my hands, now I think of it!" I held them out, stripping off the gloves and revealing the bloody handkerchiefs underneath.

Max sucked in his breath and took my hands in a gentle hold.

"I never doubted you," he said, looking at me again with that new glow. "And Father should know you well enough by now to believe you too. I think he just doesn't want to believe it. And he's still angry about what happened with Mother. I don't think he would have really kept you in the dungeons, though. He's not a bad man."

Max seemed to be pleading for my understanding so I put a hand on his arm.

"It's ok," I said. "I don't blame the king. But you have to find a way to convince him." I repeated all the details I had overheard from Ava's conversation with Joran. Max paled.

"This is horrible!" he exclaimed and I nodded dumbly. We stared at each other, completely overwhelmed by the situation.

"You have to convince your father," I said finally. I gestured at the books piled around me. "I'm reading furiously, trying to find some loophole or archaic law we can use to get you out of the engagement. From what I overheard, Rangmere won't risk a war if the rest of our allies have reason to get involved. They need at least a veneer of legality for their takeover. If we can find some way to dissolve the engagement, I'm sure Arcadia's allies will stand by us."

Max looked from me to the books. "You're going to need help. And you can't stay hiding here." I shrugged. I could only do what I could.

"Stay here for now," he continued, "and I'll find somewhere better for you." His head swayed towards me and for a moment I thought he was going to kiss me again. But then he pulled back, a sour look on his face.

"Curse this engagement!" he said and was gone.

It was hard to settle back down to reading after Max's visit but I forced myself to do it. I felt a rising tide of panic whenever I looked at the huge pile of books or thought of the Rangmeran soldiers who were hiding in the forest and waiting at the border. There were too many words to wade through and no guarantee the books even contained a solution.

The fourth time the library door opened I was so engrossed in my reading I didn't even hear it. I only realised I wasn't alone when I heard someone ascending to the balcony. The footsteps were quiet, certainly not the heavy boots of a guard, and I waited in tense expectation.

"Mathilde!" I almost cried from the relief. "You look different?"

Mathilde laughed and embraced me. "How can you even notice something like that at a time like this?" she asked.

"I'm a woman," I retorted, "I can do more than one thing at a time. I'm also trying not to let minor catastrophes like the annihilation of my kingdom interfere with my resolution to be less self-absorbed."

My attempt at light-heartedness only sobered us both.

"Prince Maximilian told me everything," said Mathilde, her expression grim. "He sent me to get you out of here."

"How are you going to do that?" I asked, alarmed at the thought of dragging my friend into the situation.

"I've apprenticed as a nurse – thus the new uniform. I was going to tell you about it yesterday but no one seemed to know where you were."

Her anger radiated from her body and I assumed Max must have filled her in on my whereabouts yesterday.

"I've brought you one of my spare uniforms. You need to change into it."

I turned around willingly and she began to unlace my dress. Within moments I was transformed from a courtier to a nurse. "It's an incredible gown," said Mathilde as she tied a scarf around my distinctive hair, "I can see why you couldn't go wandering around the castle."

Once she was finished we bundled my dress into the laundry bag Mathilde had brought for the purpose. "It was Max's idea to hide you in the hospital suite," she explained. "We're fully self-contained in case of infectious cases and there's no reason for anyone to look for you there. And we can treat your hands and any other injuries." Mathilde had noticed my cut hands and bruised, chafed wrists while she was helping me get changed.

"It's a great idea. But we have to bring these books along too." I pointed at the piles and Mathilde grimaced. "We'll just have to pile them into the laundry bag on top of the dress," she said.

The books made the bag very heavy so we took turns carrying it. I was jumpy and nervous but Mathilde told me to just keep my head down and walk confidently. "No one will recognise you," she said. "Courtiers don't really look at the servants and the hospital staff keep themselves pretty separate from the rest of us so the servants will just assume you're some new apprentice."

"The rest of us?" I smiled at her. "You're one of them now."

She flushed with pride and nodded. "I keep forgetting."

We had made it most of the way to the hospital when a sharp voice called for us to stop. We froze reluctantly and slowly turned around. I kept my eyes trained on our feet but I recognised the voice and my heart sank.

"Maid," said Lady Marissa, her voice sharp, "the cleaning in my room is just not satisfactory. This is the second time I've had to complain of it and if there's no improvement I'll make my next complaint to the queen herself." I highly doubted this but it was just like Lady Marissa to try to bully the servants. And just like her not to notice that we were dressed as hospital staff, not maids.

"And look at me when I talk to you!" she added, on a roll. I ignored her and kept my gaze focused on the floor. "I said... wait a minute, *Alyssa?* Everyone's looking for you, you know!"

I finally looked up, words of entreaty on my lips, but my gaze focused on the end of the passageway. A group of Rangmeren guards were just rounding the corner. Gasping, I grabbed Mathilde's arm and whisked her through a door to our left. We found ourselves stuffed inside a small and extremely full storage room. Leaving the door just slightly ajar I peered out into the corridor.

There were no exclamations or sounds of pursuit so I assumed the guards hadn't seen us. Lady Marissa, however, was staring at the door with a strange expression on her face. *We're lost,* I thought with despair. *I wish I had never let Mathilde get involved.*

The guards had reached Lady Marissa by this time and she had transferred her gaze to them. I was so sure she was about to betray our location that I flashed a quick look around the storage room, hoping to spot something I could use as a weapon.

"Excuse me, ma'am," said the one in the lead. "We're looking for a young lady about your age. She's got sort of red-gold hair and green eyes. You might know her. She used to be the Princess Companion."

"*Used to be?*" said Lady Marissa and my eyes flew back to her. "I hadn't heard she was removed from the post. And you should address me as *my lady*."

"Excuse me?" the guard seemed taken aback.

"I am a lady, not a ma'am." Lady Marissa's voice was at its most icy and the guard started to look nervous.

"Of course, my lady, we'll just be on our way then." The guard was so flustered he had obviously forgotten that Lady Marissa hadn't answered his question. The guards continued down the hallway, their retreat watched by Lady Marissa.

After they were gone, she trained her gaze on a statue just beside the doorway where we were hiding. "They're gone," she said, her tone as lofty as ever, and then she sailed away in the opposite direction. I stared after her in shock.

"That was unexpected," said Mathilde dryly.

I merely nodded, still too shocked to speak.

We made it the rest of the way to the hospital suite without incident and Mathilde led me straight to my old isolation room.

"Ah, home sweet home," I quipped, swinging the bag onto the bed.

We grinned at each other, relieved to have made it safely.

"The main hospital ward looked fuller than last time I was here," I said uneasily. "I think I recognised one of the men too. I'm not sure if he'd recognise me, but..." I'd been surprised to see Jonas in the hospital and wondered what he had done to get himself injured in the last two days.

"Don't worry about that," said Mathilde and I was surprised to see her still smiling. "Those aren't really patients. They're guards Max stationed here to protect you. They've been trickling in with various 'illnesses' for the last couple of hours."

This news was a relief and it allowed me to truly relax. The bed looked very comfortable and I found myself lured into it by a potent combination of exhaustion and relief from fear. It was the first time I had slept on a bed in days and my sleep was long and deep.

When I woke up I was relieved to see a tray of food and a glass of water. I ate and drank quickly and then visited the attached washroom. By the time I received my first visitor I was sitting in the chair and had already sorted the books into piles based on how promising they looked.

When I heard the door opening I looked up warily. It was Aldric who came into the room but he smiled at me reassuringly. "We thought it was better to let you sleep," he said. "Sleep's the natural healer after all. But now that you're awake I really need to look at your hands."

He advanced into the room and Mathilde came in behind me carrying a tray of medical paraphernalia. I was relieved when she closed the door behind her. I didn't want any extra witnesses to my embarrassment.

And embarrass myself I did. The handkerchiefs had dried onto my hands and the process of revealing, cleaning and stitching the cuts was very painful. Aldric was brisk and business like and kindly refrained from commenting on my tears and cries of pain.

I truly hoped he would win Mathilde. He seemed to deserve her.

After a thorough examination, Aldric pronounced me fortunate. My cuts had escaped infection and I had no other serious injuries. I expressed my gratitude and watched him leave the room, my brow furrowed.

The sight of him had triggered a thought just out of reach. For a moment I struggled to recall it but then I gave up and returned to my reading.

Chapter 30

The following days went by in a blur of tired eyes and exhaustion. I read almost without stopping and fell into bed only when I could no longer keep my eyes open. By the third day I had a constant tension headache. Slowly, slowly the read pile started to equal the unread pile in height. But I found nothing that could help us.

Max didn't come to visit but Mathilde delivered a note on my second day in the hospital.

Dear Alyssa,

I can't come in person because Ava is having me watched constantly. The instant I leave my suite, one of her entourage appears and attaches themselves to me.

I keep inventing excuses to prevent Secretary Leopold leaving with the result that Ava's 'ceremonial guard' have yet to arrive at the palace. I'm running out of ideas, though, and I'm sure she'll find another way to contact Joran soon enough.

I've confided in Felix, Nate and the Baron and Baroness. They've all promised to do their own research.

I've made some impression on Father — he now seems to view Ava with suspicion — but Mother continues to support the engagement. She keeps saying she's sure it's a misunderstanding and that Princess Ava would never hurt you.

The girls miss you but we've told them that you're visiting your family at the Blue Arrow. They keep asking me to take them down to the inn to see you and I'm going to run out of excuses for them as well. Fortunately Mother is spending time with them in the afternoons now, which keeps them distracted. It's the first time I can ever remember her doing so and it's very good timing.

I wish desperately that I could be with you, helping you, but I can't. Send me word through Mathilde if you find anything of interest.

Max

It was an almost crushing disappointment to learn that Max had made so little progress with his parents and the disappointment was only compounded by the knowledge that he would not be visiting. The heavy hopelessness was lifted only by the news that Queen Eleanor was finally spending time with her daughters. Perhaps I had managed some small good in my time at the palace after all.

By the fourth day my constant headache was joined by an ache in the region of my heart. I missed Lily and Sophie and the rest of my friends and family but I missed Max much more. Even as I searched frantically for a way to break his engagement, the knowledge that he was engaged made him seem more distant than ever before.

I felt ashamed of my weakness but whenever I closed my eyes I found myself reliving our kiss. The memory of his lips on mine was the most energising thought I had, and I wished desperately for a way to return to the exquisite happiness of that moment on the balcony. My life since then had become an endless cycle of exhaustion and fear that made that stolen moment seem even brighter.

Mathilde maintained a forced cheerfulness but I could see the cracks beneath the façade. I knew I couldn't impose on her forever. She told me that all the hospital staff were in on the secret but I saw very few of them. Since the hospital was still open for business as usual, I was forced to remain in my room.

I had always loved books because they seemed so full of endless possibility. I now began to hate the sight of them for the same reason. That constant unfulfilled possibility taunted me. The queen and Ava had settled on a late summer wedding and every day the date crept impossibly closer.

On the fifth day of my voluntary confinement I read something that gave me the first glimmer of hope. It was a small note on the complex laws and traditions that bound the kingdoms together and had been included as an explanatory addendum on an old and rather dry account of a marriage alliance. It stated that any engagement, be it royal or common, was considered invalid in law if it was found that a previous engagement existed. It did not matter, explained the text, which engagement was more formal or more public – the first engagement nullified the second. All that was needed to dissolve the second engagement was for the pre-existing fiancé to present him-or-herself with proof of their prior claim.

Such a tantalising thought was hard to let go. I realised it didn't help us at all, of course. No previous engagement, however informal, existed. But I couldn't help thinking of the possibilities and wishing that Max had entered into some sort of agreement with Marie or Celeste. It almost made me laugh, though without true amusement, to compare these wishes with my wishes at the time.

The book that contained this addendum was the last book from the pile I had deemed most promising. It was painful to close it and accept that none of the books had provided a solution. Surveying the remaining two piles I felt listless. What was the use in continuing?

Picking up each book one by one I glanced at their titles. Most were only loosely connected to the topic at hand. Pausing at one particularly irrelevant looking title I wondered why I had even pulled it from the shelf. *An Exposition on the Different Customs and Traditions Pertaining between the Kingdoms of Arcadia and Northhelm.*

Suddenly I remembered why it had piqued my interest. It had reminded me of my final conversation with Marie and I had wondered if perhaps this was another copy of the book Max had given to her. It was a slim volume and I opened it out of idle curiosity.

Skimming through its pages I realised how little Lily, Sophie, Max and I had learned of Northhelm customs before Marie's arrival. The writing was a little dry but my memory of Marie's visit kept the subject matter interesting. I told myself it was possible that some relevant international law might be hidden within its pages. I read on.

I had nearly finished the book and my mind was starting to wander when I read a paragraph that made the book slip from my suddenly nerveless fingers. I stared into space, my mind whirling, when I was interrupted by the entrance of Aldric, come to complete his daily inspection of my hands. I was quivering with excitement but attempted to maintain a casual tone of voice. "Mathilde mentioned to me once that you were here on a medical exchange."

Aldric looked up startled and nodded.

"Your accent isn't strong but it does seem familiar," I continued. "Are you from Northhelm?" I held my breath as I waited for the answer.

"Yes, I am from Northhelm," he said carefully.

"Perhaps you can answer a question for me then." I picked the book back up and found the right page, holding it out to him and pointing at the paragraph. "Is this correct?" I asked.

Clearly this was not what Aldric had expected. Cautiously he read the paragraph and then nodded again. "Yes, it is true," he confirmed. "It is a very old custom but still commonly used."

I drew in a deep breath and fell back against the chair, laughing. *We're saved!* I thought. *Saved by a book.* Aldric began to work on my hands but warily, as if he feared for my sanity. His expression only made me laugh harder.

"Can you ask Mathilde to come and see me?" I asked when he was finished. He agreed and looked relieved to escape from the room.

My own delight felt so infectious that I wondered why Mathilde looked so grave when she came in and closed the door behind her.

"I was coming to see you anyway," said Mathilde, "the news is all over the castle."

"What news?" I asked.

"Oh, you haven't heard. I'll let you read your letter first then, I'm sure it will explain it." She held out a sealed note and I eagerly broke it open.

Dear Alyssa,

Father and Mother have finally been convinced of the truth of your words and the villainy of Ava. Their reversal of opinion has not been caused by any arguments of mine but by information extracted from the guard Matthias.

Our Intelligence Chief used a very clever stratagem to gain his confidence and has received a full confession. He has confirmed everything you overheard. Unfortunately my parents know of no law to release me from my engagement or to prevent Rangmere from attacking if we choose to repudiate the connection.

Ava is aware, of course, of the change in my parents' attitude towards her and is, moreover, furious at her inability to find you. In the face of their enmity, she seems to have decided not to call any of her troops. Instead she seeks to hasten the wedding and to this end has invented a family emergency in Rangmere. She has moved the date of the wedding forward to allow us to be married before she returns home. I have no doubt she intends to return at the head of a conquering army.

Unfortunately, the wedding date has always been the purview of the bride and not the groom so there is little we can do.

The wedding will now take place in ten days' time, being the earliest date such a large ceremony can be arranged.

I can only assume from your silence that you have yet to discover anything of assistance.

Max

I looked up from the letter in shock, unable to fully comprehend the implications. "Ten days?" I exclaimed. "*Ten days*?!? But I had just found a way out!"

"You found something?" cried Mathilde.

"No, no, you don't understand, ten days won't be enough time." I calculated the time needed for a letter to reach Marie and then the time needed for Marie to return. No matter how I worked it, it could not be done in ten days. The shock left me cold.

I could hear Mathilde speaking to me but her words seemed to come from a great distance and I paid them no heed. After a while she left and I was glad to be alone.

Chapter 31

By the time the door opened again I felt like I had aged years, although in reality it had only been a few moments. It was Aldric who came in and he looked very serious.

"Mathilde says you are in shock and asked if there was something I could give you. I have brought you a sleeping draught." I ignored his words, examining his face instead.

Once again the sight of him brought back that half remembered shadow of thought. It had been tickling at me for five days now but I had shunted it aside, determined to reserve all my mental efforts for reading. Now I sat back and let the thought work its way around my mind.

It took a few minutes to burst into full life but, when it did, it turned out to be well worth the effort.

"Aldric," I said suddenly, watching him closely, "how did Marie know I was sick?" Aldric started but his confusion seemed genuine.

"I'm not sure what you mean," he said.

"When I was here last time, I received a letter from Princess Marie wishing me a speedy recovery."

Aldric nodded and regarded me warily. "I suppose someone must have written and told her you were ill," he said.

"Yes, that would make sense," I agreed and he looked relieved. "Except that the letter arrived only seven days after I first fell ill. And the network of relay-messengers who carry express royal post take a minimum of six days to carry mail between Arcadie and the capital of Northhelm. Six days one way, that is."

We stared at each other in silence while I debated my next move. Aldric's face remained calm but I noticed a small bead of sweat running down into his collar.

"Aldric," I said finally, my voice hardly more than a whisper. "I need to contact your mistress. Urgently."

Aldric remained silent.

"Princess Marie is the only hope for Arcadia now but she must arrive here before the wedding. Which means she must arrive here in nine days' time."

"That's impossible," said Aldric stiffly.

"Yes, it is – using conventional means," I replied. I stood up and grasped his arm. "Please Aldric. I know you have some means of contacting her more quickly. I need you to use that now. To save Arcadia from Rangmere." He remained silent and my pleas grew more desperate. "All I ask is that you convey a letter to her. I promise not to breathe a word to the king or his Intelligence Chief. Think how powerful Rangmere will become if they annex Arcadia! Surely blocking them is in Northhelm's interests too."

At last he stirred. "I promise nothing," he said, his words clipped short. "Write your letter but I promise nothing."

"Thank you," I cried, "thank you!" And pulling out a piece of parchment and pen I began to write furiously.

The rest of that day and the night passed in a fever of anxiety. I paced up and down my room until I was too exhausted to move and then fell into my bed and into a light, disturbed sleep. I was up earlier than ever the next morning and back to pacing. I didn't want to send word to Max of what I had discovered until I heard back from Marie. I couldn't bear to raise his hopes for nothing.

The day passed slowly. Mathilde popped her head in every hour or so to check on me and each time she looked more concerned. Eventually I gave up pacing and went back to reading. I had found one possibility of escape in my books, perhaps I would find another.

That night when I slept my rest was deep and dreamless. I had finally reached my limit of anxiety and fatigue – my body could take no more.

When I woke it took me a moment to remember where I was and why I felt a vague sense of unacknowledged doom. Strangely enough the return of memory did not bring a return of the restless anxiety of the day before. A new peace seemed to have enveloped me and I welcomed its embrace.

Mathilde was relieved to see the calm in my expression and begged me to tell her what was going on. I remembered my promise to Aldric, however, and refused to say anything. This day too passed by.

Aldric did not appear at the usual time to inspect my hands and a small bit of worry crept back under my defenses. I ignored it and returned to my reading. When the door finally opened and Aldric appeared I leapt to my feet eagerly. His face gave nothing away.

"I have heard back," he said. "She is coming. Already she has left."

I inhaled sharply and fell back, sinking onto the bed. Tears of gratitude swam in my eyes. "Will she arrive in time?" I asked. "It took her two weeks to get here by ship."

"That was a gentle voyage and round about," said Aldric. "She comes now by horseback and takes the route of the relay-messengers. She is a skilled horsewoman and very strong. She will arrive in the required eight days." I nodded. I also trusted in Marie's skill.

"I must tell Max!" I exclaimed, jumping back to my feet.

Aldric looked alarmed. "Perhaps it is best if you do not."

"But I can't leave him thinking the worst. Who knows what he might do?"

"It's not certain yet. Many things could happen to prevent her arrival. If there is any change in the attitude of the royal family it may alert Princess Ava. Who knows what fell plans she has waiting in reserve."

I was reluctant to accept his words but he was right of course. Our hope was slim enough already. I would do nothing to overset it.

I continued to read but without the feverish pace that I had previously maintained. I began a small exercise regime inside my room and felt much better for it.

Six days before the wedding I received a visitor. Mathilde ushered her into the room and when I saw who it was I gave a cry of surprise.

"Your majesty!" I swept into a deep curtsey. "What are you doing here?" Queen Eleanor approached and took my hand in a firm clasp.

"I had to see you," she said. "To apologise. It seems I have been a fool in more ways than one." I protested but she shook her head vehemently. "Our intelligence network has been working hard to discover the full extent of Ava's plans. It now seems clear that Rangmere intends a complete annexation. I fear our people will resist and that it will go hard with them. We are making what preparations we can but..." she shrugged fatalistically.

"Eleanor, there is still hope."

"Is there?" her voice was faint. "You were right about my family, by the way. It seems so horrible that I should only discover it now, when it may be too late for all of us." I led her over to the chair and sat beside her on the bed.

I couldn't contain my curiosity. "King Henry?" I asked.

She nodded. "When the truth was revealed it was a very hard blow. I was the one who had insisted on the engagement. All I wanted was for Max to have a true princess – someone who could rule beside him and make him happy. I still don't understand what went wrong. I went to Henry and offered to leave Arcadia. I have already done enough harm for several lifetimes."

I gasped. "You're not leaving!" I exclaimed.

"No," she smiled and suddenly seemed much younger than I had ever seen her look before. "My pride was finally broken down, you see. I had nothing left and therefore nothing to hide. I admitted to him all the things I had been too proud to tell him over the years. I begged him to forgive me," her smile turned radiant, "and he did!"

"And you?" I asked, delighted but not quite content to leave it there, "did you forgive him?" She looked at me with amusement and I shrugged defensively. "There's no way the situation was all your fault."

"No," she said, "we were both to blame. There were so many misunderstandings. It only took the complete breakdown of our world for us to realise it." She sobered. "It's a pity there are some things not even true love can fix."

"There is still hope," I repeated but when she pressed me I would say no more.

Two days before the wedding I had an even more welcome visitor. Mathilde let him come in unannounced and I fell into his arms. For the first time in two weeks I felt not only hopeful but happy.

For several minutes we just clung to each other, caught up in the joy of being together again. His chest felt familiar and comforting, despite how few times he had actually held me. After a long moment I drew back and looked into his eyes. The despair in them made me catch my breath.

"I had to see you once more before the wedding," he said desperately. "I've made arrangements with Jonas and some of the guards. They're going to smuggle you out of Arcadie during the ceremony."

"No!" I exclaimed, horrified. "I won't leave."

"You have to," said Max, a steely quality in his voice I had never heard before. "The only way I can get through this is if I know you're safe. Once we're married I won't be able to stop her searching the entire palace. And if she finds you, she'll be able to use you against me."

I shook my head frantically but he leaned down and touched his forehead against mine, stopping the motion. "My strength has limits, Alyssa," he whispered.

Ava's words came back to me. I suspect young Max will do anything I command if I threaten Alyssa. I whispered a reluctant, "alright."

He outlined the plan to me and I listened unhappily. My one consolation was that the imminent arrival of Marie would make it redundant. I knew I had agreed to say nothing of Marie to Max but I couldn't bear the hopelessness in his eyes.

"There's still a chance," I said.

"You've found something?" he was suddenly alert, his eyes shining.

"Maybe," I said. "I can't risk telling you anything but it's a chance at least. But I need you to promise you won't say anything to anyone else."

He was eager to know more and reluctant to promise but I eventually convinced him. Our farewell was lingering and painful and I couldn't suppress the fear that I would never see him again. After he left I spent half an hour crying into my pillow.

The day before the wedding I woke up with a flood of excitement and it took a moment for my mind to catch up. Today Marie was due to arrive. When Mathilde came in with my breakfast she seemed gripped by the same fever of anticipation.

Aldric had taken my stitches out several days ago but he came in for a 'final check-up' as well. Once he had pronounced my hands fully healed he whispered that he had had no news. "One of my contacts will meet her at the edge of the city and bring her straight here," he explained. "The hospital suite has its own exit directly on to one of the side gates in the palace wall. It's for moving quarantined patients in and out. They'll bring her through there. You'll know of her arrival almost as soon as I will."

I thanked him for the information and promised to do the hand exercises he prescribed. I even did them diligently for fifteen minutes.

When Mathilde reappeared I jumped on her. "Has she arrived?" I asked. Mathilde shook her head but showed me what was in her arms. It was my green ball gown.

"I laundered it myself," she said. "I couldn't get any of your other clothes but at least you can wear this." I smiled at her gratefully. I had expected to wear the ill-fitting nurse's uniform to my final showdown with the princess and I was glad to know I had something more elegant to wear.

But the day progressed with no sign of Marie. The possibility of a successful showdown shrank further and further from view.

When it finally grew dark Mathilde crept back into the room with a different load in her arms.

She was carrying two saddlebags and she opened them to show me an assortment of practical servant's outfits and a supply of food. "There's money down the bottom," she told me. "The prince sent it for you."

She saw the anger and despair in my eyes and said quickly, "There's still time. This is just in case." I nodded reluctantly.

I didn't sleep that night but only dozed, wakened constantly by the imagined sounds of an arrival. Each time I started up, straining to listen in the dark and then fell back disappointed.

I fell into a deeper sleep just before morning and was woken by Mathilde. "Jonas is here," she said. "He's insisting you get ready to leave. The ceremony starts in two hours."

Chapter 32

I don't know how he did it without raising suspicion but Jonas had Starfire waiting for me outside the small gate. He helped me to attach my saddlebags and then to mount. I leaned down and pressed my cheek against Starfire's head, taking what little comfort I could from her familiar presence. When I sat back up I saw that Jonas was watching me, sympathy in his face.

I hardened my own features and nodded to him. We rode out into the park. The park was large and extended all the way to the city wall. It provided a convenient route out of the city and I wondered how many others had fled from the palace this way. The park was dotted with small copses of trees and I stopped before the first of these to look back. I picked out the princesses' tower and gave it a silent farewell. I would miss Lily and Sophie and I hoped they would be safe from whatever came.

"I'm sorry I couldn't protect you," I whispered. At least they had their mother now – a far more fitting and satisfying companion than I had ever been. *Max will look after them*, I thought.

Turning around I urged Starfire forward, I needed clear eyes and a clear head if I was going to effect my own escape.

We had made it most of the way through the park when we heard the sounds of an approaching group of horses. Jonas signaled for our small party to slip back amongst the closest group of trees. I wondered apprehensively who would be riding through the park on the day of the royal wedding.

The other riders came into sight through the leaves and I regarded them in confusion. They weren't familiar and they looked like they had been riding hard. It was a group of men and several of them were heavily armed. I wondered if they were Joran's bandits and I laid a calming hand on Starfire's neck, praying she wouldn't make any noise.

The riders had almost passed us when I noticed that one of the horses at the back of the group was being ridden by a woman. In another moment I was riding forward, a cry of glad welcome on my lips. Jonas called out to me sharply but I ignored him. I spurred Starfire up to the other horse and reached my hand across to Princess Marie.

"You made it!" I exclaimed.

"I said I would," she replied with a smile that said more of exhaustion than anything else.

"I should never have doubted you! But we must hurry." I surveyed her men and her own exhausted mount. "Jonas," I ordered, "take the princess up in front of you. Have one of your men stay back to escort her guards to the palace."

One of Marie's men protested but she silenced him quickly. Retrieving a bag from one of the pack horses she allowed herself to be thrown up in front of Jonas. Still watchful but with much lighter hearts we rode back towards the palace.

It was fortunate that everyone, both inside and outside, was busy with the wedding. No one was in the park or on any of the balconies and we were able to enter through the side gate unmolested. Aldric's contact had come with us and he knocked on the door to the hospital suite in a complicated, staccato pattern.

It was Aldric himself who opened the door to us. His surprise at seeing us disappeared when he caught sight of Princess Marie. "The ceremony is about to start," he said. "Most of the staff have gone to watch."

We nodded our understanding and almost ran to the washrooms. Mathilde and one of the other nurses helped us into clean dresses. Once again I found myself donning the beautiful ball gown on my way to interrupt a royal function. I only hoped I would be more successful this time.

Marie had brought the huge gown she had worn to her welcome reception. There was no time to steam out the wrinkles but she looked magnificent anyway. Jonas formed his small troupe of guards into two lines and escorted us from the hospital.

We hurried through the deserted corridors as fast as we could go. My heart was hammering and my palms sweating and I kept shooting glances at Marie. She caught me looking at her and smiled. I noticed she was clutching a small book in one of her hands.

"Thank you," I said. "Regardless of what happens now I can never thank you enough."

"Oh, piffle," she said, making me smile. "I'm doing this for Northhelm as much as for Arcadie."

"Thank you all the same," I repeated.

So many guests had been invited to the wedding they had been forced to hold it in the throne room since it was the only room large enough to accommodate the crowd. We heard the boom of the closing doors while we were still several corridors away. I pictured Ava walking down the red carpet and urged my own feet to move more quickly.

We found the large double doors guarded by several Arcadian guards and several Rangmeren ones. Evidently Ava was nervous about interference.

At sight of us the Rangmeren guards moved into formation in front of the doors. Our own small troupe of guards rushed ahead to engage with them. The Arcadian guards at the door, however, fell back, their mouths open in surprise and confusion.

"Don't just stand there, help us," snapped Jonas, his sword clanging against his opponent's. "We fight for Arcadia."

The hesitant guards snapped to attention at his words and joined the fray. With the increased numbers, the Arcadians were easily able to subdue the Rangmerens. I wondered if any sounds from the conflict had leaked through the thick doors.

Panting, Jonas signaled for several of the guards to pull the doors open. They opened soundlessly but a harassed looking herald squeezed himself through the widening gap.

"What are you doing?" he hissed. "You cannot disturb the ceremony."

He stopped with a gasp as he found himself with a sword at his throat. "Just the man we need," said Jonas in a friendly tone. "If you could please announce Alyssa, the Royal Princess Companion and Her Royal Highness, the Princess Marie of Northhelm."

The herald gasped again as his eyes darted between us. Licking his lips, he nodded his head. Jonas kept his sword pointed into the man's back as he re-entered the room through the now fully opened doors.

The throne room was transformed with row upon row of elegant wooden chairs. The red carpet had been replaced with a white one and the rows of chairs were decorated with soft pink roses. Every seat was full and many faces were turned towards us in confusion. But I ignored the crowd, my eye drawn to the dais at the end of the carpet.

The king and queen were sitting in their thrones, facing the crowd. At the foot of the dais stood Princess Ava, resplendent in bridal white, pink roses in her hands and hair. Even from this distance I could see she looked beautiful.

But she was outshone by the man standing beside her. Max was dressed in white and gold, and he looked tall and strong in his wedding outfit. His dark hair was a shocking contrast to his clothing and his blue eyes blazed in his pale face as he turned towards the doors. My heart swelled with love and joy and all my anxiety and fatigue drained away.

The herald banged his staff and silence swept across the room. "Alyssa, the Royal Princess Companion and Her Royal Highness, the Princess Marie Christina Adrienne Camille of Northhelm," he announced, a nervous quaver in his voice.

The silence was so complete I could hear Ava's indrawn breath despite the distance between us. Marie stepped forward and I followed her. Together we swept down the carpet.

"How dare you!" cried Ava, her sweet mask slipping and then sliding away entirely.

"How dare *you*," returned Marie her voice calm but carrying across the crowd. "I came as soon as I received word. I claim the right of first betrothal."

"What?" said Max in confusion and his question was repeated by a hundred lips, a discordant echo that swept across the crowd.

"According to international law," I said loudly, "any engagement, royal or not, is considered invalid under law if a previous engagement is found to exist. To dissolve the second engagement, the pre-existing fiancée has only to present herself with the proof of her prior claim."

"Is this true," asked King Henry getting to his feet. The Master of Protocol stood up from his seat in the third row to acknowledge the existence of the law.

"I don't understand," said Max looking at me with an adorable mixture of bewilderment and hope.

"Where is this proof of prior claim?" sneered Ava. "I do not believe it exists and I will have you punished for interrupting my wedding." Her words were spoken to Marie but her eyes were on me.

Marie said nothing but held out the book in her hand. King Henry, Queen Eleanor, Max and Ava stared at it. All around I heard rustling as the crowd stood, craning to get a glimpse of what Princess Marie was holding. After a moment the king gestured to the Master of Protocol who came forward and took the book from her.

He opened it and read the inscription aloud. "To Princess Marie with my earnest wishes for an ongoing unity between our two kingdoms, Prince Maximilian." He held it open so that Max could see the writing. "That is your hand is it not, Prince Maximilian?"

"Certainly it is," he agreed, "I gave it to Princess Marie when she visited us in the spring."

"Exactly!" said Marie, triumphant. "And according to Northhelm custom, the giving and receiving of a gift between a man and a woman signifies an engagement. So I claim the right of first betrothal to Prince Maximilian. The betrothal between Princess Ava of Rangmere and Prince Maximilian is, therefore, dissolved."

The king looked questioningly at the Master of Protocol who cleared his throat uncomfortably. "That is the custom of Northhelm, certainly," he said. "It is within the rights of Princess Marie to claim first betrothal."

There was a moment of shocked silence and then pandemonium broke out. As the guests called out their surprise and confusion, Ava turned on me.

"This is all *your* doing!" she screamed, looking truly demented. She lunged towards me and Max stepped swiftly between us. But before she reached either of us she was seized from behind by the captain of her guards. I searched my memory and recalled his name, Hans.

She kicked out at him in fury but he held her firmly around the waist. His face was grim. "Rangmere regrets the termination of its alliance with Arcadia but wishes the best of good fortune to Arcadia and Northhelm. Rangmere looks forward to future good relations between our various kingdoms."

He somehow managed to give a slight bow while still holding on to the struggling princess.

King Henry nodded at him, relieved at his intervention. "Arcadia regrets any inconvenience this miscommunication may have caused the kingdom of Rangmere and its princess." He gave his own small bow in the direction of the still struggling Ava. "We also look forward to future good relations between our two kingdoms."

Hans nodded, his expression still grim, and dragged his princess out of the room through the small door behind the dais. The rest of the Rangmeren delegation followed. Jonas came trotting down the main aisle and exchanged a quiet word with King Henry.

"Jonas will escort the Rangmeren guards and their delegation out of Arcadie," said the king. "I think it's best if they leave the kingdom as quickly as possible. We will pack up their baggage and arrange for it to meet them outside the city."

All around us the throne room was in chaos. Chairs had been thrust back and a number had fallen, unheeded by the excited crowd. Nate and Felix pushed forward to exchange grinning congratulations with us all. Helena waved at me across the crowd but her path to the dais was blocked by a surging mass of eager courtiers.

Lily and Sophie, who were dressed as bridesmaids and had been seated in the front row ran forward to embrace me. I could

323

see their lips moving but couldn't hear their questions above the tumult around us.

King Henry climbed back up to stand in front of his throne. He signaled across the room and the herald banged his staff against the floor. He was forced to continue banging for thirty seconds before the excited crowd quieted and all eyes fixed themselves on the king.

"The engagement between my son and the Princess of Rangmere has been dissolved," he said clearly. "We will not be witnessing a wedding today after all. However, there is still a large feast that needs to be eaten." A ragged cheer rose from the large crowd of commoners at the back of the room. "Please proceed immediately through to the ballroom where the feast has been laid out. Queen Eleanor and I will join you there as soon as possible. Although you can no longer drink to a happy marriage, please drink to peace and unity between our kingdom and her allies." He smiled broadly at Princess Marie as he said this final line.

The conversations across the room were quickly resumed but the volume slowly began to drop as the crowd streamed out through the double doors.

Chapter 33

The king gestured for those of us standing around the dais to exit into the antechamber behind the thrones. Nate and Felix came with us and we were met there by Aldric and Mathilde. Mathilde squealed with delight and embraced me but she didn't move quickly enough to hide the sight of the two of them clasping hands. I looked at her significantly and she blushed delightedly.

"Alyssa!" cried Lily pulling on my hand. "Where have you been? And what's going on? I didn't know Max was engaged to Princess Marie!"

"Neither did I," said Max with a rueful smile. "It seems I should have read that book before giving it as a gift."

"It's a good thing you didn't," I said with my own smile.

King Henry meanwhile was clasping Marie's hand in both of his. "We owe you and your country a debt of gratitude," he was saying. "I have no idea how you knew of our predicament but you have truly come in the nick of time."

"Your gratitude would be better directed towards Alyssa," said Marie graciously. "It was she who realised the existence and significance of a prior engagement and who got word to me in time."

At these words, everyone present besieged me with questions. I held up my hands and laughingly begged them to stop. Since they wouldn't be satisfied with anything less I was forced to recount the whole story. When I came to Aldric's role I faltered, unsure of what to say.

Princess Marie cut in quickly. "Aldric was in Arcadie at my request," she said, "any gratitude you owe to me must be extended to him also." She looked straight at the king as she spoke and he nodded solemnly.

"I don't actually know how you did it," I said to Aldric.

"Carrier pigeons," he said shortly.

I laughed, amazed at the simplicity of his solution. "Of course!"

The rest of the story was quickly told but the exclamations and exaltations that followed took much longer. Everyone felt the need to relive the last few days and the ceremony, emotion by emotion. The conversation broke down into many parts and at some point the Baron and Baroness joined us and the whole story had to be explained again.

At last everyone talked themselves out. Jonas appeared to report that a whole battalion of guards was escorting the Rangmerens from the kingdom and the talk turned to the future.

The king commanded us to keep the whole story to ourselves. "There's no need to sow fear now that the threat is behind us," he said.

"Is it behind us?" I asked, voicing my concern for the first time.

It was Marie who answered. "If Rangmere were to attack Arcadia now, without legal provocation, the other kingdoms would stand with Arcadia. My coming here has clearly demonstrated that. The Rangmeren king is no fool. He won't try it."

I smiled, the last of my worries lifted.

"I can see that you were always the better choice, my dear Marie," said Queen Eleanor with a smile. "You will make Arcadia a good queen."

A sudden sharp stabbing sensation constricted my chest and I struggled to breathe. I hadn't considered anything beyond breaking Max's engagement to Ava. The desperate search for a way of escape had absorbed my entire mental energy.

The stark reality of the new situation, blindingly obvious at last, struck me like a blow. Arcadia was free but Max wasn't.

I wondered how many times a heart could break.

"Oh no," laughed Marie, cutting through my pain, "this engagement is strictly for the purposes of thwarting Rangmere. The law doesn't require that an actual wedding take place. Now that I have stated my prior claim, Arcadia is free. In the presence of all these witnesses, I now formally relinquish that claim. And I sincerely hope Arcadia won't decide to invade Northhelm for breaking the engagement."

The laughter that rang around me seemed like an echo of my own feelings. I could have hugged Marie.

"Very well, we won't hold you to it," said Queen Eleanor when the merriment subsided. "I still don't understand what happened, though. Ava was the one who felt the pea and my godmother assured me that the girl who felt the pea was the right bride for Max. The true princess."

We all stared at her in confusion. "The pea, Mother?" asked Max tentatively.

Queen Eleanor looked around at us all and sighed. "My godmother gave me a pea to put beneath the mattress of the visiting princesses. She said that only the right one would feel it. You remember the first morning of Princess Ava's visit. She complained of a lump in the bed." She looked around at us again. "I can see you all think I'm crazy but it's the reason I was so supportive of the engagement."

"Perhaps she was just feeling the loose spring?" I suggested tentatively and found all the confused looks directed at me. "You did bring the mattress back from the Winter Castle, didn't you?" I asked the queen.

Queen Eleanor nodded dumbly but Marie still looked confused. "You know," I said, turning to her, "the loose spring in the mattress on the princess's bed."

"I didn't feel any loose spring," said Marie blankly.

"Oh." Now *I* was confused. "I assumed you must have been too polite to mention it. I didn't mention it myself because I'd just been lecturing Max on polite behaviour." I threw him a reminiscent smile and he grinned in return. "I meant to say something to Mrs Pine about it but completely forgot." I shrugged. "It must have been the spring Princess Ava felt and not the pea, it's the only explanation."

A cough reminded us that Jonas was still in the room. "I was involved in Matthias' debriefing," he said and was then interrupted while we explained Matthias' role in the conspiracy to Nate, Felix, Lily, Sophie, Marie and the Liltons. Explaining about Matthias meant explaining about Rangmere's attempts to destabilise Arcadia with their fake bandits. It took a long time before everyone subsided back into silence.

Jonas, who had been patiently waiting, continued. "Yes, indeed, Rangmere had placed men wherever they could cause trouble and unrest. Even as we speak, the Intelligence Chief is in the process of uncovering them all. And, as I said, I was involved in Matthias' debriefing. Apparently Claud was spying in the woods when her majesty met with her godmother."

There was another interruption as we explained Claud to those who hadn't been at the Winter Castle.

"Claud reported the conversation to his Rangmeren employers. Given this, it seems likely that Princess Ava was lying altogether about feeling something in the bed."

Another round of exclamations was interrupted by the queen. She was ignoring the ruckus around her and was staring at me.

"I had the pea placed under the mattress in the Princess Room at the Winter Castle," she said. "I was too eager to test it to wait until our return to Arcadie. I tested the bed myself. There were no loose springs. *I* could feel no bumps at all. And the beds are always tested after they are carried between residences. Mrs Pine reported no damage to the bed when it arrived in the city.

"But Alyssa definitely felt something," said Mathilde. "I remember she mentioned it to me when we were discussing the mattresses being transported back to Arcadie."

"Then it must have been the pea she felt," said Queen Eleanor, regarding me with wide eyes.

"I don't understand," I said, "I'm definitely not a princess, true or otherwise."

"No," said Queen Eleanor, faintly, "but it seems you're the right bride for Max."

There was a moment of stunned silence and then pandemonium broke loose. Mathilde and Helena exclaimed in delight and Lily and Sophie began to dance around, yelling, in a very improper way for two princesses, "You're going to be our sister! Alyssa's going to be our sister!"

Marie just smiled but Nate slapped Felix on the back and said, "Tough luck, old fellow." Fortunately Felix seemed entirely undisturbed and was actually grinning as broadly as the girls.

"I saw it coming from the beginning," he replied, "I just thought Max was acting like an idiot and needed a bit of prodding." He seemed very pleased with his claimed foresight.

All of this I ignored.

My gaze was fixed on Max whose eyes blazed with the same joy that flooded me. In two strides he was in front of me and had swung me up into his arms. I clung to him as he twirled me around in joyful abandon. He finally set me back on my feet and leaned down to press his lips to mine. The laughs and cheers of

329

our friends and family swirled around us and I felt certain my heart would burst with happiness.

Of course, it didn't burst. It kept right on beating.

It beat away happily as a new engagement was announced to the kingdom. The news was greeted almost universally with pleasure. Lady Marissa never quite recovered from the shock but she was in the minority.

It beat on as my family arrived from the forest to grace our wedding with their presence.

And it beat particularly fast as I walked down the white carpet one last time, my eyes fixed on two spots of blue shining above a tall, white and gold figure.

It beat with joy as I snuggled inside my husband's arms as we honeymooned in his hunting lodge, deep in the woods.

And it beat on as news trickled in from all over the kingdom about the spectacular early harvest.

Queen Eleanor was gracious enough to credit us with the change in the kingdom's fortunes but I suspected her own, newly restored, true love had a little something to do with it as well.

Note from the author

Thank you for taking the time to read my book. If you enjoyed it, please spread the word! You could start by leaving a review on Amazon (or Goodreads or Facebook or any other social media site). Your review would be very much appreciated!

For free content, including a bonus chapter of The Princess Companion retold from Max's point of view, and to be kept informed of new releases, please sign up to my mailing list at www.melaniecellier.com.

Thanks for letting me share Alyssa's journey with you. If you'd like to share something of your own journey with me, you can find me on my website, on Facebook or on Goodreads. I love to interact with readers.

Happy reading! Melanie

Acknowledgements

The first thank you goes to Marc, for endlessly supporting me and helping me find the time to write. This book wouldn't exist without you!

A big thank you also to all my early readers, particularly Katie, Priya, Kristi, Rachel, Rikki and Sea, who helped shape this story and encouraged me to hurry up and get them the next chapter!

Thank you to my editors, Allan (also known as Dad!) and Lyn, who spent hours reading, editing and re-reading. Your input was invaluable and greatly improved the finished product. Any mistakes are my own!

And, of course, much thanks and praise to my model, Nicole, photographer, Steve, and cover artist and designer Claudia from Phatpuppy Art. You brought Alyssa to life and provided a beautiful introduction to the story.

Thank you also to my family, beautiful Adeline, Mum and Dad, James, Steve, Debs and Ray for surrounding me with an atmosphere of love - for both me and words.

And the final thanks goes to God, through whom all things are possible!

About the Author

Melanie Cellier grew up on a staple diet of books, books and more books. And although she got older she never stopped loving children's and young adult novels. She always wanted to write one herself but it took three careers and three different continents before she actually managed it.

She now feels incredibly fortunate to spend her time writing from her home in Canberra, Australia where they don't have a beach but they do have kangaroos hopping down the streets. Her staple diet hasn't changed much, although she's added choc mint Rooibos tea and Chicken Crimpies to the list.

Made in the USA
San Bernardino, CA
12 December 2017